CRAFT BREW

A TROUBLE BREWING NOVEL

LAYLA REYNE

Craft Brew

Copyright © 2018, 2019, 2025 by Layla Reyne

Cover Design: Temptation Creations

First Edition Editing: Kristi Yanta, Deborah Nemeth

Second Edition Editing: Sandy Bennett, Lori Parks

Second Edition

December 2025

E-Book ISBN: 978-1-962010-52-8

Paperback ISBN: 978-1-962010-53-5

Content Warnings: Explicit sex; explicit language; violence; kidnapping; discussion of past death of sibling; ailing parent; instances and/or discussion of homophobia.

ABOUT THIS BOOK

When the past comes calling, trouble's never far behind.

FBI agent Cameron Byrne is used to running toward danger, but this time it's personal. When devastating news pulls him back to Boston, he's forced to face the cold case that shattered his family decades ago. The deeper he digs, the more he realizes he can't do it alone.

Assistant U.S. Attorney Dominic Price should be the first person he calls. Except Cam isn't out to his family, and Nic's still keeping dangerous secrets while pushing him away in the name of protection. But when old ghosts and new threats collide, the only way out is together.

Reunited, they dig for the truth buried deep in Cam's past. But the closer they get to answers—and to each other—the more dangerous the fallout becomes.

The second book in the Trouble Brewing M/M romantic suspense series turns up the heat with emotional stakes, undeniable chemistry, and heart-pounding thrills, now in its second edition with a fresh cover and light edits.

ONE

"Move in with me."

Four words that should have resulted in amazing sex round two.

Not that Cam had ever uttered those words before, but from what he understood, they usually brought a couple closer, including a celebratory tumble in the sheets. Perfect as he and Nic were already there, naked and sweaty from amazing sex round one.

Nic's understanding, however, was apparently not the same as Cam's. He stiffened in his arms one second and scrambled out of bed the next. Levering up, Cam braced a hand on the mattress and watched the giant cypress inked on Nic's back sway with his mad dash to the bathroom.

"Never known you to run from an argument, Counselor!" Technically, they hadn't been arguing, but Cam knew the start of one with Nic as well as he knew the other man's taste. Arguing was what they did best, even better than sex.

"That's not what I'm doing," Nic hollered over the running water.

Cam flopped back onto the bed, staring at the ceiling. "Sure as fuck could have fooled me." A warm wet rag slapped his face, and when Cam pulled it off, it was to the sight of Nic lowering himself onto the bed beside him.

He waited for Cam to finish wiping off, then took the rag and tossed it aside. He stretched an arm over him, planting it in the mattress on the other side of his hip, icy blues staring down at him. "I'm not running."

"You told me your rental is getting demo'd and you're getting kicked out, which *thank fuck* because that place should have been torn down ages ago." Aside from its proximity to the brewery Nic co-owned, the run-down duplex made no sense for Dominic Price, federal prosecutor and son of a real estate mogul. "Seeing as you've been here every night for four months, I made the logical suggestion that you move in." He flung an arm toward the door. "And then you bolted like the sheets were on fire."

"I'm leaving for San Diego."

Shock propelled Cam up to seated again. "You're what?"

Nic leaned back just in time to avoid a head-on collision. He folded his arms, lean muscles taut as they bisected the myriad of tattoos painting his torso. "The US Attorney down there is taking paternity leave. They need someone to cover."

"And you volunteered?"

"No, they asked me."

Cam scooted back against the headboard, letting it hold him up as his world spun faster than he was equipped to handle at this hour.

It was a great opportunity for San Francisco's best Assistant US Attorney—getting out from under his asshole boss here and taking the reins of an entire operation there. Major problem for Cam, though, who after a year in the Bay Area had only recently begun to feel at home, in no small part due to the man beside him.

Anger and hurt bested professional goodwill. "Bullshit you're not running."

Nic inched closer, laying a hand on his thigh. "You'll be safer if I'm not here."

"This is about your father," Cam surmised.

Nic's diverted gaze confirmed as much. Curtis Price, once a Silicon Valley real estate tycoon, was drowning in debt, and last spring some of his lenders had come after Nic, looking to collect despite the decades' estrangement between father and son.

Cam covered Nic's hand with his own. "You said we would do this together." Nic had promised to let him help with the investigation.

"The case, yes."

"But not the moving-in part?"

"The case part has to come first." Nic turned his hand over under Cam's, lacing their fingers together. "I won't put you at risk." He was holding something back. The former SEAL trying to protect him, the FBI agent.

Growling in familiar frustration, Cam tried to yank his hand free. "I can take care of myself."

Nic held on tight. "Yes, you can, but I won't paint a bull's-eye on your back."

"Think it's a little late for that. Besides, things have been quiet lately."

"And I mean to keep it that way," Nic said. "Us moving in together? Not quiet."

"I'm not going to stop digging whether you're here or in San Diego."

"I didn't expect you to," Nic conceded. "But without me *here*"—he patted the mattress—"you can do so quietly." He leaned forward, drawing Cam into a kiss that snuffed out his anger but not the hurt.

Cam retreated, resting his forehead against Nic's. "How long will you be gone?"

"Four to six weeks."

"What about Gravity?"

"I can manage the business end of the brewery from anywhere." Nic curled a hand around the side of Cam's neck, squeezing lightly and drawing his gaze. "It's a good opportunity. I'll have my own office and can set the agenda. Take cases that matter, not just the ones that guarantee a win. You know as well as I do that this is how DOJ works. We go where we can make a difference, where we're needed."

Like Cam had been needed in San Francisco so he'd left Boston behind.

And now Nic was needed in San Diego. But what about the people who needed Nic here? Was this thing between them not affecting Nic the way it was affecting Cam? "What happened to building something?" he whispered hoarsely.

Nic's determination faltered and he twisted away, his back to Cam as he braced his heels on the bed's foot rail. "I've never been good at construction. I'm better at demo."

"That's bullshit too," Cam said, anger resurging but redirected for Nic, not at him. "Look at Gravity, at your USAO teams, at your work with the Bureau."

"It's too good, Boston. You, *us*, most of all. And the last time I had it this good . . ." Glancing sideways, Nic's eyes were brimming with remembered pain. "I made a mess of things and lost it all. I can't let that happen again. I can't lose you and everything I've already built here."

His breath hitched, torso heaving, and Cam's attention was drawn again to the giant cypress on his back, to the spindly limbs that curled over Nic's shoulders and to the mysterious *GS* in the center of its trunk. *His biggest mess*, Nic had once said. And now Nic didn't want to make another. This was affecting him, maybe more than it was affecting Cam. And if Cam wanted a shot at building more, he couldn't push right now. That would be a mistake he'd regret. He needed to give Nic the space to find his answers. "Okay, Dominic. Go to San Diego."

Nic huffed a relieved sigh, shoulders dropping and curling forward. "You gonna let the argument go, just like that?"

Trailing a hand over his back, Cam slid to his side and rubbed his cheek against Nic's, the brush of scruff against his own electrifying. "I'm thirty-six," he rumbled in Nic's ear. "Not a fucking teenager. I'm going to miss you like crazy, but this is a two-way street, one I'd like to keep driving on with you, the same direction." He grasped Nic's chin and angled his face toward him. "Do what you need to clear the roadblocks." He palmed Nic's cock with his other hand. "And fuck me good before you leave."

"Christ, I'm an idiot," Nic growled, right before he did exactly as Cam asked, proving himself smarter than he gave himself credit for.

———

Five weeks later, Cam was wondering who was smart and who was the idiot. He was leaning toward them both being the latter, phone and video calls a poor substitute, especially as they'd both had less and less time for those owing to work. He glanced at the ever-growing stack of admin paperwork on his desk, the pile teetering precariously. Assistant Special Agent in Charge came with more than just a pay raise, not that the extra cash went far in the Bay Area, especially when he was trying to keep up with a bunch of fucking millionaires.

A new mail notification flashed at the bottom of his screen and Cam groaned aloud, anticipating more busy-work. Double-clicking the icon, he was halfway to hitting Print, his normal routine for admin emails, when he realized what it was—next week's federal court calendar for San Diego. He'd set up the alert when the new month had rolled over without a firm word from Nic as to when he'd be home. Looking at the latest court calendar, which didn't have D. Price on it anywhere, Cam deduced his answer was *soon*.

Which meant he needed to get his ducks in a row, namely on the case he was supposed to be working with Nic. Things had remained quiet during his absence, but with Nic returning, he'd be putting himself back in the line of fire should his father's lenders get impatient again. Cam wouldn't let him get hit. He'd committed to never losing someone else he loved, which now included Nic, the miserable weeks apart making that conclusion irrefutable even if he hadn't let Nic in on that bit of information yet.

Pushing back from his desk, Cam left his office and strode through the bullpen. Bypassing the elevators, he continued down the long hall to "the cave," the interior boardroom that had been converted into the cyber agents' domain. He wove through the server racks to the workstations in back, finding the agent he needed at her desk, a wobbly pencil bun visible above three oversized monitors. While the other agents paused and acknowledged him, the rapid-fire *tap-tap-tap* of Agent Lauren Hall's nails didn't let up.

"If you don't mind?" Cam said, tilting his head toward the exit.

The other agents gathered their things and scurried out, the flurry of movement finally attracting Lauren's notice. Brows drawn and eyes narrowed, she looked stumped and seriously sleep-deprived. She was turning in her swivel chair, popping out her earbuds, when Cam plopped down behind the adjacent desk, the visitor chairs in front of hers made useless by the wall of screens.

"Something you can't hack?"

"I don't want to talk about it."

Well, at least he had better news for her. "Nic's on his way back."

Her big blue eyes brightened, a spark of excitement—she was fond of poking the prickly bear and just generally fond of Nic—but then she reined it in, asking cautiously, "How do we feel about that?"

While he and Nic hadn't told any of their friends about their relationship, Lauren had intimated she'd figured something was brewing between them. They hadn't confirmed or denied.

"Like I need something to show for a month of work," he answered.

She pressed her lips together like she wanted to say more.

He glowered.

She rolled her eyes, then spun back around to the monitors, some of the long brown waves coming loose from her bun. "Curtis's bank accounts continue to dwindle," she said.

While they hadn't been actively investigating, they had set up alerts on Curtis's accounts and installed extra security at the properties he still owned.

"Any new loans?" he asked.

"Several. He's barely afloat. Most were refis except this one." She rotated the monitor closest to Cam so he could see the document open on the screen.

He rolled his chair closer, squinting at the long-form deed of trust.

"It was made back in May," she went on. "But only recorded this week."

May.

Five months ago, when the threats against Nic had quieted.

Her rainbow-painted nails directed his attention to the property description line. "You recognize that address?"

"Fucking hell. That's the mansion in Hillsborough."

"Yup, and the same company holds the mortgage on the office building in Burlingame."

"Please tell me you've cracked that."

The mortgage holder had a generic company name as did many real estate lenders and investment companies. Nic had claimed not to know who it traced back to. Cam didn't buy it, suspecting that's what Nic had been holding back.

"That's where things get interesting," Lauren said. He waved a hand, prompting her to go on. "There are other affiliate entities with loans on other Price properties and at the top of each company's org chart is Vaughn Investments."

"Who runs that?"

Her dark brows raced all the way to her hairline.

"I'm supposed to know?" Cam said.

"Vaughn Investments is run by Duncan Vaughn."

"Who's he?"

"Only one of the biggest real estate investors in the Valley. He's like, all over the weekly business journal, opening this or that new project. I can't believe you don't know who he is."

"I haven't lived here my whole life, remember." He also avoided the local business journals and other reminders of how little money he made relatively. In any event, his mind was making a more troubling connection. "So you're telling me one of this area's biggest real estate investors might be behind the threats against Nic?"

She nodded, not looking the least bit surprised. "I'm still tracing funds, but I doubt there's any 'might be' to it."

"Why's that?"

She rapped her nails on the desk in a mock drumroll. Good news did not follow. "Because Duncan Vaughn is Silicon Valley's version of a gangster."

———

The gate agent called for Zone 5 passengers to board, and Nic heaved himself out of the vinyl chair with a sigh, in no hurry to race the other passengers to hell. Ninety minutes of cramming his six-foot-three self into coach, then at the end of his journey waited a new apartment, a mountain of unpacked moving boxes, and a dark-haired, dark-eyed Bostonian whose mood Nic couldn't predict after five weeks apart.

Don't run to your death, the SEAL saying went. When he'd been a SEAL, Nic took the saying seriously. Calm, methodical, well-scoped-out missions saved lives; uninformed, reckless ones cost them.

He still took it seriously post-military. Accepting Cam's offer to move in with him would have been reckless, no matter how much he'd wanted to say yes. With his father's creditors looming, Nic might have been running them both to their deaths. He wouldn't have that, wouldn't risk Cam. So, as Cam rightly accused, he'd run the opposite direction, making true the other SEAL saying inked on his torso.

The only easy day was yesterday.

Because each day away from Cam had hurt. He'd missed his Southie drawl and hungry kisses, his bed with the so-worn-they-were-soft sheets, and even his big-as-a-dog cat named Bird. He'd also missed their friends who'd been steadily expanding Nic's world beyond Gravity and the US Attorney's Office. He'd missed them all—his life—more than he cared to admit. But facing them anew after he'd cut and run, no matter how good the reason, was going to make yesterday, as miserable as it had been between trial and transitioning cases, somehow easier.

"Excuse me, Mr. Price?"

Nic turned toward the lilting British accent, finding an unfamiliar older gentleman standing behind him. Gray hair styled, expensive suit tailored, he carried himself with the impeccable air of a professional butler or steward, Nic familiar with the sort from when his father had had a staff of more than two. The stranger also carried Nic's checked suit bag over his arm.

"That's me," Nic said. "Is there a problem, Mr. . . .?"

"Chase. Jeremy Chase," the man said with a polite nod. "You've been rebooked onto another flight." Jeremy held out a business card emblazoned with a star and clover logo Nic knew well. "I think you'll find it a much more comfortable transport to San Francisco."

Nic took the card, flipped it over, and read the note on the back. He couldn't tell from the two-word order—*Follow Jeremy*—if the author was furious with him or not. Commands were her normal default. But there was no doubt that what she was offering, even if it came with a side of recriminations, would be more comfortable than Seat 25D. He pocketed the card, shouldered his messenger bag, and grabbed the handle of his carry-on. "The lady wants me to follow you, Jeremy."

"The lady is best not ignored."

One side of Nic's mouth hitched up. "Too true."

Jeremy led him out of the main terminal and into a waiting town car. They drove around to a separate terminal on the south side of the airport and directly into a hangar where a G-5 was being fueled and readied for takeoff. At the top of the jet's stairs stood imposing, beautiful Melissa Cruz, in a dark pencil skirt and cream-colored shell. Formerly a Special Agent in Charge at the FBI and more recently Chief of Security for Talley Enterprises and bounty hunter on the side, she was definitely not a woman you ignored if you wanted to keep all your bodily bits.

"Price," she greeted, when he reached the bottom of the steps.

"You gonna give me a lift?"

She crossed her toned brown arms, biceps flexing. "I shouldn't after that disappearing act you pulled."

Recriminations it was, then.

"But I'm the last person to judge," she added. "You had your reasons."

Jeremy, who'd finished loading his luggage, closed the hold door just as the pilot called from the side window, "Ms. Cruz, we're ready to go."

"Thank you," she returned. Then to Nic, "Your reasons, as it turns out, were also well-founded."

Interest and apprehension warred. "You've learned more?"

With a nod, she beckoned him to follow her inside, and Jeremy held out an arm toward the stairs. "Mr. Price, if you would, please."

He climbed the steps into the luxury private jet, and Jeremy secured the door behind them.

"Anything else, Agent"—Jeremy paused, correcting himself with a smile that Mel shared—"Ms. Cruz?"

"We're good, Jeremy, thank you."

The steward, who must have known Mel from her Bureau days, disappeared behind the cockpit door.

Nic sank into one of the swiveling leather chairs and strapped in. "Where'd you find Alfred?"

"Stole him from commercial," she answered with a smirk.

"Well done."

Thanks to priority takeoff, they were airborne in less than ten minutes, and Nic was out of his coat and tie five minutes after that, tossing them into one of the other empty chairs. He stretched out his long legs, laced his hands over his middle, and leaned back in the plush seat, eyes slipping closed. There were difficult conversations to be had, Mel had intimated as much, but he couldn't help taking a brief respite for himself.

Definitely better than commercial. "How are you, Nic?"

Respite over.

He righted his head and swiveled to face the couch where she sat, one knee crossed over the other, red-soled designer heel bouncing. "Tired but it was a good stint there."

"You considering having your own office one day?"

"It's tempting," he admitted.

Being out from under Bowers's thumb had been re-energizing. Having his own team, choosing his and approving the team's cases, being able to direct efforts toward causes within Justice's purview that were of particular interest to him versus merely trying to clear cases, had reminded him why he'd gotten into this in the first place. Besides his gift for arguing, as his SEAL XO had put it.

In five weeks, he'd made a difference, a bigger one than a single prosecutor's caseload. There was no shortage of abusers to introduce to the full weight of the law and doing so at the opposite end of the state from his asshole boss had been all the better. But the opposite end of the state had kept him from the things he'd missed most—Gravity, friends, Cam.

"I'm not sure where my future lies if I'm being honest."

"Gravity?"

"Some part of it, most definitely." But all of it? What about the courtroom?

"Kegs won't keep your bed warm at night," Mel said, making the next leap to the bedroom.

He chuckled. "I was going to say something noble about the carriage of justice, but marriage seems to have turned you into the matchmaker."

She poked him in the knee with her heel, smiling and unrepentant. "I want to see my friends happy too."

If that constant ache he'd felt in the vicinity of his chest the past month was any indication, Nic knew what would make him happy. But he wouldn't let his happiness come at the expense of those he cared for.

"I need to know how to protect the future," he said. "No matter what or who is in it."

The seat belt light dinged off and the pilot interrupted to report they'd reached cruising altitude. When the intercom clicked off, Mel unclasped her seat belt and stood, gesturing to the chairs a row back on either side of a table. "Then I need to bring you up to speed," she said, all business.

And the business wasn't good.

Thirty minutes later, the table was covered with documents and Nic was pacing the length of the cabin, his hands in his hair, which had more gray in it every day. Warp speed, if this shit kept up. "That's why they laid off."

"Mostly likely. But this"—she nudged the damning deed of trust on his childhood home—"won't keep them at bay forever. Not when Curtis still can't pay his bills. The debts will outweigh the equity before long."

"Did Vaughn take out insurance on it?"

From the folder of horrors that had produced only bad news, she pulled out another sheet of paper—an insurance certificate on the house. His gaze shot to the declared value box, and all the moisture in his mouth vanished. Double the assessed value, last time he'd checked the county land records.

He ran his hands down his face, groaning. "It's as good as doused in lighter fluid." He had to get his father and the staff out of there.

"Have you had any more calls?" Mel asked.

Nic shook his head. No more of the distracting calls from an *Unknown* number, the first having rung right as Vaughn's goons attacked him. He pointed at the deed of trust. "Now we know why."

"Not necessarily."

"Swear to Christ, Cruz, you pull another nightmare out of that fucking hat"—he glared at the folder—"and I might just throw it out of this plane."

"How you gonna do that?"

"I'll get creative."

She laughed, then pulled two pieces of paper from the Folder of Doom. He growled. "Easy, Price." She set the papers on the table. "Jury's still out on these."

"Tell me where the calls originated from, and I'll be the judge of that."

She smirked and pointed at several highlighted entries on the first sheet—his phone record. "These are the unknown calls to you, all from a single burner phone like we suspected."

"Did the calls originate from the same location?"

"Appears so. Took a bit of digging, but I traced them back to Jacksonville, North Carolina."

Bracing his hands on either side of the table, he stared at the second sheet.

A map with a cluster of pinpoints, all in a familiar location.

"That's Camp Lejeune." He'd been based at Little Creek in Virginia, then Coronado in California, but he'd done joint special operations training with the Marines at Lejeune. Numerous times. "Someone from when I was in the service?"

"That would be the logical conclusion."

Was a former teammate in trouble? He knew of at least one who was there in the area, an instructor now. Or a Marine he'd crossed paths with? From his time as a SEAL, then in the JAG Corps, he had colleagues across branches, and if there was one thing the military engrained in him, it was never leave a teammate behind. He had his own teammates' names inked on his skin because they hadn't left him behind when he'd been injured in the field. If one of them was in trouble now . . . And was that trouble the Duncan Vaughn sort? If it were, he'd either been betrayed or someone was up to their neck in shit with Vaughn. Shit they probably didn't grasp the full danger and extent of. "You got enough fuel on this thing to take us to North Carolina?"

"I do. But it's one in the morning there, and I've got a husband at home who will not be pleased if I'm gone another day."

"Cruz."

She covered his hand, which had formed a death grip on the table's edge. "Priorities, Price. The base would've called you if it was serious. Or the caller would have left a message."

"Maybe." If it was something that would be escalated that high officially, then yes. If not, then no. And if the calls were connected to Vaughn, he doubted the matter would go through the base at all.

"Let me dig," Mel offered. "Determine if it's connected while you deal with the other issues first."

She was right. The problems—with Vaughn and his father—were known.

Possibly—probably—worse and most definitely immediate.

As was his need to see a certain federal agent.

He loosened his grip and straightened. "All right, let's go home."

TWO

Priority departure, yes.

Priority landing, not so much.

They circled an hour before finally touching down at SFO, and by the time Nic hit the elevator for the hipster-infested hive complex he now called home, it was midnight. His disgust, amplified by the K-pop playing in the elevator, was almost enough to distract him.

Almost.

Key an inch from the lock to his third-floor unit, he looked down and noticed the scuffs on his oxfords, visible in the light streaming out from under the door.

The scuffs he didn't care about; the light stopped him cold.

Maybe the complex's management had been in for maintenance or inspections. But they would've given him notice of that; they legally had to.

Glass shattered inside the unit.

Nic snatched back his key, dropped his bags, and

reached for his sidearm. Maintenance wouldn't be in his apartment at this hour.

He visualized the one-bedroom floor plan. Small faux wood foyer, bathroom and bedroom to the left, laundry on the right, a carpeted hallway that led to the main living area and kitchen. The glass had shattered from somewhere deep inside the unit—not in the foyer or bathroom. With the rest of the area carpeted, it had to have been in the kitchen. If he entered quietly, he wouldn't be heard or seen in the entry hallway. He could sneak up on the intruder before they knew he was there.

He pressed the door handle down—unlocked—but when he pushed the door, it didn't give. The deadbolt was still engaged. Sliding his key in gently, he rotated it right, millimeter by millimeter, minimizing the *click* of the lock being thrown.

Weapon in hand, he eased open the door and snuck inside.

And with one deep breath, he realized his caution was unnecessary. The aroma of beef stew tickled his nose and a string of curses, long on the vowels and short on the Rs, reached his ears. He'd know that voice anywhere, and the ache in his chest eased a little at hearing it live and in person again. B&E culprit identified, Nic holstered his weapon and collected his bags, dropping them in the foyer next to a stack of moving boxes. He shut the door and unclipped his holster, setting the weapon atop the boxes. "Boston, you okay?"

"Fucking finally." Cam appeared around the corner, and Nic nearly stumbled at the handsome grin that greeted him. "Got hungry unpacking your shit, so I threw some stew on." He lifted a dish-towel-wrapped hand. "Until this happened."

The shattering glass.

"Bathroom, now," Nic ordered. From the foyer stack of boxes, he lifted off the top one marked *Bedroom* and dug through the *Bathroom* one for a first aid kit.

"You gonna fix me up?" Cam crowded his side, the heat of his body and the smell of his beer on Cam's breath throwing Nic for a loop. The painted-on tee that showed off his ripped chest and arms and the ratty jeans that hung low on his hips spun him further. Cam looked good in a suit, but Nic liked him best dressed down, unusual for his tastes.

But this was Cam—*Boston.*

Nic tore his eyes from the outline that was making itself known under those threadbare jeans and stepped toward the bathroom. "Well, you did get injured unpacking my shit," he said with a smile tossed over his shoulder.

"Missed that," Cam replied, voice gravelly.

Dark eyes liquid warm, body heat magnified in the small space, he was too tempting for common sense. Nic had counted on a night alone to get his thoughts in order, to decide how best to warn Cam of the new dangers Mel had uncovered, and to practice his apology for running scared, just as Cam had correctly deduced.

But with Cam right here, all Nic wanted to do was sample his beer on Cam's lips—his favorite taste in the world.

Fuck.

He grabbed Cam's hand and shoved it under the faucet instead.

"Ouch!" Cam yelped. "That's fucking hot. And not in the good way!"

Chuckling, Nic adjusted the temperature and carefully brushed out the tiny shards of glass, cleaning the relatively minor cut.

"Way to kill the mood, asshole," Cam grumbled, then proceeded to kill it further himself. "You didn't tell me you were coming back."

Nic dried his palm and dabbed on antiseptic. "I was in trial until yesterday."

"That why you didn't call?" Hurt belied Cam's words, even as he stepped closer.

Nic's hands shook as he ripped open two Band-Aids and stuck the strips together, big enough to cover the cut on Cam's palm. "In part."

"In part?"

Nic pressed the Band-Aids over the cut and smoothed down the sticky ends. He curled his hands around Cam's, turned it over, and brushed his thumbs over the backs of his knuckles. "I was still trying to figure out how to say I'm sorry for being an ass. For running."

"So you admit that's what you were doing?"

Nic lifted his eyes to Cam's swirling dark ones, equal parts hurt and need with a chaser of indignation. "I said it, didn't I?"

Taking the last step closer, his front pressed to Nic's side, Cam curled his other arm behind him, laying a hand on his lower back. "Then that's all you need to say." The warmth of his words blotted out the hurt and indignation in his eyes and the warmth of his hand seared through the cotton of Nic's dress shirt.

Nic fumbled the antiseptic he was trying to put away. Cam grabbed the tube, dropped it in the box, and closed the lid. He moved it off to the side, and Nic let himself be shifted between the faux-marble vanity and Cam's hard, hot body. Everything he'd missed, everything he didn't deserve, was pressed up against him, magnifying the torture. Nic's heart and breath stuttered. "I'm sorry, Boston."

"Apology accepted," Cam whispered, then lower, "Now, I just need my dick in you."

Groaning, Nic angled his face in, lips prickled by the enticing scruff, tongue tasting skin, sweat, and man. "Fuck, I missed you."

Cam cupped the other side of his face, holding him there, cheek to cheek. "Missed you too, baby." He lowered the hand on Nic's back, hauling him off the vanity and grabbing his ass, bringing them dick to dick.

Nic couldn't have stopped himself from thrusting if his life depended on it.

Same as he couldn't stop himself from begging. "Boston, please."

Plea granted, Cam's mouth came down on his, hard, and Nic claimed the taste he craved, lips devouring and tongue thrusting into the other man's mouth. He chased after it, again and again, until he was out of breath and had to draw back.

Smiling, Cam nipped along his jaw and trailed kisses down his neck. "I set up the bed."

Another thrust, chasing that idea as eagerly as he'd chased Cam's kiss. "Sheets too?"

He felt Cam smirk against the hollow of his throat. "Of course."

"Awfully confident."

"Thought you liked that about me?"

"Oh, I do, Boston." He ran his hands through the dark

brown strands of Cam's hair, tilting his head back and forcing his gaze. "The food?"

"Instant Pot."

"I don't own an Instant Pot."

"Housewarming gift."

Meaning Cam understood. And he'd said he'd been unpacking him.

Here.

He wasn't going to pressure him to move in.

All of Nic's lingering tension, the fears he'd been holding inside, been holding on to for the past month, fell away. He breathed deep—

And almost choked. "Do you smell that?"

Inhaling, Cam's eyes widened a second later in recognition, and they both spun, looking up to the air vent above the door. Smoke was billowing out from between the metal slats. "What the fuck?"

The building fire alarm blared in answer.

———

Cam raced into the living room and grabbed his gun and badge off the window ledge. He was back in the foyer by the time Nic came out of the bathroom with two soaked pillowcases.

"Makes it easier to breathe," he said, holding one out to Cam. "We're going up?"

Cam nodded; no question. He was a first responder already on scene who could rescue trapped residents or help coordinate evac. This was his job and judging by the determined look in Nic's eyes, he considered it his too. Cam didn't bother trying to convince him otherwise. He might be a lawyer now, but the soldier resided just beneath the surface. If Nic could be on the front lines, he would be, and there were only a handful of others Cam trusted as much as Nic to have his back. He took the pillowcase from Nic, folded it into a triangle, and tied it bandanna-style around the lower part of his face.

After Nic did the same, he dug two flashlights out of another box and handed one to Cam. "You're more recently trained in evac procedures. You lead."

Smoke was slowly seeping into the third-floor hallway, not a full-on pour like through Nic's vents yet, so the other residents were more disoriented than panicked. Woken in the middle of the night, driven out of their units by the alarms, they struggled to find their way to the exits in the dim hallway, the emergency lighting and signs not as bright as they should be.

"This way, folks!" Cam shone his light up at the glossy white ceiling, moving it around like a beacon. "Let's go, let's go, let's go!" he hollered in his agent voice.

People began to hustle, taking his orders seriously.

"Boston!" Nic called from where he stood holding open the stairwell door, ushering people through. "We need to get upstairs!"

"I got it here!" A third voice entered the fray. A young man in uniform was shoving his way through the crowd, flashing a badge. "Shante Bridges, Redwood City PD. Just got home from my shift. You cops too?"

"Assistant Special Agent in Charge Cameron Byrne." He flashed his FBI badge, then aimed the beam of his flashlight at Nic. "And that's Captain Dominic Price, retired SEAL and federal prosecutor." He normally wouldn't prioritize, much less reference, Nic's rank, but

Cam didn't want to waste time arguing who would take lead here.

Shante caught the drift. "Go on, then. I got it here. I'm sure they can use your help upstairs."

"Thanks, man." Cam slapped his shoulder, then hurried to join Nic in the stairwell. Using his bigger body to cut a path along the rail, Cam climbed the steps in front of Nic, the smoke getting thicker the closer they got to the fourth floor. The crowd, however, was thinning out.

Cam understood why when they reached the fourth-floor landing and heat blasted his face. "Fire must be on this end."

"It's right there!" shouted a woman running past them, dragging a bleary-eyed kid behind her. The next man pointed to the elevator side of the stairwell. "It's the corner unit!" he hollered, then thundered down the stairs, picking up the kid for the woman, who thanked him profusely.

"Right above my unit," Nic said, redrawing Cam's attention. "We need to make sure it's clear."

Cam nodded and they moved into the hallway where they were blasted by another wave of heat. People were running away from this end, away from the corner unit that was clearly the source of the fire, dark black smoke billowing out from around the door's edges. Cam laid his hand on the door—blistering hot. Cursing, he snatched his hand back and kicked at the door with his foot.

It didn't budge.

"You smell that?" Nic said beside him. "Underlying the smoke."

Cam sniffed and nearly hacked up a lung, but yeah, he smelled it. Taken together with how hot that door had been to the touch, there was only one conclusion. "Accelerant."

"Has to be. Meaning we gotta get everyone out of here now." Nic banged on the door with his fist. "First responders! Is anyone in there? First responders, open up!"

"It's empty," came a thin, wobbly voice from across the hall.

Cam spun, gaze following the direction of the voice to a little girl in the opposite doorway. Dressed in Wonder Woman pajamas, she couldn't have been more than eight. Tears streaked down her face and as a coughing fit overcame her, she covered her mouth with her hand.

"I got this," Cam said to Nic. "Make sure the other units are clear." Nic nodded and took off down the hall, banging on doors, while Cam crouched in front of the little girl. "Hey, sweetheart. What's your name?"

"Amali."

"Amali, my name's Cam, and that's my friend Nic." He shone his light at Nic, who was rustling stragglers out of their units and directing them to the far stairwell. "We're cops," he oversimplified. "We need to get you out of here."

She grabbed Cam by the hand and tugged him inside the unit. "I can't leave Nani." In the living area, an older woman wheezed and struggled to stand from a wheelchair.

Cam glanced at the pictures on the walls. Amali with a mom and dad and her grandmother, her Nani. "Where are your parents?"

"Wedding," the older woman said. "Sacramento. On their"—she broke into another coughing fit— "way back."

"Boston!" Nic called from the door. "Hall is clear. We gotta get out of here."

"Help me!" he hollered as he darted into the kitchen. He grabbed the hand towels off the fridge door, wet them, and was coming back into the living room as Nic charged in.

Cam tossed him a towel and was going to offer to carry the grandmother, but Amali had already attached herself to his leg.

"Don't leave!"

"We're not, sweetheart."

"I've got Riya," Nic said, tying the cloth over the older woman's mouth, whose name he'd also apparently gotten.

Cam knelt and did the same for Amali, then picked her up in his arms, shifting her onto one hip.

"Stairwell across the hall is closer." Nic adjusted Riya in his arms. "Open some doors for me."

"Amali, I want you to hide right here." Cam patted his chest and Amali shoved her face into it. "We're going to run, okay?"

She nodded, and Cam hauled ass to the door, Nic on his heels. He held his breath and charged across the hallway. Visibility was nil, the air roasting, and Amali screamed in his arms, but they made it across the hallway in one piece, unburnt. He slammed open the stairwell door, his own eyes watering from the smoke, and Nic barreled through behind him. Shante was waiting for them on the third-floor landing.

"We're clear up there!" Nic said. "All clear here?"

"Clear, Captain."

"Let's get out of here!"

Cam couldn't agree more.

THREE

It was closer to sunrise than sunset when Nic emerged from a cloud of steam in Cam's bathroom, a far cry from the cloud of smoke they'd staggered out of earlier with Amali and Riya. Heat and smoke had nipped their heels every step of the way, but they'd made it to the ground floor, Shante throwing open the door to glorious fresh air. And to Amali's tearful, thankful parents who'd been waiting outside. He and Cam had gotten the reunited family seen to, then, after a couple hits off a shared oxygen mask, they'd assisted the actual first responders until residents had been allowed back inside. Nic, however, was barred from staying in his unit. Between the smoke that had poured through the air vents and the overflowing water from the sprinklers in the upstairs unit, Nic's new home had been deemed uninhabitable. He'd only been allowed in to quickly grab essentials, most of which were still packed in his suitcases by the door.

He'd grabbed his luggage while Cam had packed up the Instant Pot, the stew preserved under the locked pressure lid. As much as Nic wanted to sleep, he also wanted to eat, his body thrown out of whack from the travel and unplanned all-nighter. Maybe food would also make the difficult conversation he'd avoided earlier—the one about what an idiot his father had been—go down easier.

Cursing him, Nic yanked on a borrowed tee, rolled it down to the top of his sweats, and ran a hand through his damp hair. Situated well enough, he strolled across the open dining area and into the kitchen where Cam stood ladling stew into bowls, his cat winding around his feet.

Cam's dark eyes twinkled up at him, surprisingly awake for four in the morning. "Beer to go with?" he asked with a nod to the fridge.

He'd showered first while Nic had been on the phone with the arson investigator, filling him in on what they'd detected at the scene. Nic had also made it known they wanted to be kept in the loop. *Because it was his home*, he'd claimed. Because it was a nasty welcome home present, he suspected.

"I'll get it," Nic said, ignoring the hissing orange furball. He and Bird had been on good terms before he'd left for San Diego. Apparently, he was going to have to win the beast over again.

Food and drink in hand, they bypassed the dining table for the deep-cushioned couch in the living room. Digging in, Nic hummed as the rich flavors of the stew hit his tongue. "Thank you for the housewarming gift," he said a few spoonfuls later. "Even if we are enjoying it at your place."

Cam shot him a sideways grin. "I'm just glad it survived. Otherwise it would've been cup of noodles."

"Wouldn't be my first time."

"Military?"

"Law school."

Cam laughed mid-slurp of stew, and Bird pounced on the spray, licking it up off the floor.

Nic smiled, amused and more content than he had any right to be. "You didn't have to do this."

Dark eyes, dimmer now, slid his way. "My apologies for presuming."

Nic lowered his spoon and forced down the bite that lodged in his throat. "I'm the one who owes you an apology. Thought we established that."

"Confession," Cam started, and Nic whipped his gaze back up, not sure where Cam was headed with that lead-in. "This is also me softening you up. I'm Irish," he said, gesturing with his spoon at the clover on his Celtics T-shirt. "We attack through the belly."

"Go on."

Dropping his spoon in his empty bowl, Cam leaned forward and set it on the round leather ottoman. He stopped halfway back, elbows resting on his knees. "It's about your father."

"What'd you find?" Nic set his bowl next to Cam's for Bird to lick clean. Cam had said he was going to keep digging, but had he found out more than Mel? And had he tipped off Vaughn doing so? "Were you quiet?"

Cam nodded. "We didn't approach. Just dug into financials and legal records."

"This is what you were softening me up for?"

"No, I was softening you up for what we found. You're not gonna be happy when I tell you what your father's done."

Meaning they'd gotten at least as far as Mel had. "The mortgage on the house," he said, grimacing.

"You knew?"

"Mel gave me a lift back from San Diego. Brought me up to speed."

"Do you know *who* holds that loan?" Cam's tone clearly indicated he did.

But first . . . "*We* didn't approach?"

"Lauren."

Nic had guessed as much; he'd already drawn her in himself last spring.

Ultimately, though, she answered to Cam, and her ace hacking skills, together with Cam's investigative prowess, had led them to the same discovery Mel had made. "Duncan Vaughn."

"He's a gangster, Nic." Cam raked a hand through his hair, dark brown made black by the lingering dampness. "He must be the one behind the attacks last April. He's come at you three times already."

Two snipers and a hit-and-run. Plus one Cam didn't know about.

"Four times. Five, maybe, if that fire in the unit above mine tonight was arson. Which is why I've tried to keep you out of this."

Cam's eyes grew wide, swirling with worry and smarting from betrayal. "Four or five? And how long have you known it's Vaughn?"

Nic put a hand on Cam's knee to keep him from bolting upright. He left it there as he filled Cam in on his first run-in with Vaughn's goons. The two bruisers had tried and failed to jump him in Gravity's parking lot a week before a sniper had pinned him and Cam down there.

"You've known it's been Vaughn this entire time?"

Standing, Nic grabbed his wallet off the table, took out the card the goons had given him, and handed it to Cam. "They were clear about who they worked for."

Cam turned the card over in his hand, running a thumb over the embossed lettering. VAUGHN INVESTMENTS. He glanced back up, the betrayal in his eyes eclipsed by the worry. "Fuck, Nic. This is serious. We need to report this."

"I can take care of myself, Boston."

Cam shot up off the couch, standing nose-to-nose with him. "Don't be fooled by that lie I told earlier. I'm the LEO here."

"I'm not going to report this."

"Why the fuck not?"

Bird scampered off the ottoman with a startled *meow*, surprised by his owner's outburst. It was enough to break their stare-down and poke a hole in the rising tension. Taking Cam's hand, Nic sat on the edge of the ottoman and tugged Cam back down to the couch. He wasn't the enemy —Cam could be an ally—if Nic explained why he'd taken the steps he had. Why he'd kept things quiet, beyond merely wanting to protect him.

"I'm not going to report this because I still think they were just threats, not actual attempts on my life."

"Bull—"

"And because the FBI is already investigating. I don't want to fuck up that case, and I don't want to be walled off any more than I already am."

Cam pressed his lips together, stewing. "We're walled off too," he said after a moment. "I can't access the files on Vaughn or Curtis."

"All of us are, including Aidan. Conflicts of interest."

Which was putting it mildly. Aidan Talley, Cam's partner, was the San Francisco Special Agent in Charge. He was also Cam's best friend's husband, Mel's brother-in-law, and the man Nic had once dated. The Irish ex-pat was the center of the wheel that held them all together. "Assistant Director Moore has the files. He keeps them on flash drives in a safe in his private residence. He's the only one who can grant access."

It took Cam less than a second to draw the same conclusion Nic had earlier. "Shit, the same flash drives I stole that one time?" Cam, undercover with a wanted heist crew, had had to steal flash drives out of the AD's personal safe to prove himself. "Fuck, fuck, fuck. Becca said they were for another client. Vaughn?"

Nic nodded. "I'd put my money on it."

"But we gave them back."

Nic shook his head this time. "I'm pretty sure I saw Lauren copying them after the bust, before we gave them back."

"That's what she's been working on all these months. She can't crack 'em. It's driving her nuts." Slumping into the cushions, Cam ran a hand down his face and over his stubbled jaw. Nic wished for this conversation to be over so he could run his fingers over it. "I can talk to AD Moore," Cam said.

And then he was right back in it. "No!" The word came out harsher than Nic intended, and Bird skittered on his nails the rest of the way out of the room. "Shit, I'm sorry, that came out wrong." He spread his legs on either side of Cam's knees and laid his hands on his thighs. Containment with a side of contrition. "I haven't slept in almost twenty-four hours. Hell, I haven't really slept well in over a month."

Cam's hands landed on top of his. "In five weeks?"

Nic smirked as irony reared its head. The very house he'd run from was now his refuge. He was here now; he wasn't going anywhere. No use denying how much he'd missed it. "Yeah, Boston, since I left your bed. That what you want to hear?"

"That's exactly what I want to hear," Cam said, voice practically a purr, but when Nic tried to slide his hands higher, Cam stopped them. "First, though, I want to hear why you think we can't talk to Elton Moore about this."

He should have known Cam wouldn't let it go. Groaning, he tipped from the ottoman onto the opposite end of the couch. "I already told you."

Cam shifted to face him, bending a leg and planting a foot in the cushion, arm resting on his knee. "The real reason, Dominic."

"The first sniper, who had my picture, struck mid-operation. The car that hit me, mid-op. And the second sniper was waiting when we pulled into Gravity that night, after we left the Federal Building."

"Vaughn has someone on the inside," Cam said, tying it all together. "Someone who knows when and where we'll be."

"On our operations, no less."

"Perfect cover. We thought they were connected to the case at first."

Nic nodded. "Which is why the only people I trust at the Bureau right now are you, Aidan, and Lauren."

"It could also be someone in your office."

Cam's *someone* sounded a lot like Bowers to Nic's ears,

and given how far up their asses his boss had been on that case—how he'd been clued in to every one of those events where Vaughn had simultaneously struck—Bowers was at the top of Nic's suspect list too. "Oh, I know. It could be more than one person in both offices. Vaughn's spent a lifetime accruing favors and leverage."

"We'll get Lauren to run financials."

"I was going to do that, but then the threats quieted and I didn't want to tip Vaughn or his sources off."

"The threats died off because your dad mortgaged the house."

And they were back to that unfortunate turn of events. "Count on Curtis to make the wrong decision."

His father's history of wrong decisions was a major reason why Nic strived so hard to make the right ones, even if they were the opposite of what he wanted. Case in point, avoiding anything too serious, like cohabitation, with the man on the other end of the couch. If Nic had his way, he'd happily spend every day and night in this house with Cam, preferably in his bed.

But he never wanted to go the way of his father or repeat the mistakes of his own past. He'd thought he'd been making the right decision decades ago—the one his heart had demanded—but the ensuing mess had jeopardized more than one person's future. Until he'd made the right call and broken his heart in the process. Since then, Nic had kept dalliances casual, never wanting to hurt someone else by making the wrong decision.

Then Special Agent Cameron Byrne had walked into his life, and his heart had begun making demands again. If Nic made the wrong call, if he trusted the wrong person, or if he trusted his single-minded heart, both their lives could be in danger.

"I don't think it's the wrong decision to trust AD Moore," Cam said, as if he could hear his thoughts. "El's been nothing but upstanding since I transferred out here. Even after I stole from him." He waggled his eyebrows, and Nic appreciated his attempt to lighten the nosediving mood.

"Let's see what Lauren turns up. If he's clean, we'll consider it."

"I can live with that," Cam said with a satisfied smile.

That turned wicked on a dime.

Levering up, Cam knee-walked to Nic's end of the couch and threw a leg over his lap, straddling him. "Now, I need to know if there's something—someone—else you can live with?" With the both of them sans boxers under their sweats, Nic because he was out of clean clothes and Cam because he just liked going commando, the instant warmth of Cam's dick against his own through the thin cotton distracted Nic. For a second. Before the implication of Cam's words cut through the flare of lust.

He tried to scoot away, but Cam caged him in, hands braced on either side of his shoulders in the cushion behind him.

"Boston," he warned.

"Just for now, until you're cleared to move back into your unit. I need to know you're safe, and right now, you're safest here with me."

Nic's objection was on the tip of his tongue—that his presence here wasn't safe for Cam at all, a major reason he'd run in the first place—but then Cam rolled his hips and the fog of lust clouded his better sense again. "Playing dirty," he growled.

"I'll show you dirty." Cam lifted a hand out of the cushion, spit in his palm, and without any posturing or pretense, without foreplay or teasing, went straight for Nic's waistband and wrestled free his hardening cock.

Nic gasped, hips rocking forward. "Dirty's right."

It got dirtier when Cam yanked out his own cock and clasped them both in his spit-slick palm, hot and tight. He stroked and listed forward, forehead resting against Nic's.

Mouths close, Nic claimed the lips and tongue he'd been deprived full ravaging of earlier. Cam countered, fighting to lick every dark corner of Nic's mouth.

"Dirty and desperate," Cam breathed, the words puffed against Nic's lips.

Scorching to his ears. "A month with nothing but my own hand and dick, after four with this gorgeous one here." He twisted his hand on the down stroke, and the blaze burned hotter.

Unable to hold his head up any longer, Nic let it fall back on the couch cushions. He could hold something else up, though. He added his hand to Cam's around them, Cam's spit and their precome making it easy to stroke hard and fast. Judging by Cam's pitching hips and his teeth sinking into the tendon of Nic's neck, it was just the kind of dirty he had in mind.

"Missed you," escaped among the *fuck yeahs*, *fuck mes*, and *harders*. Nic was just as desperate, just as tired of solo jack-offs and contorting himself in showers. So unfulfilling when he had this waiting for him here at—

Nic yanked the wheel of his thoughts off that path, veering off-road instead, tumbling in sensation. Moaning, he threaded his fingers through Cam's hair and held that delectable mouth against his skin as he thrust up into their grip, harder and faster still.

Driving them to finish at record pace.

Apart for too long, the time to climax was too short, a desperate race to their finish. But the perfect dirtiness of their come splattering them together was the most fulfilled Nic had been in months.

He couldn't fathom this decision being wrong.

———

Cam was still sprawled across Nic, reveling in his favorite hard body back beneath him, when the rumbling under his ear shook him out of his haze.

Sitting up, he laughed as Nic half woke himself on another snore, struggling to lift his head and open his eyes.

"Sleepyhead," Cam teased as he yanked Nic's tee and then his own the rest of the way off and tossed them onto the floor. He dragged a hand through their come and spread it over Nic's tattooed torso on full display. Over the rainbow frog and trident, the SEAL mottos and emblems, his teammates' names, the kill count Nic worked so hard to atone for every day. Dirty and beautiful. The most beautiful man he'd ever known. "Maybe I shouldn't have kept you up so late."

Nic bounced his knees, toppling Cam back into him. "Worth it." They indulged in a lazy kiss that lasted until a cautious *meow* preceded an *oomph* at the other end of the couch. "Fuckin' Bird," Nic grumbled.

Chuckling, Cam pushed upright, waved the cat off, and wiped his messy hand on his sweats. "We should clean up."

"Times like these," Nic said, chin lolling on his chest, "I feel the ten-year age difference."

"Nine, at least until next month." Cam ruffled his hair, more gray mixed in with the brown. "See it too, old man."

Nic shot him a one-eyed death glare. "Watch it, Boston."

"Silver foxes are hot."

Nic tried to topple him forward again, but Cam clambered off him, slapping his hip. "All right, Counselor. Sleep."

Nic heaved to his feet, then bent, collecting the bowls Cam had set aside. "Let me help wash these. Won't have to do it in the morning."

Half asleep, Nic didn't think to clean himself first or to react to the domesticity of his own words, but Cam's insides blazed, stoked by the simple gestures. He didn't expect to have Nic here again so soon, and he wasn't going to pressure him into staying permanently if that wasn't what Nic wanted. Now, though, Cam had unexpectedly gotten what he wanted, at least temporarily. He only regretted that it had come by way of suspicious circumstances.

Picking up their T-shirts, Cam wiped himself down and followed Nic, stopping at the end of the granite-topped bar separating the kitchen and dining area. Nic stood in front of the corner sink, cleaning himself off with a hand towel. Cam admired the long, lean lines of the former soldier and the exquisite tattoo that spanned his back. Five months and Cam still didn't have an answer as to who *GS* might be either.

"You're staring," Nic mumbled, as if he had eyes in the back of his head. Or just a halfway decent pair of ears. He tossed the rag out the garage door to where the washer and dryer were and gave his ass a shake.

Cam's dick roused. "Don't tempt."

He shook his ass again, and Cam was halfway across the kitchen, dick leading the charge, when "Sweet Caroline" blared from his phone in the adjacent office.

That was the ringtone he'd assigned his family members back in Boston. He should hurry to answer it, before the call rolled to voicemail, but he was rooted to the spot, cinder blocks for feet. Why were they calling him in the middle of the night? Had something happened to one of his brothers? Keith was home on leave so less likely him. Bobby or Quinn? Or their wives or kids? His parents? Cam's stomach sank. Nothing good came from calls at this hour. He knew that well enough after ten years as an agent.

The ringer cut off abruptly. Maybe just a butt dial then. He blew out the breath he'd been holding.

Then sucked in another when Neil Diamond started crooning again.

Nic appeared in front of him, all trace of sleep gone. "That's your family's ringtone, correct?"

Cam nodded.

"They're three hours ahead," Nic said. "It's morning there." He rubbed his hands over the goose bumps that had risen on Cam's arms. "Don't jump to the worst-case scenario."

"Says the attorney."

Nic lifted a hand, cupping his cheek. "Do you want me to answer it?"

"No," he answered too quickly, causing Nic's brows to snap together. That was a situation he'd explain to Nic and his family later, if and when Cam won his argument about their future. Right now, he needed to deal with the present. He covered Nic's hand with his, lowering it. "I've got it but thank you."

And I've got you, said Nic's unrelenting grip.

In the office, Bobby's face lit up the phone screen. Cam yanked the device off the dual charger where it was plugged in next to Nic's and answered it just before it rolled over to voicemail again. "Hey, Bobby."

"Did I wake you?" His older brother's voice sounded rough, scraped over.

Cam's stomach plummeted. "No, I was up. Phone was just in another room. It's early there."

"And late there." Bobby cleared his throat. "Listen, need you to book a flight home. As soon as you can."

Cam squeezed Nic's hand harder. "Home? What's going on?" Nic drew closer, laying a hand on his back.

"It's Ma," Bobby choked out.

Cam swayed into Nic's body and would have dropped the phone if Nic hadn't covered his hand, helping hold it to his ear. "What happened?" Cam managed.

"I can't . . . Cam . . ."

Bobby's voice broke, and all Cam could do was shout "Bobby!" into the line, desperate to know more yet cut off while there was muffled shuffling on the other end of the line. "Somebody tell me what's going on!"

Nic's hand on his back circled his waist, pulling him back against his chest. "Give 'em a second, Boston." He was clearly close enough to hear what was going on and no doubt close enough to feel the shaking that had started in Cam's knees.

"Cameron, you there?" Quinn, his oldest brother, came

on the line, his voice likewise rough but steadier than Bobby's.

"Q," Cam said, making his fingers work again and clutching the phone tighter. "Please tell me what's going on." In his periphery, Nic, with his free hand, reached out and drew his phone off the dual charger, texting someone.

"Ma had a heart attack."

Off balance again, Cam gave more of his weight to Nic. "Is she okay?" he asked, voice a choked whisper.

"She's in ICU."

"What happened?"

"She woke up early feeling off," Quinn explained. "Told Dad she felt a bit nauseous. Maybe a bad cannoli." Cam wanted to laugh, it was totally something his mother would say, but all he felt was sick. "She went into the bathroom, and Dad heard a crash a minute later."

"Did she break anything?"

"Mercifully, no, but given her age and the severity of the attack, they're gonna have to do a bypass. Maybe multiple. The docs are worried about her throwing a clot and having a stroke."

Which could happen at any minute. Like had happened to their aunt Linda two years ago when she'd passed. His mother could be gone at any minute, and he was stuck out here in California, clear across the country.

A five-hour plane flight away.

Fuck!

The arms around him grew tighter, as if sensing the spiral, and Cam realized Quinn was calling his name again. "Cameron, did you hear me?"

"I'm sorry, hear what?"

"We're at Tufts Medical. You need to get here as soon as you can."

"I'm on my way." He lowered the phone from his ear, trying to hit End but his hand was shaking too badly to manage it. Same as his knees again. Fucking hell, he was an FBI agent. He'd seen worse.

Get it together!

But this was his mother.

Nic's hand closed over his, ending the call and trying to slip the phone free.

"No!" Cam snapped, fighting for the phone. "I need to book a flight." Never mind that his motor functions weren't a hundred percent right then.

Ignoring him, Nic tugged the phone free and tossed it onto the desk next to his, which was lighting up with texts. "You need to breathe, Boston." Both arms sliding around him, Nic held him closer and leaned them back against the doorframe. "I've got you. Just breathe with me."

He hadn't even realized he'd been on the cusp of hyperventilating until he forced himself to inhale and exhale with Nic, at a much slower, deliberate rate. Doing so, the adrenaline-ready tension ran out of him and the shaking knees would have taken him down if not for Nic's sure hold. "My mom . . ."

"The rest of the family is there with her," Nic said. "And you will be too."

But would it be soon enough?

FOUR

Nic swung into the same airport parking lot he'd left seven hours ago, barely getting his truck parked before Cam's hand went for the door handle. He put a hand on Cam's knee, urging him to wait. It was understandably the last thing Cam wanted. Cam would have been on the first flight out to Boston this morning if there'd been any seats left. Nic had been checking while Cam had talked to his brothers, and when all the flights had come up booked, he'd phoned a friend instead—Cam's best one, who'd want to know what was going on and who'd recently married a man with access to his family's company jet.

Seven-thirty was as soon as the Talley Enterprises jet could secure a takeoff, and it had been just enough time for them to shower and pack. And to repack. When it had become clear that Cam was throwing any and everything into his bag, including Bird, Nic had shooed him out of the bedroom with the cat and rearranged things in an orderly fashion.

It was the least Nic could do with Cam wavering

between locked down and a mess. He'd go from barely speaking, holding the words that scared him in check, to rapid-fire verbal vomit on the mundane and work-related. The security codes for the house, Bird's feeding routine, his open Bureau cases.

The twenty-minute drive to SFO had been worse, Cam muttering under his breath repeatedly, "Should've never left."

Cam reached for the door handle again, and Nic squeezed his knee. "Just wait. Aidan and Jamie aren't even here yet." He hoped it sounded more like an observation than the plea it was. He didn't want to make Cam feel guilty for leaving. He might have only been six at the time, but Nic remembered the pain of losing his mother. He could only imagine what the threat of losing one who'd been with Cam for thirty-six years was doing to him. But Nic selfishly wanted another minute or two alone with him. A seven-hour reunion, half that time lost to a fire, and now they were going to be separated again. "Are you sure I can't go with you? I'm not due back in the office until Monday, and I can—"

"Jamie's going with me," Cam said, gaze aimed out the passenger window.

That rankled, even though it rationally shouldn't. Jamie was Cam's best friend, he'd spent summers during college with Cam's family, and it was another month before his basketball coaching duties kicked into high gear. And he had ready access to the aforementioned jet.

Still, Nic wanted to be the one who was there for Cam. "I can—"

"No, Dominic." It was his pulling-rank voice. The one he trotted out whenever he sidelined Nic on an op for his protection. But that didn't make sense, nor did Cam's added, "I can't do that to them right now."

"Do what?" Expose them to Nic and the danger around him? Cam was the one who wanted to run toward that fire, which hadn't followed Nic to San Diego. It seemed contained to the Bay Area where Curtis could witness the destruction firsthand. Leverage worked better that way. Nic had no reason to think the danger would follow them to Boston.

Nic didn't have a chance to follow up, the roar of an engine and the peel of tires cutting through the heavy silence. Aidan's gleaming black Aston Martin tore into the parking lot faster than strictly necessary.

"They're here," Cam said, using the distraction to get the jump on Nic, finally thwarting his delay tactics and climbing out of the truck.

Nic banged the heel of his hand against the steering wheel, cursing himself for wasting the last few minutes arguing instead of kissing. Hustling out, he called after Cam, who, bag slung over his shoulder, was halfway to Jamie already. They met at the side of Aidan's car, Cam dropping his bag and Jamie yanking him into a crushing hug.

"It's gonna be okay," Jamie said, and Nic cursed himself again for not offering the same reassurances. He hadn't wanted to lie to Cam—he didn't with his witnesses either—but while that had served him well in the courtroom, he didn't like it one bit when it created more distance between him and Cam.

The slam of the trunk lid snapped Nic out of his thoughts and a rumpled Aidan appeared at his side, guiding Jamie's rolling suitcase. His husband was walking ahead with Cam, their arms slung over each other's shoulders. "Thanks for giving Cam a lift here," Aidan said.

"Thanks for giving him a lift there."

They passed through the terminal doors, and Aidan ran a hand through his disheveled auburn hair. "Jamie said you were there when Cam got the call."

"Apartment above mine flooded. Was crashing at Cam's."

A partial lie, and judging by Aidan's narrowed eyes, he wasn't buying it. Before he got the chance to investigate further, Jeremy met them inside the terminal. If Nic didn't know better, he wouldn't have guessed the impeccably put-together steward had come off the same flight as him a mere seven hours ago.

"Gentlemen," he greeted them. "I'd be happy to take your bags." Cam handed off his, and Aidan rolled over Jamie's.

"We'll be ready when you are," Jeremy said, efficient and polite, and correctly gauging the subdued mood. This was not an impromptu guys' weekend away.

"We're square on cases?" Cam said to Aidan.

"We had our status meeting yesterday. We're square. Go to your family."

"Thank you," Cam said, then exited out to the tarmac, seemingly in a fog.

As the newlyweds exchanged their almost-indecent goodbyes, Nic slid past them, following Cam outside. He spotted the Talley jet on the tarmac, Jeremy waiting by the steps. "Mr. Price, good to see you again."

"Likewise, Jeremy." He gestured up the stairs at the open cabin door. "I think I might have left something on the plane last night."

Jeremy held out his hand. "Go right ahead, sir."

He took the steps two at a time but ground to a halt inside the door. Across the cabin, Cam stood by the mini-bar, arms braced on the polished wood, torso heaving with deep, labored breaths. Nic glanced over his shoulder; Aidan and Jamie hadn't emerged from the terminal. Stealing a moment while he still had a chance, he crossed the cabin and wrapped his arms around Cam from behind.

Cam stiffened at first, but after another hitched breath, he relaxed into the hold, and Nic hugged him tighter, same as he'd done earlier. He nuzzled the nape of his neck, inhaling deep. "I wish you'd let me go with you," he whispered.

So I can make sure you come back.

Cam's "I do, too" was so quiet Nic barely heard it. But it landed like a kick to his chest.

"Then why—"

Cam rotated in his arms, silencing him with a quick, hard kiss. "Please wait until I get back to move on Vaughn."

Maybe he *was* worried about the mess Nic's family was in somehow reaching his in Boston. "Is that—"

"Your turn to be quiet and careful. I can't be there dealing with my family and worrying about you back here. Just wait to make any moves, please."

Nic nodded because at least Cam was talking about returning. "Okay, we won't move on Vaughn until you're back."

Cam lifted his hands, framing his face. "And think about telling Aidan, at least about the mole inside the Bureau. And go to Moore. I trust him."

"Shh, Boston." Nic laid his hands over Cam's. He was rambling again, worrying about him and Vaughn instead of what was truly terrifying him. "Don't worry about me," Nic reassured him, making up for the earlier lost opportunity as best he could. "I'll fly under the radar. I'll be safe. You worry about your family."

"You are—"

Using Cam's own moves against him, Nic kissed him quiet, silencing the demanding flutter of his own damn heart as well.

"Call me if you need me," Nic said. "I'll be on the first plane out. Or I'll phone a friend again if need be."

"Thank you for doing that." One corner of Cam's mouth hitched up, and it was the best thing Nic had seen since the call from Bobby. "Kind of nice having rich friends sometimes."

"They do come in handy."

Except for when they were traipsing up the stairs. Loudly.

As if in warning.

Nic stepped out of Cam's arms just as Jeremy came through the door, Aidan and Jamie on his heels. "Did you find what you left, Mr. Price?"

Behind Nic's back, Cam slipped his keys into his hand. Nic held them aloft, pretending they were his. "Got 'em."

The pilot poked his head into the cabin. "Report from the flight deck. We can be up in five if we taxi now."

"Go," Aidan said, giving Jamie a last kiss. "Love you, Whiskey."

Jamie slapped his ass as he turned toward the door. "Love you too, Irish."

"Anything," Nic said to Cam, "you call me."

"Be nice to Bird."

"I can't promise he won't answer to 'Joe' when you get back."

Cam's answering smile was worth every second he'd spend taking care of the furry beast.

"Later, Boston."

"Sooner, Price."

———

They'd been in flight an hour, and despite the plush leather seats, Cam hadn't been able to get comfortable for a single minute of it. Thoughts raced through his mind, and while he could normally harness that energy for good, today his thoughts kept slipping out of his grasp, spiraling.

He scrubbed at his face, the beard he hadn't had time to shave itchy.

Maybe a couple hours of sleep would help shut down his jumping thoughts. Jamie wouldn't mind, engrossed in whatever he was watching on his screen. He reached down to retrieve the pillow he'd tossed aside earlier and found a monochrome blue tie underneath it.

His favorite of Nic's, the one that perfectly matched his eyes.

Picking it up, he wove the cool silk around his hand, mentally contrasting it with the warm and sticky body he'd dragged his fingers over a few short hours ago. It had been a roller coaster of a night, or rather morning. Nic arriving home, the fire, their reunion at Cam's place, then the call from Bobby. Nic had steadied him in the wake of the unexpected blow, helped get him to the airport with the same focus and efficiency Cam depended on when they worked cases together. And now Cam was leaving him in the middle of a messy one, the shit with Vaughn still up in the air. He felt pulled in two different directions. Who would have Nic's back while he was in Boston?

He couldn't sleep until he knew Nic was safe too. Mel was already on Team Nic. Time to officially add more players. He pulled his phone out of his pocket and texted Lauren. **Need a favor.**

The text registered as Delivered but not Read yet. This time of morning, she was probably mid-commute to the office. He set the device on the armrest and went back to staring at the clouds, sleep a long-lost cause.

"You keep at it, you're going to tear a hole in Nic's tie."

Cam's gaze shot to the man across the aisle. Headphones off, Jamie was no longer focused on his laptop screen but on the piece of fabric clutched in Cam's hands. "It's not—"

"Well, I hope you're not mooning over one of my husband's ties. Or one of Danny's, assuming you value your life." Mel would probably end it if Cam's thoughts had ever strayed that direction. "And seeing as Nic was on this plane last night . . ."

Cam forced his fingers to uncurl from around the tie, smoothing it out on his lap. "I just needed something to do with my hands."

"Right." Jamie shut the laptop and set it aside. He ruffled his light brown hair and propped an elbow on the armrest, chin in his hand. "That why Nic was with you when Bobby called this morning? And don't give me that bogus apartment flooded excuse."

"It's not bogus." Nor was it the entire truth. Cam tossed the tie into the adjacent seat. "Why did I ever convince you to join the FBI?"

Jamie ignored the dig, too focused on his other line of inquiry. "Seriously, Cam, what's going on with you two?"

"This you trying to distract me?"

"In part. Now stop deflecting." He gave Cam the fess-up look, the same one he was used to getting from his real brothers.

As much as Cam wanted to tell his friend that he was falling in love with one of the best men they knew, he didn't want to have that conversation without getting Nic's okay. They'd agreed to keep things quiet while they were "building something." Past complications and present uncertainties had made them both cautious. Construction, however, had been halted while Nic was in San Diego. Last night, they'd started swinging hammers again, but once Nic learned the real reason Cam hadn't wanted him to come to Boston, would he take away his tools and renewed affection, leaving the project forever unfinished?

"We got close on the Kristić case," Cam hedged. Not a deflection but not the whole truth either.

Jamie called him on it immediately. "Close?"

"He's a good friend."

"Cameron."

"Jameson."

The big man chuckled, rolling his bright blue eyes. He turned serious a second later, dropping his arm and leaning forward. "I know this is going to sound horribly egotistical, and feel free to tell me to shut up—"

"Shut up," Cam said with a smirk.

Jamie shot him the middle finger. "But if this is about my past dustup with Nic over Aidan, don't let it be."

Cam tilted his head, encouraging Jamie to continue. This

particular air needed to be cleared, be it now or in the future Cam still hoped for with Nic.

"That's ancient history," Jamie said. "And it was Aidan's fault, not Nic's. I've made my peace with that." He glanced down, rubbing his thumb over the emeralds in his platinum wedding band. "I made my peace with Nic too at the wedding. Hell, I even helped upgrade the security at Gravity. From everything I've seen, he's a good man."

"He is." Cam knew that down to his bones. Nic was a better man than he let on or gave himself credit for. Striving to atone for the sniper's kill count inked on his skin, taking a special interest in abuse and exploitation cases, holding himself back from Cam for fear of making their friends uncomfortable. And for fear of repeating whatever mistake the cypress tree and *GS* on his back represented.

Cam's buzzing phone saved him from saying more than he should.

"Bobby?" Jamie asked.

Cam shook his head. "Lauren."

Anything, her reply text read.

"Everything okay?" Jamie said.

"Case we're working on." Not exactly but that was more than Jamie needed to know. "Just making sure she's set."

Another text popped up. **Aidan told me about your mom. Hope she pulls through.**

Thank you.

Favor?

Nic knows we know about DV. Work with him, he texted. **And call in Mel if you need backup. She's been helping him.**

She replied with the thumbs-up emoji.

Cam, however, needed to be sure she understood the

gravity of the situation and the full scope of his ask. **I need you to have his back, Lauren.**

On it.

That's what he wanted to hear.

And then because she was Lauren . . . **Well, not on it, on it. That's more your job**, she added with a winky-face.

Cam laughed for the first time in hours.

FIVE

Cam's nieces and nephews were waiting for him at the hospital doors, charging him with shouts of "Uncle Cam!" For a few blissful seconds, Cam forgot the frustrating hours it had taken to get here, forgot that he'd been a continent away when his family needed him, and just reveled in having his family in his arms again. The reunions continued upstairs in ICU, Quinn and Bobby greeting them in the hallway with back-slapping hugs.

"Was hoping you'd show up with a girlfriend," Quinn said to him.

"Hey!" Jamie mock protested. "What am I, chopped liver?"

"We knew you'd be here," Bobby said. "You're family."

Cam wondered if his brothers would say the same about Nic eventually.

Once they got over the shock of him bringing home a man. As far as they knew, he was straight. He hadn't told his family he was bisexual. He'd only dated girls in grade school, and he'd kept his college conquests contained to campus, not bringing anyone home. He'd let the years pass without correcting his family's assumptions. It had never seemed like the right time, and now definitely wasn't it. That's why he'd turned down Nic's offer to accompany him. If Cam had had what he really wanted, it would be Nic by his side, hand on his back, keeping him steady like he'd done early this morning. Meeting his family, especially—

"Where's Keith?"

"In with Mom and Dad," Bobby said, leading them into a nearby lounge. "He's due back at base tomorrow. Supposed to ship out sometime next week."

His younger brother was an active-duty Marine stationed at Lejeune, though he'd spent more days deployed than on base during his service so far. "Can he get his leave extended?"

"Tried," Quinn answered. "Not looking good."

Unless you knew someone with juice. Like a former SEAL sniper, JAG Corps captain, and federal prosecutor. Granted Nic was Navy, but USMC technically fell under the Navy's umbrella. He bet Nic knew some higher-ups there too. "I've got a friend with connections."

Phone in hand, Jamie, following his train of thought, was already heading back into the hall. "I'll call Price."

"The former special forces prosecutor?" Bobby said.

Cam nodded. He'd mentioned Nic to Bobby when he'd called his brother for a gut check on last spring's under-cover assignment. That case had required him to tap into the less-than-legal past he and Bobby had shared and worked so hard to put behind them. They'd lost their sister because of it, Cam and Bobby out on a job the day Erin went missing while walking home alone from the library.

She'd been presumed dead for two decades now, but the wound they'd inflicted on their family had never fully healed, especially Keith's. He and Erin had been born only nine months apart, five years after Cam.

Behind the rest of them in age, Keith had latched on to his mother after losing Erin. Cam didn't want to think what losing her would do to him.

"How's Mom?" Cam asked.

"In and out," Bobby said.

Cam's heart soared, buoyed by the first bit of hopeful news in hours. "She's been awake?"

"Wouldn't miss an opportunity to remind Dad to take his meds," Bobby said.

"Or tell me how to run our fishing boats," Quinn added. "Like I haven't already been doing that since Dad retired."

That sounded even better. His mom was awake and aware enough to nag. "Don't get too excited yet," Bobby cautioned, motioning him to sit.

He filled him in on their mother's status, bringing Cam back down to reality. She was conscious and stabilized but it was a temporary reprieve. She was being scheduled for surgery—no, surgeries, plural—starting with a double bypass. Cam propped his elbows on his knees, spinning head held in his hands. There would be risk at every step of the way, keeping them on pins and needles for at least the next week, then after, during her recovery.

When he'd be back on the opposite coast.

Fuck.

"She's awake now."

Cam dropped his arms and looked up, meeting his youngest brother's blue eyes across the table. He was struck by how similar Keith's bearing was to Nic's, but that was the only thing the two military men had in common. Just under six feet, Keith had a bruiser build like Cam's, like their mother's, and at thirty-one, he still had his fresh face and headful of dark hair.

"She's asking for you," he said, voice clipped, bubbling with the low-level resentment that had taken root the day Erin disappeared. Since the big brother he'd worshipped had let him down and cost him his sister and best friend.

They'd never been close again.

Didn't mean he didn't want to have his little brother safe and sound in his arms again, especially when Keith regularly put his life on the line. Cam stood and drew him into a hug. "I'm glad you're here."

Awkward as it was, Cam didn't hold the embrace for long, but then Keith clasped his upper arm, keeping him close. "Don't do what she asks," he whispered. "This family has been through enough."

This family, spoken like Cam wasn't a part of it.

He was still trying to digest the words, his stomach tossing and turning, when he nearly ran into Jamie in the hallway.

"He's right here." Jamie held his phone out to him.

"I'll get your brother's leave extended," Nic said, no greeting and no hesitation. Just getting things done for him.

Cam's rioting insides calmed a little. "Thank you."

"I wish you'd let me do more."

Cam angled away from Jamie, hiding his blush at Nic's softly spoken words. "You got any Gravity distributors out here?"

Nic's deep laugh warmed his insides, soothing him more. "I'll check my list."

"Seriously, Dominic, doing this for Keith will go further

than you know." If Cam could take the threat of imminent deployment off Keith's shoulders, then he'd feel like he was at least here for his brother now, like he hadn't been before.

"I'll get right on it."

"Thank you."

"Jamie said you're at the hospital."

"Yeah." He raked a hand through his hair, pacing the area to the side of the elevators. "Getting ready to go up and see Ma."

"Call me later. Let me know how she's doing."

"Will do."

"Boston," he said, voice brooking no argument. "Call me."

Cam felt the urge to salute, which he hadn't done since his Bureau swearing-in ceremony. "I will. Now go."

He hung up and handed the phone back to Jamie. They were outside his mother's room when his own phone buzzed with an incoming text. Reading it, he couldn't help but smile. True to his word, Nic had sent him a list of Gravity distributors in the Boston area. His uplifted mood, however, was short-lived, disappearing as he entered his mother's room.

Edith Byrne was a fisherman's wife and mother of five, a stout Southie who took no shit off anyone, especially her husband and sons. She was loving, she was tough, she commanded any room she walked into, and she was the high standard Cam held anyone he'd dated up to. She'd been the glue that had held their family together after Erin disappeared. Her only daughter gone, presumed dead, she'd saved her husband from the bottle he'd almost drowned in and wrestled all her sons onto the right path. Seeing that woman, his mother, laid up in a hospital bed looking frail and helpless, hooked up by wires and IVs to a dozen monitors and machines, was going to haunt Cam's nightmares forever.

His dad rose from the chair next to her bed. His salt-and-pepper hair was mussed, his Sox polo wrinkled, and his blue eyes were bloodshot and red-rimmed. He was the picture of misery. Cam hadn't seen him like this in twenty years.

"Cameron," he said, hauling him into a firm embrace.

"Hey, Dad."

"Missed you, son."

Lump stuck in his throat, Cam couldn't make the words come out, so he held on tighter. Fuck, he'd missed them more than he'd realized.

"Kenneth," Jamie said, laying a hand on the older man's shoulder.

"Jameson." Ken shifted his attention and hugs to Jamie. "It's good to see you too. Thanks for coming out with Cam."

"Nowhere else I'd rather be."

"Always such a good boy," Edye said from the bed.

She held out a shaking hand and Cam clasped it between both of his. "He's married now, Ma. He's never going to run away with you."

His mom was also an incorrigible flirt, though there was no question her heart belonged one hundred percent to her husband and kids. Cam still liked to tease, especially since she'd been a little starstruck by the too-handsome Whiskey Walker.

The hand on her stomach turned over and she flipped him the bird. But the way her one finger wobbled belied the thin veil of humor and normalcy that had settled over them.

"How you doing, Edye?" Jamie bent over and pecked her cheek.

"Better now," she said with a wink.

Jamie glanced over his shoulder at Cam. "You do come by it honest." He smiled, likewise trying to lighten the mood, but Cam knew Jamie well enough to see how forced it was. How much he was hurting too at seeing his second mother like this.

"I'd be doing better," Edye said, "if you'd take my husband downstairs so he can eat and take his meds."

"Now, Edye," his father said.

"Now, Ken," she returned.

His father, like the rest of them, knew better than to argue.

Cam waited for them to step out before dragging the chair closer to the bed. His mother tried to push herself upright, and Cam patted her arm over the wires and IVs. "Nuh-uh-uh." He fished out the bed controls from where they'd slipped between the mattress and bedrail. "You have a button for that."

She glared with eyes the same dark shade as his and reluctantly took the controls, adjusting her position. "You look tired."

Always looking out for everyone else, never for herself. "Was helping a friend move last night."

She swiped at her gray bangs. "She pretty?"

Cam bit back a laugh. No one would ever describe Nic as pretty. Ruggedly handsome, yes. But pretty? Never, not with cheekbones cut like glass, eyes like ice, and lips just this side of thin, which, when pressed together, made him look like he was deciding your fate. In many cases, he was. Pretty didn't even describe him when dressed in that light gray suit Cam loved so much or when covered in come.

"Sharp, intense, older," he answered instead.

"Good," Edye said with a nod. "Will keep you in line."

He did chuckle at that, and so did she, until her laugh got caught in a cough, her heart monitor skipped, and Cam panicked, reminded that this wasn't his usual healthy, firecracker mother. She'd had a heart attack, and she had the fight of her life ahead.

"Mom," he started, his voice cracking.

She cut him off, reaching out a shaking arm toward the bedside table. "Hand me, please."

On the table were a few of his dad's things—glasses, watch, and keys—together with his mom's reading glasses and one of her books. He slid the paperback off the table, turned it over, and smiled. He remembered this series—the ones with Scottish tartans and brooches on the covers. They were her favorites, the spines so cracked you could barely read them on the shelf.

She'd read them dozens of times, to herself and aloud to her kids, to the point Cam could still remember the engaging, sweeping tales of love and family.

"You want me to read to you?" he asked.

"I'm not blind," she griped.

"Glasses then?"

She shook her head and held out her hand. Cam passed the book to her, and she opened it, shaking loose a laminated library card.

A duplicate of Erin's that she'd had made from the original in Cam's wallet.

Edye used her copy as a bookmark, always there to remind her of her daughter, who was likewise a ravenous reader. In Cam's wallet, the card served to remind him of the place he should have been then and the rules he lived by now so as not to make any life-shattering mistakes again.

"Solve it," his mother said, snapping him out of his thoughts.

He didn't have to ask what she was referring to. It was the reason he'd decided to join the FBI. But the unsolved case of Erin's disappearance was cold for a reason. He'd been unsuccessful, like every other detective or investigator who'd touched the file over the past twenty years. "I've tried."

"Need to know," she said, increasingly winded. She set the book in her lap and laid the card over her heart, tapping it. "No time."

He laid his own hand over his mother's, struggling for words. "We don't know that. The doctors—"

"No time." She closed her eyes and a tear slid down her cheek. "Need to know if she'll be there waiting for me."

Cam's head swam as his heart drowned. He had to lay his head on the bed and make himself breathe. His mother's fingers carded through his hair, coaxing and calming. "Please, Cameron."

Dragging in a breath and sucking back his own threatening tears, he righted himself and squeezed his mom's hand. "I've tried. My entire career." She was the last person he ever wanted to disappoint again but he'd hit a brick wall on Erin's case, time and again.

She flipped the book to the last page and held it out to him. Taking it, he was surprised to find the normally blank couple of pages at the back filled with his mother's meticulous handwriting.

Dates, locations, and details.

He looked back up at his mother. "Are these case notes? When did you start this?"

"The past year, after you left. Kept you both close." She tapped the side of her head. "Kept this going too."

Something else he came by honest.

He stared at the scribbled-on pages, running his fingertips over the amateur sleuthing his brilliant mother had been doing.

She covered his hand, stopping its movement. "Need to know."

He couldn't disappoint her. Especially if this turned out to be the last thing she asked of him. Not when he'd failed her before.

"Are there more books with notes?" he asked.

"That series." The words were thin, a battle to get out. "Started rereading. By the bed at home."

He clutched the book in one hand, her hand in his other. "I'll try."

She squeezed, a fraction of her normal strength. "Hurry."

SIX

Nic sat at his brewery office desk, phone jammed between his shoulder and ear, reviewing the details of the proposed new brew Eddie had left for him as on-hold jazz competed with live punk rock for headache-inducing dominance. Weekend nights at Gravity were open to the public, and they did it up right with bands and food trucks to bring in more customers and keep the mood lively. This time of year, when the days were long and warm, they were packed, patrons filling the event space, tasting bar, and picnic-ready back lot. As a result, they were running through their stock faster than expected, which meant his co-owner and former SEAL teammate was busily brewing. All good problems to have, minus the headache.

The hold music stopped, then after a click, "Captain Price?"

He juggled the phone from shoulder to hand. "Here, Lieutenant."

"Apologies for the wait."

"Not a problem." It had been five minutes, which was shorter than he'd expected, considering the day and time.

"Sergeant Byrne's leave has been extended until the end of the month."

"Thank you," he said, breathing a sigh of relief. "And please give my thanks to the admiral."

"He says to thank him in person at his retirement party."

There was a smile in her voice, and if there had been anyone there in the office with Nic, they'd see the smile on his face too. Sounded just like Admiral Bailey. And like an event not to be missed even though Nic usually avoided those sorts of things. "I'd be honored."

"Invitation's in the mail," she confirmed.

"Lieutenant, one more thing."

"Yes, sir?"

"I've had some *Unknown* calls from a burner that trace back to Jacksonville. I'm concerned it might be a former teammate trying to reach out." For good or evil, he still wasn't sure about the calls, but either way, this was an opening to learn more about them.

"Send me the details," she said. "I'll have someone at Lejeune check it out."

"Thank you, Lieutenant."

"Have a good night, Captain."

She hung up and Nic set the phone down, marveling at the efficiency of it all. He missed that sometimes in civilian life. He glanced down again at the papers, and when the chemical formulas swam before his eyes, he called it a night. Stuffing them back in their folder, he stood and crossed to the Beers of the World map on his office wall, swinging it open to reveal the in-wall safe behind it. He entered the code, popped open the door, and set the folder on the shelf with the other brew formulas. The call with naval admin still on his mind, he withdrew from the lower shelf the zipped leather pouch with the US Navy crest embossed on the front. It was worn, scratched, and far from the fancy display case in Eddie's office, but it was just as special. It had arrived anonymously shortly after his commissioning, and he'd carried it throughout his service. He didn't know who it was from—maybe his estranged father given that he'd recently learned Curtis had been keeping tabs on him—but he did know his service medals and ribbons felt at home inside it. This was where they belonged, safe and sound and only taken out on the rare occasion Nic wore his dress blues, which he'd have to do for the admiral's retirement ceremony.

It was the least Nic could do for the man who'd rescued him from the second-lowest point of his life. Injured on a SEAL Team mission seven years into his service, he'd been knocked out of combat duty short of a full term and short of a completed college degree, which he had been slowly accumulating remote credits for. Laid up in the Naval Medical Center, he'd been out of his mind with worry and fear that he was going to have to take a medical discharge and go home. Except he didn't have one after being disowned by his father for being gay. He'd enlisted the day after his high school graduation, never intending to go home again.

As it'd turned out, his SEAL Team XO had gone to Officer Candidate School with then-Captain Bailey of the Navy JAG Corps. Nic had driven his XO nuts with his tendency to argue, something he hadn't stopped doing since the day he'd stood up to his father. He'd saved two lives that day, lost his first love, grown a backbone, and gotten a fist to the face from his father. No argument could end as badly as that one had. So he hadn't stopped arguing, and he'd been good enough at it to earn a recommendation to the JAG Corps even without his college or law degree yet.

Bailey had flown out to San Diego and offered him a way to stay in the service, finish his education, and argue for a living, for the Navy and beyond.

In that "beyond," Nic had seen the path of atonement he'd needed for the sins he'd committed before and during his service. So yeah, he could schlep across the country and put on his dress blues and ribbons for the soldier who'd saved him. And who'd just pulled some strings with the Marine Corps to help Cam's brother.

Nic snapped the tote closed, zipped it, and secured it back in the safe.

Returning to his desk, he picked up the phone and texted Cam. **Keith's leave is extended until the end of the month.**

As tired as Nic was, and as late as it was, he didn't expect a response from Cam, who was three hours ahead and had to be even more wiped than him, but his phone vibrated in his hand before he put it back down. **Thank you**, read the text from Cam.

Nic was tempted to call—he wanted to hear Cam's voice —but what kind of day had it been for him? Where was he? And what right did Nic have to take precious family time away from him, especially when Nic had been the one to take himself away for the past five weeks. **How's your mom?** he texted instead.

I'll call tomorrow.

That didn't sound good. He started to type back but bubbles appeared, indicating Cam was typing, so he waited.

I'd call now, but . . . After a second, a picture popped up. Cam, wearing a Captain America T-shirt, was on what looked like a sofa bed surrounded by sleeping children in superhero pajamas.

Whereas Nic wasn't a kid person, Cam was great with them. He effortlessly interacted with Aidan and Jamie's nieces and nephews, and there was no denying he looked happy to be where he was, despite the bed being several feet too short.

There are these things called hotels, Boston.

I'll check in tomorrow, Cam replied. **Wanted to spend tonight with family.**

Fuck, he'd said the complete wrong thing even if it had been in jest. How was he so good with witnesses and so dysfunctional when it came to personal relationships? **Sorry, I shouldn't have suggested—**

It's fine, Dominic.

He circled the desk and collapsed in his chair. He should let Cam go, but he didn't want to lose the connection yet. **How are you?**

Better now. He sent a smiley face, then added, **Have a pint of Pils for me.** Gravity's pilsner was Nic's favorite, the stout Cam's.

Redwood Stout is back next month. Imperial in December.

Thank fuck. Can't wait.

Nic took comfort in Cam's implication that he'd be back. Would that still be the case tomorrow? He hoped so.

Okay, can barely hold my eyes open here, Cam texted.

Nic needed to let him go, at least for now. **Night, Boston**.

Another picture popped up, of a groggy Cam with his lips puckered in a kiss. **Night, baby.**

The ache in Nic's chest stole his breath. The picture, the words, everything he wanted, everything he lo—

No, he couldn't think that word. Not if it added Cam to Vaughn's hit list and not if there was a chance he wouldn't get to act on it. Cam had looked so comfortable in that puppy pile with his family. What did Nic have to offer him besides death threats and fear of commitment?

As if on cue, his assistant manager knocked on his office door. "Hey boss," she said, poking her head in. "Those two guys you told us to be on the lookout for are here."

Shit.

Rising, he considered getting his Beretta out of the safe but then dismissed the idea just as quickly. It was packed out there with adults and children. Not a situation for a firearm. Even trained as a sharpshooter, he could miss, or worse—and more likely—the goons could miss, and innocent lives would be lost. That wasn't something he was willing to risk, not now that he was a civilian and had a choice. Besides, these two had come at him before and he'd taken them down. He could do it again. Would enjoy doing so. Maybe it would relieve some of the tension that had only waned when he was in Cam's arms.

Following Ang into the event area, he easily spotted the two goons at the tasting bar. Shiny suits, trainer-honed physiques, and three-figure haircuts. Their displays of wealth were a poorly worn facade. There was nothing fake, however, about the wealth and power rolling off the man standing between them. Nic halted in his tracks, mouth going dry and skin prickling with remembered desert heat, his learned responses to danger. What he'd said to Cam once about image not matching reality here in Silicon Valley held true. No better example than the polished and poised man at the bar.

With a headful of blond hair and a trim runner's build poured into bespoke jeans and a fitted linen dress shirt, the man looked like a menswear model.

One closer to Nic's age than to his father's. The man rotated half around, peering over his shoulder at Nic, and the sparkling smile and warm brown eyes only added to the effect. He looked like a fit dot-com millionaire who was out cruising for a date.

He did not look like a gangster.

But Duncan Vaughn was exactly that, so Nic approached with caution, weaving through the crowd and considering with each step what he needed to get Vaughn to say for his case. He patted his pocket for his phone, intending to turn on the recorder, then cursed himself for leaving it on his desk. He couldn't turn back now without it being obvious. That said, even if the conversation wasn't on the record, Nic could try to extract the leads he needed.

When Nic came face-to-face with Vaughn and his goons, he stood at attention, feet shoulder width apart, hands clasped behind his back. He puffed out his chest and eyed the goons with open hostility. "Thought I made it clear you two aren't welcome here."

"You made your point perfectly clear," Vaughn said. "Rather spectacularly." He smiled, wide and easy. It was one of the most photogenic grins Nic had ever seen, second only to Jamie's. "I had a mind to recruit you, Dom."

Good thing he'd left his weapon in the safe. Nic might

have pulled it right then. As it was, he balled his fists and gritted his teeth. "It's Nic, and I'll never work for you."

Vaughn stepped closer, lowering his voice to a conspiratorial whisper. "I didn't necessarily mean work, Dom."

Nic fought to control his surprise. In every press picture Nic had ever seen of Duncan Vaughn and at every event or function where they'd both been in attendance, Vaughn had always had a beautiful woman on his arm. Pictures, Nic knew well enough, could lie or omit. Apparently, there'd been a pretty big omission when it came to Duncan Vaughn if Nic had read that leer right. He was equal parts revolted at being the unexpected target of the man's interest and intrigued by the potential in to Vaughn's circle. He had to tread carefully. Let Vaughn continue to direct this conversation while he picked up more leads.

"So what stopped you?" Nic asked.

"Your father convinced me to give you some space."

"The mortgage on the house."

Vaughn smiled wider, and Nic fought another wave of surprise. He'd thought Curtis had taken out that mortgage to save his own ass, not Nic's.

"Why are you here, Vaughn?"

"Your father's falling behind again."

"Because you've taken everything."

Vaughn pointedly looked around the tasting room. "Not everything."

Nic dug his nails into his palms, forcing himself not to lash out. He kept his cool every day at work and in the courtroom, had learned to do so in the military. He could do it here. "I told them, and I'll tell you, Curtis didn't give me a dime for this place. And if you think to try to pull something here, good luck getting past the security."

"I'm sure Ms. Cruz and Mr. Walker did their finest work."

A good guess, Nic's association with both was known, or someone had been spying. Perhaps Duncan's inside source at the USAO or FBI. Nic's thoughts were derailed when Duncan produced a Zippo lighter, flicking it open and closed. "I'm already in here now. Wonder what would happen if I threw this into the back bar."

He rolled the spark wheel, and a flame blazed to life.

Nic snatched the lighter out of Vaughn's hand. Worth the burn.

And worth whatever force Vaughn's goons brought against him, the both of them lunging forward.

Vaughn spread his arms, blocking their advance. Calm, as if his little threat and flurry of action had never occurred. But it was more than enough for Nic to cut this parlay short, no matter what leads he'd hoped to get out of this. He just wanted the gangster out of his fucking brewery. "What do you want?" he demanded.

"What your father took from me."

"And what was that?"

He smiled again, only this time the flirtatious invitation was gone, replaced by one hundred percent shark. "Everything."

SEVEN

"Fourteen total?" Jamie shouted up the stairs.

"Fifteen." Cam rounded the corner from his mother's bedroom, last book in hand. "Thank fuck it was one of the shorter series."

Jamie stared at the stack of books at his feet. "Shorter?"

Chuckling, Cam loped down the stairs, meeting him in the foyer by the front door. "There's one up there in her boxes that's fifty plus."

"When we were younger, she always had a book in her hand."

"We couldn't afford cable and rabbit ears didn't always work, so these"—he set the last book on top of the stack—"were her—*our*—soap operas. She'd read them aloud to us."

Jamie glanced back up at him, worry in his too-blue eyes. "Are you sure you want to do this? Open up these wounds?"

"I opened these wounds four months ago." When he'd gone undercover on a case, exercising the breaking and entering skills he'd learned as a teen working with Bobby, first at a chop shop and then for the criminal enterprise operating out of it.

"That was just you," Jamie said. "This is your whole family."

"For once, pretty boy is right," Keith interjected, stalking in from the kitchen. "You really gonna put us all through this again?"

"She begged me."

"I know what she asked. She told me to let you."

"Keith . . ." Cam took a step toward him, then stopped when his brother held up a hand between them.

"I was eleven when we buried our sister's empty casket. None of us need you bringing that up again just to appease your guilty conscience."

Cam stumbled back. Keith wasn't saying anything he hadn't thought himself, but to hear it out loud and with so much hurt in his brother's voice . . .

"You sure about that?" Jamie said.

Keith shot him an angry glare, snarling. "You stay out of this."

And Cam shot forward again. "Don't you dare talk to him that way. He's as much a part of this family as the rest of us."

"But he's not. Why's he even here?"

"Because I need all my brothers with me." Cam jabbed Keith's chest with his index finger. "Including you."

Keith's eyes widened. "You made the extended leave happen?"

Cam removed his finger from Keith's chest and waved it between him and Jamie. "*We* made that extended leave happen."

"Then please, brother"—he clasped Cam's shoulder and the anger in his blue eyes morphed into pleading—"don't make me spend my extra time here remembering the worst thing that's ever happened to me and this family."

Cam couldn't hold his stare. He had to look away for the prickling at the corners of his eyes.

Keith squeezed his shoulder with a whispered "Please," then turned on his heel and left out the back, the screen door off the kitchen banging shut.

"He's got a point," Jamie said, and Cam swung his gaze back around. "We have to hope for the best and prepare for the worst. In either case, do you want to spend that time investigating Erin's disappearance? What good will it do?"

Cam scrubbed his hands over his face and plowed them into his hair, pulling at the strands. "She needs to know, Jamie. We all do."

"*If* you can solve it."

Cam blew out a shaky, uncertain breath and let his arms drop to his sides. "I have to."

———

With both assistant managers on at Gravity tonight, Nic took off early, hoping to catch up on sleep before he started back at his old office tomorrow. Arriving at Cam's place, he fought with the front door lock for a good minute before finally getting the sticking thing to turn. Inside, a fluffy ball of orange streaked across the living room, dashing into the dark hallway.

"Oh, come on, Joe." He closed the door behind him and flipped on lights as he crossed the room. "You know you like my company."

Hands braced on either side of the hallway pocket door, he looked left and right. No sign of him. Shaking his head, he tossed his wallet and spare change on the media cabinet and double-tapped the whole home light switch by the kitchen, turning on every light in the house. See how the damn cat liked that.

"Get in here, Joe!" He rinsed out the food bowl he'd left in the kitchen sink and grabbed a can of wet food out of the pantry. "Giving you the good stuff for dinner."

He'd just popped the lid when his phone vibrated in his pocket. He set the can aside and pulled out his phone, smiling at Cam's face filling the screen. "Boston," he answered, "your cat won't come when called."

A deep chuckle sent heat rolling through Nic's body. "What name are you calling him?" Cam asked, accent thicker than yesterday.

Wanting to hear more of the smile in his voice, Nic tapped the can on the counter and shouted, "Here, Joe."

A fuzzy orange-and-white face with big green eyes peered around the hallway door. *Meow.*

Nic dumped the gravy-like contents of the can into the bowl, and Bird slinked toward the kitchen. "Yeah, that's right, Joe. You want this."

"You're gonna ruin my fucking cat."

"Nah, I'm just teaching him a better way."

More of that smile and laughter. Nic counted it a win. Crouching, he pushed the bowl under Bird's twitching nose and scratched behind the cat's ears. On the other end of the line, Cam's laughter subsided and Nic heard foghorns in the background. "You down by the water?"

"Taking a walk before I head to the hospital for the night shift."

"How's she doing?"

"Better today than yesterday, but tomorrow's the first surgery. Bypass. She's got risk factors for blood clots and stroke. Docs are worried."

"How's your dad handling everything?"

"Worried sick and regretting every minute he didn't spend with her before he handed over the reins to Quinn." It didn't sound like Cam was only speaking about his father. The earlier wave of warmth inside Nic broke, cooling as it fizzled out. "Thank you for getting Keith some extra time."

"It was the least I could do. Is there anything else I can do?"

Cam was silent and the receding wave chilled to ice in Nic's veins, a glacier leaving destruction in its wake. Done with his food, Bird jumped up on the counter and nudged his fingers, as if he could sense Nic's distress.

Maybe also that of his owner on the other end of the line.

"Cam, tell me," he ventured. "I know something's bothering—"

"Mom wants me to solve Erin's disappearance, in case she dies."

Nic jerked in surprise, startling Bird. "Christ, Boston."

"Sorry, that was blunt, but I'm tired of checking every word, and I can't . . ."

"No, hey, I wasn't cursing at you but for you."

"No one wants me to do it, especially Keith, but she begged me, Nic, and I promised."

He was starting to ramble like he had Saturday morning. This was tearing him apart already and it was only going to shred him further, no matter the result. Cam had to know that. Nic wished he was there to step behind him, to lay a hand on his back or wrap his arms around him. To ease his breaths if not his burdens. The best he could do three thousand miles away was try to talk—or argue—it through with him.

"Will you feel better if you solve it?"

Cam let out a big sigh, and Nic took that as a good sign, some of the tension escaping. "I think we all will. Just hurts like hell dredging it up again."

"But it's never really been buried, has it? It's always been there just beneath the surface."

Nic knew something about that himself, a phantom tingle racing up his spine, climbing the trunk of the giant cypress and spreading out to the tips of its branches. A reminder of the biggest mess he'd ever made, inked on the surface of his skin, the memories buried beneath it never far from his heart and mind.

"No, it hasn't," Cam said, bringing Nic's attention back.

"Keep your promise, for all your sakes."

Cam's family, unlike his, would be better for the truth, whatever it might turn out to be. No one's life would be lost uncovering it.

"If you need my help," Nic added, "I'll be there."

"Just talking has been more help than you could imagine." Voice softer, the ice melted before it reached Nic's chest, letting loose a cascade of warmth instead.

"Boston . . ."

Cam cleared his throat and sniffled. "Listen, I gotta go."

"All right, keep me posted."

Nic hit End and at once felt adrift. He was in Cam's house, caring for his cat, wondering if he was coming back, hoping their paths would eventually cross in the same place, and, most of all, cursing himself for wasting five weeks in San Diego.

"I am not the brightest," he confessed to Bird, scratching again behind his ears. The big cat's purrs almost muffled the jiggle of the front door lock.

Almost.

The sticking lock gave Nic enough time to grab Bird by the scruff, duck behind the kitchen corner, and draw his sidearm. The door gave way, and in its wake followed a string of Gaelic curses. Nic came out from around the corner. "Fucking hell, Talley."

Aidan took one look at him and doubled over, cackling.

"What's so fucking funny?"

Tearing up he was laughing so hard, Aidan left one hand braced on his knee and pointed at Nic with the other. "You, the cat, the gun. Funniest fucking sight ever."

"Fuck you and close the fucking door." He waited for Aidan to do so before putting the hissing cat down and holstering his weapon. "I was protecting Joe in case there was a firefight."

Aidan wiped his eyes, snickering still. "I thought the cat's name was Bird."

"I refuse—"

"Wait, why would there have been a firefight? And are you still staying here?"

Not wanting to get into either of those conversations, he avoided both questions, hands on his hips. "Why are you here?"

"We didn't know if you'd be here, so Jamie sent me to feed Bird." He matched Nic's stance, squaring off with him mid-living room. "Answer the question."

Fucking lawyer. Combined with FBI credentials, he was

relentless. Nic could still probably out-lawyer him, but at this time of night, after a too-long weekend already, he just wanted Aidan to leave. He turned back to the kitchen, collecting Bird's bowl and taking it to the sink.

"Nothing you need to be concerned about."

"Same thing I didn't need to be concerned about last spring?"

Aidan had previously learned about the first sniper attack. He didn't, however, know about the other threats Vaughn had leveled.

Setting the washed bowl aside, Nic turned and leaned back against the counter, fingers curled around the lip. "I'm handling it."

"I can help."

"I'm trying to minimize collateral damage, Talley."

"The cat I get. I, however, can take care of myself."

"I can't ask—"

"You're not asking, I'm offering." Aidan took two whiskey glasses down from the cabinet and poured two shots each from the bottle of Jameson Cam had left out on the counter. "You and Cam have helped me on how many cases? Now with Cam gone, I'm down a partner and you're down a team member in whatever off-book op you're running." He handed a glass to Nic. "As your friend, your family, and an SAC who can pull some strings, let me help you. Please."

Nic considered the gold liquid he swirled inside the glass. Considered that Cam might not be here much longer to drink it with him. Considered that what Aidan offered was family, friendship, and the sort of juice Nic would need to build his case against Vaughn.

He glanced back up, lifting his glass. "Meet me at mobile command tomorrow night at nine."

Aidan smirked, clinking his glass against Nic's. "Does she know you call it that?"

Nic tossed back his double shot and slammed the empty glass down on the counter. "No, and if you tell her, I'll kill you myself."

EIGHT

Cam pushed open the hotel room door with his hip, careful to keep the box of doughnuts balanced on his one hand and not lose his grip on the hand truck he was hauling with the other.

Jamie hustled over, relieving him of the doughnuts and opening the door wider so Cam could roll in the stack of boxes. "What are those?"

"My case files."

"On Erin's disappearance?"

He nodded. "Had them in a storage unit here."

Cam dropped the boxes in front of the long, narrow desk that stretched the length of the suite's living area. His mom's books were stacked underneath it and taped to the walls above were giant poster-sized sheets of paper.

Jamie handed him a mug of coffee, then dropped into the chair in front of his laptop. "Give me two minutes to finish setting up."

"You know . . ." Cam shoved half a doughnut in his mouth, chewed, and washed it down with the coffee. "I'm surprised this isn't like the movies where you throw around a computer screen projection with your hands."

Jamie waved the hand not working a mouse. "Work with what we got."

Scarfing down the rest of the doughnut, Cam stood next to him and read the title of each sheet taped to the wall.

Timeline. Victim. Suspects. Evidence. Additional Notes.

Faced with it all again, the doughnut settled like a brick in Cam's stomach. His discomfort must have shown.

"Last time I'll ask," Jamie said, leaning back in his chair. "Are you sure about this?"

Looking at those sheets again, Cam had a moment of doubt. Did he really want to dive back into this mess? Into his worst failure? He glanced again at the books beneath the desk. He didn't have a choice. "It's what Mom needs."

"Okay." Jamie grabbed a doughnut and a marker. "Let's see how far we get before you're due back at the hospital."

As they worked their way through the timeline first, Cam couldn't help remembering each wrong decision he'd made the day Erin disappeared. His dad's boat had been stuck out on the water with mechanical issues, and his mom had had to leave twelve-year-old Erin at the library. Cam was supposed to pick her up, but Bobby had told him about a chance to score some real cash. He'd been saving up for a car, embarrassed to pick up his dates in the family junker. It was only dusk, so he'd figured Erin would be safe walking home. He'd told her as much when he'd called the library. He'd also told her to tell Mom that Cam had picked her up and dropped her off, just like he was supposed to do. Erin had been hesitant, but Cam had bribed her with the promise of a cream horn pastry. Erin had left the library, forgetting her library card at the checkout desk, and old man Wilkinson had seen her two streets from the house, cutting down the alley they always took to sneak in the back door. She'd never made it home, and Cam hadn't eaten a cream horn in the twenty years since.

A black hole in the timeline and no clues at the scene to help fill it. No sign of a struggle—no blood or pulled hair or ripped clothing. She'd either known her attacker, been forced to cooperate, or been drugged. There had also been no security cameras to catch it on tape and no witnesses to say what they might've seen other than Mr. Wilkinson, who was now deceased.

She'd vanished into thin air. Assumed kidnapped, then when she hadn't been found after two years, presumed dead.

The possibility remained, albeit small and unthinkable, that Erin had simply left, but she'd had no reason to do that. She'd been a happy kid, loved her family, and, on the phone with Cam that afternoon, had been reticent to walk home alone. Those were not the signs of a runaway.

Unfortunately, there were few other signs either.

As he and Jamie filled in the suspect list next, their leads continued to dwindle. They cross-checked each potential suspect who'd been identified in the past investigation and crossed out more than half of them as dead or in jail, including several members of rival B&E crews. It was a harsh reminder of where Cam and Bobby could have ended up if they hadn't gotten their shit together. By the time lunch rolled around, he and Jamie were eating white clam pizza and flipping through his mother's books again, looking for any new leads. Most of her notes were information Cam and other detectives had collected and discarded over the years. Tips, interviews, wild shots in the dark. A mother, just like a brother, desperate for clues, but the tangential rarely connected to the concrete.

With a frustrated groan, Cam tossed aside the book in his hand and lay back on the floor, staring at the ceiling. "What did she think we'd find in these?"

When Jamie didn't reply, Cam lolled his head his direction. All of Jamie's focus was on the book in his hand. "What are these?" he asked, turning the book to Cam and holding open the front cover.

"Character names," Cam answered. "From the book. She used to write them there so she could keep the family tree straight."

"But these don't match." He tapped with his index finger, holding the cover open. "The listed names are not the characters' names."

"They can be for the series, not just that one book."

Jamie shook his head. "Cam, listen to me, none of them match. And they're all female."

Cam righted himself and reached for the book he'd earlier tossed aside. It was the typical family tree sort in that one, but in the next book he grabbed from the stack, it was a nonconforming list like Jamie's. "The names in this one don't match either. And I recognize some of them." Especially the ones that had been crossed through. "They're missing persons cases that we evaluated and discarded as —" Cam froze at the name halfway down the page, a line struck through it.

"What is it?" Jamie said.

He turned the book around, open, and held it out to Jamie. "Anyone's name look familiar?"

Jamie's eyes widened at the halfway mark, same as his

had. "Holy shit, Rebecca Wright? Is that the same Rebecca Wright from the case last spring?"

"I think so. I remember an old missing persons report in her file."

Twisting, Jamie grabbed his laptop and brought it to his lap, fingers flying across the keyboard. Cam scooted to his side and waited for the search to run. Mentions of the heist case dominated until Jamie added "Boston or Massachusetts" to the search parameters. On page two of the refreshed results, they got a hit. A missing persons report filed in Waltham, and it was their Becca all right. Same jet-black hair, same dark eyes, same cocky, confident expression.

"Did you know she was from around here?"

Cam shook his head. "No, she didn't have an accent at all." That said, her ex-girlfriend was a linguistics expert. "She was reported missing when she was fourteen."

"Only two years older than Erin. She didn't ping the investigation?"

Cam shook his head. "We didn't connect her to the case because she was found shortly thereafter. A runaway."

"Well, your mother did for some reason."

"Mom was making lists too," Cam said. "Of similar cases."

"And crossing out the names on girls who were found, like Becca. Do you recognize the other names? The ones not crossed out?"

Most but not all of them. And those were Cam's first real lead in twenty years.

———

A stack of work was waiting for Nic when he returned to his office Monday morning—some of his own cases, some of Bowers's—including a motion he had to argue on less than an hour's prep. Even flying by the seat of his pants, it felt good to be back in his home courthouse, the judges and clerks happy to see him again.

Outside the courthouse though, he couldn't say for certain whether the tall, suited Black man standing in the sun at the bottom of the steps was happy to see him.

But then that hard, take-no-bullshit scowl broke into a gleaming white smile and the man was transformed. Morphing from imposing federal agent to an absurdly attractive man who knew how to flash that smile to get exactly what he wanted, including a Bureau Assistant Director's position. Helped that Elton Moore was also supremely competent at his job.

"You think they appreciate weather like this in San Diego when they have it year-round?" Moore spread his arms, showing off his massive wingspan.

The guy did not look like a bureaucratic desk jockey.

"You're right." Nic made his way down the courthouse steps. "This is something only us Bay Area natives can truly appreciate."

"That's what I told my ex-wife. She moved back to Georgia where they have"—he curled his fingers for air quotes—"real seasons."

"They can keep the snow."

"Not gonna argue that one, Counselor." He nodded to the courthouse behind Nic. "You win your motion?"

"Of course."

Moore laughed, full and loud. "You always were a cocky son of a bitch."

"Won you more than a few cases."

"That you have."

The chitchat was cordial—he and Moore always had been, each respecting the other's talents—but Nic couldn't help wondering what the Assistant Director was seeking him out for today. A case? Or the case Nic wasn't supposed to be working? Only one way to find out. No use beating around the bush. "Something you need, El?"

"Walk with me." Moore extended an arm toward the food trucks parked around UN Plaza. A little after noon, it wasn't too crowded yet. "Pick your poison, Price?"

"I've got a staff meeting at one."

"Just need fifteen minutes of your time." The AD was obviously stewing over something. "Promise it'll be worth it."

They grabbed sushi burritos, and Nic followed Moore over to the water fountain. Pigeons scattered as they claimed one of the empty concrete benches. Nic didn't miss the AD's strategic choice of seats. There were other people around—nothing to see here—but the fall of water from the fountain would make it impossible for anyone to eavesdrop on their conversation.

Nic unwrapped the foil from his burrito and took a bite, crunching through crispy daikon and pickled carrots and cucumbers to reach the rice and tempura shrimp, all the flavors mixing with the sriracha mayo. He swallowed down the bite, then fixed Moore with his best questioning-the-witness stare. "What's going on, El?"

"You tell me," Moore said, throwing the inquisitor's stare right back at him. "Why have you been meeting with your father's executive assistant? And don't tell me it's a sudden interest in joining the family business."

Nic couldn't stop the bitter laugh that escaped.

The corners of Moore's eyes crinkled, letting on that he was fighting a knowing smile. "Yeah, I didn't think so."

Nic took another bite, deciding whether or not to trust the AD. Aidan and Cam both did, the latter urging him to go to Moore, especially if Moore had more facts on Vaughn and Curtis that they could use. At the same time, Moore was a skilled interrogator and an astute political climber, having played the game masterfully so far, becoming one of the youngest serving ADs. Nic had to tread carefully. "You've got eyes on the family office?"

Moore took a bite and nodded.

"My father too?"

Nodded again.

"Me?"

He swallowed and swiped a napkin across his mouth. "Not unless you're suddenly getting into the family busi-ness. A source tells me you're not."

Nic let out a breath, relaxing. Ten to one he knew who that source was, and if she trusted Moore, if she had ques-tioned him and come to that conclusion, including about this, then Nic trusted her instincts. "That source a certain bounty hunter of our mutual acquaintance?"

One side of Moore's mouth hitched up. "Bail enforce-ment agent."

Nic chuckled. "Sure, if that's what we want to call her."

Moore's smile faded and he set his burrito aside. "You know what you're getting into here, Price?"

"I think I'd know more if I saw the FBI's file on the matter."

Moore seemed to consider him now, deciding whether or not to trust him and Mel. Reaching the same conclusion

Nic had, he withdrew a flash drive from his pocket. "Give that to Agent Hall. Should be what she needs to crack the encryption on the flash drives she copied last spring."

Nic wiped off his hands before taking the jump stick. "Who encrypted them? Walker's the only person I know who can outcode Hall."

"And Walker would have given you the key." That devastatingly handsome smirk reappeared. "Which is why I had Walker's mentor at MIT encrypt them."

"Why are you giving this to me?"

Moore leaned forward, forearms resting on his crossed legs. "Because you're a good attorney, Price. You were a good soldier too. You don't deserve to have your name dragged through the mud for something you didn't do. You need to be the one to shut it down, but you need to be careful. Vaughn has sources everywhere."

Nic narrowed his eyes, parsing through the AD's words. He didn't want to offend but he had to ask. "Your office?"

Not offended in the least, Moore nodded. "Talley's and Byrne's conflicts weren't the only reason access was restricted on this matter."

"Do you know who?"

"No, we couldn't figure it out, which is why I'm authorizing you to bring in Talley for the mole hunt. I don't want that shark Vaughn infesting my waters."

So this wasn't just about helping him. Moore wanted to clean up his own shop too, to make sure the way was clear for his next step up the ladder.

Seemed like a mutually beneficial arrangement to Nic. They both had skin in the game.

Nic pocketed the flash drive. "I was already planning to loop Aidan in."

"Good," Moore said. "But there's a leak in your shop too."

"I think I know who." The same person who'd known where he'd be each of those times a threat had been leveled against him. The same person who had ridden his ass particularly hard as of late.

"Don't be so sure." Moore scooped up his leftovers and stood, Nic doing the same. "He was my first guess too, but we didn't find anything to connect him. Some people like your boss are just assholes."

If not Bowers, then who was the asshole helping Vaughn? That's what Nic needed to find out before the gangster decided threats were no longer enough.

NINE

Captain Diana Pritchard sauntered toward the front desk of the Boston Family Justice Center, smile dazzling as she caught sight of Cam. "Well, well, well, if it isn't Agent Hard-Ass." That had always been Di's favorite nickname for him for multiple reasons. Dressed as he was in a suit and tie, Cam had been hoping for the professional one, but by the way Di's big brown eyes raked him over, she was definitely contemplating the less professional context, which he'd admittedly welcomed when he'd been younger, hot-to-trot, and unattached.

Then her gaze shifted to Jamie, and Cam might as well have been invisible. She pushed through the swinging counter door, whistling. "Damn, sugar, where you been hiding him?"

"In San Francisco with his husband," Cam answered, and Jamie brandished his wedding band.

Her face fell so fast it was comical. "Well, that's a fucking shame."

"Di, Jameson Walker." Cam gestured between the two.

"Jamie, Diana Pritchard, Captain of BPD's Family Justice Group."

Jamie held out his hand, flashing his good-ole-boy smile. "Captain Pritchard."

"Di, please," she said. "You a fed too?"

"Former. Consultant still, on occasion."

She shifted her assessing gaze back to Cam. "What are you doing back here? Just showing your boy around?"

When he'd worked kidnap cases for the Bureau, especially those involving missing children, Cam frequently worked with Di's group, the matters often crossing over. As they did again now.

"Personal matter," he said. "Looking again into some missing persons cases."

Di's expression softened, the mother of four coming out in her. There was a reason she'd dedicated her career to the Family Justice Group and a reason the officers working under her were some of the most loyal and hardworking in the department. "You going there again?" She'd found him more than once in the basement archives, combing through Erin's file. After enough times, she'd made him an unauthorized copy. *If you're gonna obsess,* she'd said, *at least be in stumbling distance of your own bed so you don't keep falling asleep here.*

"Special request," he told her now. "Mom's in the hospital."

"Oh, sugar." She pulled him into a hug. "She gonna be okay?"

"She had a heart attack. Bypass surgery today, maybe more later this week."

"So you're here distracting yourself."

"That, and she asked me—"

She raised a hand. "Say no more." If anyone knew the lengths to which grieving parents and family members would go to find the truth, for better or worse, it was Di. As captain of the FJG, she oversaw human trafficking, domestic violence, and crimes against children cases, many often involving runaways. "But won't the FBI and missing persons databases have more info?"

"We've put in all the usual requests," Jamie said. "They're compiling files and uploading for us to review."

With special emphasis on the names they'd relayed from his mother's books and on any reported within the past year since Cam had been on the West Coast. "We wanted to review BPD's files too," Cam said. "Since missing persons are usually reported here first."

"I got you." She held open the swinging counter door and led them through the bullpen. Their path of travel was frequently delayed by officers interrupting to greet Cam, but they eventually reached the basement stairs. "Timing's good," Di said, leading them down. "Superintendent's at headquarters."

"He owes me a favor or ten," Cam said.

"Don't doubt it," Di replied. "But now's not a good time for feds to be poking around BPD and missing persons cases."

"Why's that?"

"Officer over in D-4"—she looked over her shoulder at Jamie—"that's District Four."

"South End," he said with a nod.

She halted and Cam nearly ran into her. "You sound Southern and look California . . ."

"Grad school at MIT, and I spent summers here all

through undergrad." He jutted a thumb at Cam. "With this one."

She waved a hand and continued down the steps. "Okay, you're local. So over in South End, Officer Murphy's daughter, Shannon, went missing day before yesterday. We're trying to keep it in house, at least for now."

"Randall Murphy?" Cam asked.

She shook her head. "Little brother, Billy."

"They're Southies," Cam told Jamie. Then to Di, "Like you said before, the feds have more resources that can help."

She raised both hands as they walked down the hall to archives, which took up the back half of the building's basement. "Preaching to the choir, sugar, but they got their reasons." She pushed open the swinging doors, and the lights automatically flipped on.

Standing among the four wooden worktables, Cam eyed the rolling racks of files stretching endlessly the opposite direction. A sad sight in and of itself—so many cases—but the very files he needed access to.

"You remember where everything is?" Di asked.

"Yep, other than the coffeemaker." He'd noticed it missing from the kitchenette.

"Upgrade." Waggling her brows, she opened a cabinet door to reveal a single-serve espresso machine.

"Look at you," Cam teased. "Gettin' all fancy."

"Was the least I could do for the archives and evidence clerks." Always taking care of her people. "You in town for a while?"

"To be determined."

"All right, just don't fall asleep down here. Lights go out automatically now." She gave him a wink as she stepped past him toward the doors. "You boys let me know if you need anything."

The doors swung closed behind her and Cam sat at the table by the window, picking at the nick his own fingernail had carved there over the years.

"How's it feel to be back?" Jamie asked, claiming the chair across from him.

"Better than it should," he admitted, and that was a problem.

———

The first time Nic visited "mobile command," it had been a bright spring morning, right at the start of this mess with Vaughn. Five months later, they were meeting under the cover of darkness and Aidan, rather than Mel, stood on the deck of the yacht with Irish and American flags flying from its stern.

"I see I'm late for the party," Nic said, climbing aboard.

"Nah, I just got here myself." Aidan gestured for him to follow and headed toward the deck stairs. "You heard from Cam today?"

"Not yet. He has the night shift with his mom, so usually later."

Aidan glanced back, smirking. "You know his schedule."

Nic pushed him down a step, and Aidan chuckled. A throat cleared from across the living area, and Nic looked up to find a reproachful Mel leaning out of what should have been the bedroom. "Lauren's got something," she said, then vanished back inside, muttering "children" under her breath.

"Into mobile command we go," Nic said with a grin.

Aidan held a finger up to his lips, half shushing him, half holding back his laughter.

It was an accurate description, though. Befitting a Chief of Security for a major shipping company, and bounty hunter on the side, Mel had retrofitted the main cabin with a wall of monitors and high-speed computers, satellite connections that ran up to the roof, police band radios, and an AmSec 8000 safe, courtesy of their heist crew case. Who knew what was behind that armored door.

Even with all the gear and four people, the area was relatively spacious. "Moore's key worked?" Nic asked Lauren, who was working at the bank of computers.

"Like a charm." Her glittery red nails flew across the keyboard, and the screens filled with PDFs. "We've now got the full FBI files on your father and on Duncan Vaughn."

Nic grabbed one of the rolling chairs and kicked the other over to Aidan. "Do I need to bring you up to speed?"

"Saved you the trouble," Mel answered instead.

As easy as that, and Aidan was still here, still willing to help. His surprise must have shown. Sighing, Aidan clasped his forearm, squeezing. "For the last fucking time, Dominic, you're family."

Still hard to believe, given his limited knowledge of the same, but it was getting harder and harder to deny. And Nic didn't want to. "All right, then," he said with a nod. Then to Lauren, "Anything in Dad's file we didn't know about already?"

"There's an outlier account. Neither Vaughn nor your father's other lenders seem to know about it."

"Curtis has been careful with this one," Mel interjected. "All we've got so far are records of microtransactions.

Small, non-triggering amounts being taken out of other accounts and deposited into this cloaked offshore one regularly."

"How regularly?" Nic asked.

"Every month for over ten years until last April."

Exactly when the *Unknown* calls had started. Because the payments had stopped?

"You're thinking about the calls," Mel said, as if reading his mind.

He nodded. "I have someone in Navy admin looking into them."

"Could be related," Mel said. "But that's an awfully convoluted path to get five thousand to someone in North Carolina."

"Five thousand total?" Those were microtransactions.

"Five thousand a month," Lauren corrected.

Aidan whistled. "That's over half a million by now."

Not so micro, but in his dad's investment heyday, five thousand a month was Curtis's dining-out budget.

"For what?" Nic said. "Or for whom?" *He* made the least sense where Curtis was concerned. "That's a decent-size rainy-day fund he's kept hidden."

"Assuming no one's tapped it already," Aidan said. "Do we know that yet?"

Lauren shook her head, strands coming loose from her pencil bun. "Like Mel said, it's cloaked. We're still trying to find it. We've just got the withdrawals going to the same place. We have to pull back the cloak and find the account."

"Keep digging," Nic said, then moved on to the more immediate problem. "What more have we learned about Vaughn?"

Lauren pinged a few keys, and FBI documents on

Vaughn zoomed forward on the screens. "He's connected to half a dozen arsons and at least two murders. Not to mention all the extortion cases he's suspected of being involved in."

Nic rolled closer, squinting at the screens. "How has he not been charged?" Aidan asked.

"It's all hearsay," Nic answered, catching on fast to the pattern of evidence before him. "No one's caught him in the act."

"He's threatened you."

"Me, an interested party. Just like every other person he's pressured into not testifying or answering the feds' questions."

"But you're not like all those other people, are you?" Mel tried and failed to hide her smile.

"No, I'm not, but I need more than this"—he pointed at the screens—"to charge him. Bowers will never move on Vaughn based on my word alone."

Lauren spun in her chair, facing him. "You do realize who's the prosecutor who stalls us out all the time, right?"

"Oh, I realize, but I need a paper trail Bowers—or the Deputy AG, if I go over his head—can't refute."

"We think we've found the start of one." Mel waved him over to the metal desk running the length of the opposite wall. She spread a stack of bank statements out in front of him. "Your father's assistant has been most helpful." She tapped a French-tipped nail by the payor's name on the first sheet. "This is the account that paid off his bank home loan." She tapped at the second. "The same payor also paid off the subordinate lenders on your father's building in Burlingame. One of Vaughn's entities."

Nic gestured at the other sheets. "And who do all these other accounts belong to?"

"Federal employees."

Nic's mouth went dry, and Aidan gasped behind him. "Vaughn's got that many people on payroll?"

"Do any of them trace back to Bowers?" Nic asked.

"We isolated his accounts first, and no," Lauren said, clearly disappointed. "We're working on the others."

Nic glanced at Aidan. "Only a handful of people have been on each case and would know where I was."

Aidan nodded. "We'll run the list as soon as we get it."

It was a break, a better one than they'd had in months, but it still involved exerting pressure on pawns Vaughn already had under his control. Nic, however, had a direct path to Vaughn if he chose to play the queen on the board. "There might be another avenue open to us."

Mel crossed one leg over the other, heel bouncing. "What's that?"

"Vaughn approached me at the brewery Saturday night."

Lauren slumped back in her chair, staring open-mouthed at the ceiling. "And y'all complain about me always hiding the ball."

Nic would've laughed if Aidan didn't look like he was about to spit nails.

At him. "That's what you wouldn't tell me last night."

"I'm sorry," Nic said. "Won't happen again."

"What did he say?" Mel asked, calm and assessing. This was a friendly team-up meeting and yet Nic still felt like she was interrogating him.

"He made certain . . ."

"Threats?" Aidan supplied.

"Overtures."

"To what, come work for him?"

"Not exactly." His cringe must have given him away, because Lauren's blue eyes went round as saucers and her mouth fell open in a silent *Oh.*

"You want to use yourself as bait," Mel likewise surmised.

"If I can get him to actually confess on record . . ."

"By seducing him." Aidan, very not calm, shot out of his chair, sending it slamming back into the metal table. "You're walking a thin line of entrapment."

"Entrapment requires I induce him to commit a crime he wouldn't otherwise commit. He's gonna commit a crime. I'm not talking him into anything."

"No," Aidan said, pacing in front of him. "It's just you talking yourself into an early grave."

Nic stood, squaring off against him. He wasn't angry or upset. He was actually humbled by Aidan's concern, by his commitment to protecting his family, including him.

But the same held true for Nic. "Vaughn's gunning for me, my livelihood, and my family." He punctuated the last word with a significant glance around the room at the members of his family gathered here. "If I don't start talking soon—if I can't find a different song to sing—then I'm going to be dead anyway. And I refuse to take any of my family to the grave with me."

TEN

Run out of his mom's room by the night nurses, Cam traded the chair by her bed for the one in the hallway. She'd come through the bypass fine, though she was still mostly asleep, only waking once during his shift—he checked the time on his phone—which ended shortly. He was starting to fade too after a day of searching through books and archives. Not even the atrociously uncomfortable hallway chair was stalling the nodding off.

He checked his phone again. Almost midnight there; he'd still be awake.

Nic picked up on the second ring. "You on night shift again?"

"West Coast time, relatively," he said around a yawn. "Dad can go home and sleep, and Bobby and Quinn can be with their families."

"You need to sleep too."

"Keith comes on at three. Only God and the Marine Corps know what time zone his body is set to. I'll sleep then."

Nic laughed, low and soft. "I remember that, never quite sure where or when you are."

Cam slouched in his chair, closing his eyes against the florescent lights and white walls. He could commiserate with them both. Not quite sure where and when he was. He needed to be here with his family, and today at the station, he was reminded of the people he missed working with. But Nic's voice, his laugh, made Cam want to be someplace different too. He felt grounded in Nic's presence, adrift without him.

"Hey, Boston, you still there?"

"Yeah, sorry." He opened his eyes and ran a hand through his hair, tugging it as if he could tug himself into the here and now. Awake. "Zoned out there a minute."

"That thing I mentioned about sleep . . ."

"Zip it, smart-ass." Nic laughed again, and Cam hated to have to upend the easy mood of the only easy conversation he'd had today, but he needed an update worse and a distraction worse still. "Anything new on Vaughn?"

"You don't need to worry about that."

Cam gritted his teeth and righted himself in the chair. "I'll worry about you if I goddamn want to."

"I said you don't need to worry about that because I brought in Aidan and AD Moore like you suggested."

Cam unclenched his jaw and released a giant sigh. "Thank fuck." He'd still worry, no stopping that, but this was progress. More people on the team meant maybe they'd fix this shit with Vaughn and Curtis before more bullets flew. At Nic.

"We've got the full FBI files now," Nic went on. "We're following the money, looking for Vaughn's Bureau and

USAO sources. Fucking game of whack-a-mole but we'll get there."

"And when you do?"

"Pressure, and if I make a run at Vaughn directly—"

Cam launched out of his chair. "If you do what?"

"It's fine, Boston."

"The fuck it is," he shot back, hand braced on the opposite wall, trying to stop himself from punching through it. "I should be there."

"You should be right where you are. I can take care of me."

"He threaten you again?"

"Not so much. He showed up at Gravity."

Cam's arm gave out and he sagged front first into the wall, banging his forehead on the plaster. "Fuck me."

"Listen, Cam. Aidan and Moore have my back now too, in addition to Mel and Lauren. We got this. Now, tell me how it's going there with your mom."

He flattened his palm and counted to ten, biting back the argument on the tip of his tongue. Nic was right. He had all the team assembled there except him and Jamie, who were here. If they really needed them, they'd say so, Aidan especially. Didn't make it any easier knowing the guy he was falling for could make one wrong move and Cam would be across the country where he couldn't do a damn thing about it. But fucking argue. And what the fuck good was that going to do at three in the morning but piss the both of them off.

He took a deep breath and pushed off the wall. "She's fine. Bypass surgery went as well as could be expected. Now we wait for her to stabilize before they assess if another operation is needed."

"That's good. What about Erin's case? You and Jamie make any progress?"

He dragged his feet back across the hallway and collapsed again into the chair, waving at the nurses on the way out of his mother's room. "We were at the Family Justice Center today, going through old missing persons cases. Trying to find links."

"You didn't do all that before?" Nic asked.

"Yes, I did, but fresh eyes and a fresh list from Mom."

"Your mom?"

"It's been her pet project the past year. She's been making notes and missing persons lists in her old romance novels."

"No shit?" The admiration in Nic's voice made Cam smile.

"No shit, and you'll never guess who one of the names was." He didn't keep him in suspense long. "Rebecca Wright."

"You're shit—" He cut himself off, and Cam could picture Nic drumming his fingers on the nearest surface, deep in thought. "Actually, I remember that. There was a missing persons report in her file."

"From when she was fourteen. Two years older than Erin."

"But she didn't stay missing. False alarm as far as we understood."

"And the two matters are probably unconnected but given her similar appearance and age when she disappeared . . ."

"You want me to question her?"

"If you've got time."

"I'll make time."

That feeling of being too far from shore walloped Cam again. The anchor was right there but out of reach, the current pulling him back the other way. Unfortunately, he had to go with the current, back out to sea for the time being, especially with Bobby and Keith stepping off the elevator at the end of the hall. "Fuck, I gotta go."

"Everything okay?"

"Keith just got here," he said, standing.

"Good, go get some sleep."

The genuine concern in Nic's voice tamped down his instinct to snark. "Thank you for following up," he said instead, meaning it both ways. "And let me know what Becca says."

"Of course. Later, Boston."

"Bye for now," Cam replied, and the words felt wrong the second they left his mouth.

Nic hung up before he could correct them. But would giving his usual sign-off be fair? Could he answer *Sooner, Price*, when he had no idea when sooner would be?

"You look like you ate something sour," Bobby said.

Keith, without a greeting or second glance, went directly into their mother's room.

Cam's gaze followed his younger brother until the older one in front of him spoke. "He's angry."

"He's been angry for two decades."

"Because of what we did."

Grim-faced, Bobby tilted his head toward the other end of the hallway. They were halfway down the hall before Cam asked, "What are you doing here? You're supposed to be home sleeping."

"Sat up talking with Keith, then gave him a lift here."

"Don't you have to be at work in the morning?"

Bobby waggled his dark brows as he ducked into one of the lounges. "Benefits of being the boss." He ran his own private security company, an ironic yet appropriate gig for a former B&E guy. "Besides, you're the one who looks like he needs sleep."

"Everyone keeps telling me that."

"Because it's true," Bobby said as he poured coffee for them both. "How are you, really?"

"Tired," he admitted, eagerly taking the cup, and Bobby smiled wider. "The case—"

"Don't want to hear about the case." He pulled out a chair at one of the lounge tables, and Cam claimed the other across from him.

"You're angry too."

"No," Bobby said, surprising Cam. "I understand why she asked and why you have to look. You're doing us both a favor."

"But Keith . . ."

"He'd be just as angry if you were here looking over his shoulder." He took a long swallow, then leaned back in his chair. "I meant, how are you doing? After that case last spring? With work? With San Francisco? You haven't really mentioned to anyone how life's going for you out there."

"I'm not the one we need to be worrying about right now."

Bobby laid a coffee-warmed hand on his forearm. "I'm not worried. I just want to know and to not think about our mom's condition for five minutes."

There was a reason he and Bobby were closest. They thought so much alike, for better or worse. "The case was hard. I can't go into details."

"Understood. But you made it through okay?"

"Yeah, I have a good partner and good friends. They kept me grounded through it." The heist case had been rough, having to dig into his old life to save another, and there'd been more than a few close calls. Worth it, though. "I was able to help someone else's sister too."

"That's good, that's good."

"I haven't broken our promise, Bobby." After Erin's disappearance, they'd promised each other never to slip back into the life. It had been hard for Cam on that case to ignore the adrenaline rush each time he cracked a safe, coming right up on his red line multiple times, but he'd stayed on the right side of it by remembering the promise he'd made to Bobby and the people counting on him.

"I know that," Bobby said with a nod. "How's San Francisco?"

"Fucking expensive." Cam groaned and scrubbed his hands over his face. "And fucking swarming with Giants and Warriors fans. Though get this. Nic, the former special forces prosecutor"—he lowered his voice because God forbid anyone hear the blasphemy he was about to utter—"is a fucking Kings fan."

Now it was Bobby's turn to groan loudly.

Cam laughed. "He's also determined to rename Bird, Joe."

"And this guy's still a friend?"

More than, but Cam still wasn't ready to have that conversation, not while they were all so tense. "He also brews a wicked good beer," he said, sticking to a safer topic.

"Hmm, good man to have around, then." Bobby searched his face, a little too knowing, and Cam stood, heading back to the coffeepot. "Anyone special in San Fran?" Bobby asked.

Cam almost bobbled the pot. "A few dates here or there but with work . . ."

"No one at work?" Bobby continued to dig, damn him.

"After Aidan and Jamie's office romance, no." It technically wasn't a lie.

Bobby shrugged. "Worked out for them. Jamie looks happy."

"He is, and I'm happy for him."

"You deserve to be happy too, Cameron."

The words and sentiment were so heartfelt, Bobby's blue eyes so concerned, that Cam could tell this wasn't the first time Bobby had had this conversation. For some reason, the matter of his love life, or lack thereof, was a family concern worth discussing. "Why's everyone on my ass and not Keith's?"

"'Cause he's nothing but piss and vinegar. You're more sweet and sour." Bobby shot him a wink. "We have hope for you."

Cam chuckled, but it petered out as he thought about his angry little brother. And the hand he'd played in making him that way. "I don't want Keith to hate me more than he already does."

"You bring Mom peace, he won't."

Cam feared the other possibility more. If he couldn't solve his sister's disappearance, all he would've brought any of them was more unrest.

ELEVEN

Jamie's rainbow-colored file folders had seemed like a good idea when Cam first returned from the hospital. Cases had been color-coded by district, then organized by year and status. Everything else in the hotel suite's shared living area had been a disaster—soda cans, Kit Kat wrappers, and scribbled-on notepads covered every surface—but the facts he'd needed were at his fingertips. Hours later, sitting on the hotel room floor surrounded by his own all-nighter detritus, the bright folders were more frustrating than anything. A reorganization of facts he'd been through a time or twenty before. Add to that the other loop running in his head, replaying over his talk with Bobby and his call with Nic, and it had all become a headache-inducing blur. Resting back against the couch, he laid his head on the cushions and closed his eyes.

When he opened them again, it was to a rumpled Jamie in team sweats and an FBI tee standing over him. "Did you sleep?"

"I wasn't sleeping."

"Your snoring woke me up."

Cam righted himself and sure enough, it was at least an hour brighter in the room. "Okay, so maybe I slept a little."

"I think you need to sleep some more."

Cam waved him off, then waved at the folders. "Thanks for putting some order to this."

Jamie sat on the couch next to his shoulder. "I see you've put more order to them."

"Gut instinct, basically." He pointed to the pile on the left. "Possibly related." Then to the pile on the right. "Not likely related." Unfortunately, the new names on his mother's list had all fallen in the not-likely-related column.

"What are the possibly related factors?" Jamie asked.

"Age, description, neighborhood, and other similarities. The same thing that tagged them as related before."

Jamie dropped onto the floor next to him and drew the possibly related stack closer. "Setting aside the first three, which I get, what other similarities?"

Cam opened the first folder and handed it to Jamie. "Brandi Maynard, abducted on the way home from the library." He picked up the next two. "Two girls from the same middle school but not Erin's." The three after that were the same socioeconomic status as their family, blue-collar working class. The next had left behind a gemstone necklace—not a topaz like Erin's but a ruby.

Jamie flipped through the folders, then set them aside. His baby blues were skeptical when he looked back over at Cam. "Those are rather disparate."

"Which is why age and description are the better bet, plus one." He took the folders back, tossed out two and added three more from the possibly related stack. "Eight disappearances over the past twenty years where the victim is between twelve and fourteen, with dark hair and dark eyes, from large families that are barely scraping by."

Jamie nodded. "Same as Erin."

"Eight cold cases spread over two decades. We could never tie them all together. Hell, two had brothers who also went missing."

"So the girls were deemed runaways too."

Cam nodded, scrubbing a hand over his beard. Then voiced what he must. "All of which assumes Erin wasn't a runaway too."

Jamie shifted, drawing up a knee and angling toward him, elbow propped on the couch. "Do you really think that about your sister?"

God, he wished he did. As terrible as it would be to learn his sister had voluntarily left, had turned her back on her family and stayed away for two decades, it would be better than learning for certain she was dead. But the latter was far easier to believe. Things had not been easy for their family back then—Dad always out on the boat, then stressed over managing the other boats when he expanded, Mom running a tight ship on a tight budget at home—but Erin was their princess, worshiped and adored by her parents and brothers. She'd never wanted for anything, except the one day she'd wanted Cam to pick her up and he'd been selfish instead. "No," he croaked hoarsely.

Jamie rubbed a hand over his shoulders, soothing, while he recited back the pertinent case details, giving Cam something else to focus on. "So then we assume she was taken because she fit a profile the kidnapper targeted."

"Is still targeting," Cam said, making a connection he hadn't considered until they'd laid it all out. It was right there in front of him. A case that wasn't cold. He shot to his feet and grabbed his laptop, heading for the table.

"What've you got?" Jamie asked, following him.

Brushing aside Kit Kat wrappers, he made a place for the computer, opened a search window, and called up BPD's roster. "Remember what Di said yesterday about the officer with the missing daughter?"

"You said you knew the family."

Cam nodded. "I went to school with Randy, the oldest. This" —he opened an officer profile page—"is Officer William Murphy, whose daughter is missing."

"Dark hair, dark eyes, daughter could be the right age if he married young." Jamie yanked out his phone, tapping away at it, while Cam searched social media sites for Shannon Murphy.

"Yep," Jamie said. "Per Social Security, he's thirty-two, married at eighteen, and had Shannon when he was nineteen."

"Making her thirteen." Cam stood back from the screen, giving Jamie a view of Shannon's online profile picture. She was a pretty girl, with big dark eyes, long brown hair, and a bright smile.

"She looks like her dad," Jamie agreed.

Cam drew up another picture, one of his sister he had saved on his laptop. "And if you didn't know better?" he asked Jamie.

"I'd say she could easily be mistaken as Erin's sister."

———

Nic waited in Cam's office, looking at the framed pictures on his windowsill. A basketball team photo from Boston

College. One with his family, all of them in ugly Christmas sweaters. A photo of him and Jamie, arms slung over each other's shoulders, on a fishing boat. Cam was smiling wide while Jamie's expression was somewhere between grin and grimace, face a sickly shade of green. One of Cam, Danny, Jamie, and Aidan in their tuxes at the wedding.

Nic hadn't been in the wedding party, but seeing that picture, he felt a certain sense of disappointment that he wasn't in it. He'd been holding himself back from his newfound family and more than a little of him regretted it now.

But not the kiss that day. Nor any of the kisses since.

Every day he'd spent in San Diego, he'd missed Cam. This separation, however, was somehow worse. Even knowing what he did, that there were leaks in both their shops and that the safest course of action would be to stay apart, Nic wanted to be there for Cam, as a team member and more.

He'd have to settle for what he could do here. At least Cam had asked for his help, which he was more than happy to give. Grabbing the file he'd assembled off Cam's desk, he made it as far as the door before his phone rang. He retreated into the office, pulling out his cell and recognizing a DC-area number.

"Nic Price," he answered.

"Hold for the Deputy Attorney General," a woman said, and a moment later, the line clicked over. "Morning, Price," the Deputy AG greeted. "Thanks for taking my call."

"Of course." Not that he'd been given a choice; the man was his ultimate boss, after all. One he actually liked, unlike his immediate supervisor. "What can I do for you, sir?"

"You can take the US Attorney position in San Diego permanently."

Staggering, Nic reached out a hand to steady himself, narrowly avoiding Cam's framed diploma on the wall. "I'm sorry, what was that?" he managed around the shock.

The Deputy AG chuckled. "I should be the one apologizing for that abrupt lead-in. I've been on the Hill all morning and have to go back this afternoon."

"Then you're the one in need of condolences." He pushed off the wall and circled behind Cam's desk, tossing the file on the blotter. "You caught me off guard is all. Daniels just got back." Daniels had been the US Attorney he'd filled in for last month.

"He dropped the news today that he's leaving year end for a private practice position." The Deputy AG didn't sound too surprised; it wasn't an uncommon occurrence, more money and more flexibility in private practice. "Your name's at the top of the replacement list."

"I'm sure there are more qualified—"

"Beg to differ. You closed cases faster than Daniels, and they were cases the staff there wanted to work on. Three calls in with the SD AUSAs and all of them recommended you for the job. I'm sure the others will do the same."

"I'm honored, sir." Nic rested back against the edge of the desk, thumb drumming a steady beat against the wood. He appreciated the admiration and respect of his colleagues —there really was no higher honor—and they'd been a good team there in San Diego. But looking again at the pictures on the window ledge, he couldn't deny he had a good team here too.

More than a team. Family.

He'd spent half his life a virtual nomad—going wherever the Navy sent him. His life was settled now, here, with Gravity, the family Aidan had somehow sucked him into, and Cam. But with homesickness growing louder in Cam's voice each time they spoke, could Nic afford to ignore this offer?

Did he want to stay here if the most important part of his team—of his family—were to leave? And there was no denying everyone would be safer if Nic wasn't here. He'd proved his point this summer and on his first night back with the fire.

"The confirmation hearings won't be easy," he said, reminded of the skeletons that would no doubt be shaken loose.

"Is that a yes, then?" the Deputy AG asked.

"It's not a no," Nic said, hedging. He needed time to think and to see how other things shook out. "Can you give me to the end of the week to decide?"

"By all means but the sooner we can strategize on the hearings the better."

"Understood, sir." He thanked him again for the offer, then arranged with his secretary for a call on Friday.

When he hung up, it was to the *whoosh* of blood in his ears, held at bay somehow during that brief yet momentous conversation. This was not a decision he'd anticipated having to confront so soon. Mel had vaguely hinted at it on the plane ride back—had she known?—but he'd not known of the opening, hadn't even contemplated it in the current political climate. Truth be told, if he could have any position, it would be the one Bowers held, here in San Francisco with his friends and family and Gravity. But that position wasn't open and even if it were, would staying here put all those people and things he valued most in more danger?

"We're ready."

Turning, Nic found Lauren waiting in the doorway. "She's here?"

"Holding Room Two."

With a witness in holding and Cam on a clock that could stop at any minute, a decision, much less deliberation, on San Diego would have to wait. He had to focus on the here and now.

Taking a deep breath, he grabbed the folder again and followed Lauren across the FBI bullpen, sparsely populated at the lunch hour. She handed him a comm device that she would use to feed him analytics from the room's biometric equipment. "You sleep any last night?" she asked, glaring up at him.

"Not much." He tucked the comm in his ear. "You?" he asked her back as she trudged into the observation room. She looked as tired as he felt, now helping on this matter, digging into Vaughn, and covering who knew how many other cases. She was FBI-San Francisco's best hacker, a top-notch analyst, and more than capable in the field. Great for job security; hell on sleep.

"Nada." She returned with two coffees, a third visible on her desk in the room. "That's why God invented Starbucks."

"I don't think it was God who did this," Nic said, claiming one of the cups. "More like the devil."

She shrugged. "On zero hours of sleep, I'm not choosey."

Nic nodded at the other cup in her hand. "Who's that one for?"

"Becca." She waited for Nic to tuck his folder under his arm before handing it to him. "I guarantee she hasn't had good coffee since you put her behind bars. It'll grease the wheels a bit, hopefully."

"Good thinking." She wasn't a crack analyst for nothing. "All right, let's do this."

Nic pushed the door open, revealing Rebecca Wright sitting on the other side of the table, looking radically different from the heist crew ringleader he and Cam had busted. Maybe it was realizing she'd been played by her client on that job. Or maybe it was the orange jumpsuit versus her leather boots and bustier. But sitting there, purple streaks gone from her limp black hair, sans makeup, in an oversized jumpsuit and with one hand chained to the desk, she looked far removed from criminal mastermind and far younger than her thirty-one years.

But her dark eyes still spit fire and cased every corner of the room and everything in it, including him. Assessing, needing to be in control, no matter how tiny the confines. "Well, if it isn't the attorney my girl picked over me."

"She picked her sister over you."

Becca tried to hide her flinch, but Nic saw it and the monitors read it, Lauren reporting so in his ear. It was a good test, if unplanned.

"Your ex and her sister are doing well." Nic pushed a cup toward her. "If that matters to you."

She took a dainty sip, pretending like it was any other coffee. "I realize I might not have treated her well."

"Sucks being betrayed, doesn't it?"

Becca took a longer swallow, unable to fight the flutter of her eyelids. "What would you know about betrayal?"

"More than you think," he answered, and ignored the intrigued flare of her eyes. "We're not here to talk about that."

"Why did you spring me from the joint? I know it was for more than just good coffee."

Sitting back, he crossed one leg over the other, hands in his lap, giving her as much space as the room allowed. "You went missing when you were fourteen."

Her movements were measured as she set the cup down without answering.

"There's a missing persons report filed with the Boston PD."

"You act like this is news," Becca replied. "I had a record. It must have been in my file."

"It was, but we weren't focused on it. We need to know more about it now."

Forearms on the table, she wrapped her hands around her cup. Nic was surprised the cap hadn't popped off already. "Why?" she asked. "What's happened?"

"Why do you care?"

She clammed up again, hiding behind another sip. She was clearly holding something back, but the coffee hadn't been enough to secure her cooperation.

"She wants to play," Lauren said. "Let her."

He needed to tell her more, but how much more before he risked compromising an active investigation? But it wasn't really. And it had been a while since she'd worked a job. Her brain used to regularly put pieces together much the same way his and Cam's did, just on the other side of the law. Lauren was right. He had to offer Becca a chance to solve the puzzle too.

"We're working a case." He withdrew a stack of pictures from the folder and spread them out on the table. "Eight missing girls over twenty years in Boston and the surrounding areas. All of them bear a striking resemblance to you."

She looked at each picture, then back to him. "What's it matter to you?"

He slid the last picture out of the file, a pen rolling out with it. "This is Agent Byrne's sister. She's been missing for twenty years."

"So Hot Stuff really was from Boston? I didn't know if that accent was real or his cover."

"Southie, born and bred," Nic said. "You're from a few neighborhoods over but you have no accent."

"Because I trained myself not to use it."

Nic startled at the full-blast Boston drawl. Not exactly like Cam's but close.

"We're not all lucky enough to be born in accent-free California," Becca said, cutting through his shock. She reached for the pen and Nic tensed, ready to draw his sidearm if she tried to use the pen as a weapon. She put it in her mouth instead, speaking around it. "Trick for enunciating words and masking an accent."

"Why'd you need that trick?"

She dropped the pen out of her mouth, pushed the photos aside, and pulled the missing persons report toward her. "I wasn't taken. I left."

Not surprising, seeing as she was sitting here before him and there were no follow-ups or charges related to the old missing persons report. Nic, however, continued to push, searching for any connection, no matter how tenuous. "Who were you running from?"

She tapped the "Filers" box with the pen. "Them. My parents."

Nic drank his coffee, waiting her out. He'd had enough experience with witnesses to recognize Becca was ready to tell this story. She'd started down the road and couldn't turn back, but she had to go at her own pace. And Nic had to let her.

"I wasn't the easiest kid," she said after another minute.

"I would have never guessed."

She glared at him over the rim of her cup. "I came out to them as bisexual when I was twelve. One of my uncles thought that meant I was a slut—that he had free access—and my parents let it happen."

Nic raged internally at the abuser and the enablers. All too common a scenario he saw in his work and in his own past.

"After two years," Becca said. "I was done."

"How'd you get out?"

"I was already into some shit. Friend of a friend introduced me to their crew. They took me in."

"Just like that?"

"I'd already been told I was a slut. An abomination. I did what I had to."

"I was told I was weak." Self-esteem trampled by his father, would Nic have done the same if he hadn't already known the love of a good man? Of a good woman who'd put herself on the line for him? If he hadn't passed that enlistment office every day?

"So you ran off and became Captain America?"

He chuckled at the too-apt description and at the memory from the other night that flitted through his mind, of Cam in a Captain America T-shirt.

"Coming out to a big family like mine," Becca said, "did not go well."

"Mine was small but I ran away too." He wasn't given a

choice to return home. Not that Becca should have, given the toxic environment she described. That toxicity had rooted itself deep, affecting her relationships. "The way you treated your girlfriend—"

"Was wrong," she acknowledged. "I fell into the trap of the abused becoming the abuser. Betrayal and jail have made me see that clearly. And I regret it, more than she'll ever know."

"I'll see what I can do about moving you somewhere more comfortable if you give me the names of the crew members who took you in."

"I already told you I wasn't kidnapped."

He gave her a significant glance, one outcast to another. "You'd be surprised the connections we find sometimes."

TWELVE

Di was right about it being all hands on deck at the D-4 station house. From the conference room where he sat with Jamie, Cam watched the flurry of bullpen activity. There was also a Sox game tonight, and with Fenway being in District 4, they'd be coordinating police presence.

His phone on the table buzzed. Picking it up, he read the text from Nic. **No luck with Becca.**

"Shit, Becca's a dead end."

"Then we better pray this one isn't," Jamie said with a nod to the door.

Following his line of sight, Cam tracked a wrecked-looking Billy Murphy and his captain, Bo Smith, through the bullpen on their way to the conference room.

"You think they'll play ball?" Jamie asked.

"If he loves his daughter, he will." Cam stood, Jamie rising beside him, as Smith entered the room, Murphy on his heels.

The officer, however, stalled over the threshold. "Cap, I thought you said we could keep the feds out of this."

"We're here in an unofficial capacity," Cam said.

"You're Keith Byrne's brother, right?" Murphy asked.

"That's right," Cam said. "He was a year behind you. I knew your brother Randy. I'm not going to do anything to hurt your family. I want to help."

"Give 'em a chance, Billy," Smith said. "Cam's one of the best agents I've worked with. He'll bring Shannon home."

Cam fought back a retort. He hated making promises like that—after a decade of this work, he knew cases didn't always end well—and the fact that Shannon was already missing over twenty-four hours wasn't a good sign. But he couldn't say any of that without upsetting Murphy more and without jeopardizing his own case.

He gestured toward the table. "Hear us out, please."

Murphy stepped the rest of the way inside, and Smith shut the door behind him as Jamie introduced himself.

Once they were all seated around the table, Cam started in easy, asking Murphy, "How long have you been on the force?"

The officer picked at the cuffs of his sleeves. "Just over two years."

"Last case I had with you guys was, what?" he asked the captain. He knew the answer—he unfortunately never forgot a case—but that's not what the question was about. He needed Murphy to see and believe the rapport Cam had with the department and with his captain.

"About three years ago," Smith replied. "Nikka Wallace. Missing almost a week. You brought her home."

"I can find Shannon myself," Murphy said to Smith. "We can. We don't need the feds."

"The FBI has more resources," Jamie countered.

Murphy's dark gaze whipped back to them. "Thought you said you were here in an unofficial capacity."

"Unofficial yes but not without resources." Cam pulled the folder he'd laid in the middle of the table closer and withdrew the top picture. "This is my sister, Erin. She disappeared twenty years ago on her way home from the library. She was twelve." He pushed the picture across the table to Murphy.

"I remember that," he mumbled, drawing the photo closer. "She looks—"

"A lot like your daughter." Cam spread the remaining photos on the table. "So do these other girls who have gone missing over the past twenty years."

Murphy's dark eyes widened. "But I thought—"

"Thought what?"

Jamie leaned forward, taking on the role of bad cop, though still soft playing it relatively. "There's a reason you don't want the feds involved, isn't there?"

It was the perfect setup for Cam to swoop in and save the day. "Do you remember me and Bobby when we were teens?" He pointed at himself, smile self-deprecating. "Not exactly law-abiding citizens."

Murphy hung his head, tugging at his sleeve again. "She's into some shit. I thought that's why . . ."

"It still may be," Smith interjected. "But if it's not, if it's got something to do with these other disappearances, don't you want the best helping us find her?"

"We can handle this delicately," Cam said. "I've got skin in this game too. I want to find out what happened to my sister, and I want to help find your daughter."

"But if there are charges against her. Or—"

He cut himself off, and Cam sensed there was a "me"

about to follow. It wasn't only Shannon who was into some shit. Shit that could very well be unconnected to Erin or the other disappearances, but it was the best lead they had. And a girl was missing regardless.

Cam needed his best people on it, needed a certain one here who'd handled a similarly delicate matter before. Maybe Nic could maneuver the local federal prosecutors from San Francisco, but if Cam knew him, and he did by now, Nic wouldn't abide sitting on the sidelines. Cam had already asked that of him enough, and this was not a case where there was a threat to his life.

He'd want to be in the middle of this, helping. He'd jumped at the chance to interview Becca and now here was a chance for him to be directly involved if Cam just asked. Except every part of that ask was dangerous, especially the part that would bring Nic to Boston. That would throw his family into further turmoil.

Because as untethered as he was beginning to feel, Cam would grab hold of Nic the second he walked through the door and not let go. A big part of him wanted Nic here. There'd be no hiding, assuming Nic didn't turn his back when he found out Cam had been the one hiding all along.

But could Cam afford not to make the ask? He was a kidnap-and-rescue agent. He had to use every lever he had at his disposal to rescue Shannon Murphy, even if throwing that lever turned his own world upside down. And hell, he'd done that already, reopening his sister's case. If helping Shannon could lead to finding out what happened to Erin, didn't he owe his mother and family that too?

"I need to make a call," he said, pushing back from the table. "There may be someone who can help us."

He slipped out of the conference room and into Di's

office, shutting the door behind him as he dialed Nic's number.

"I'm sorry I didn't have better news for you," Nic answered after the first ring, jumping straight into conversation as was their way. As much as Cam loved hearing his voice, he hated hearing the disappointment in it.

"It was a long shot. Which was why we didn't identify a lead there the first time. She was a runaway, plain and simple."

"Still, I wish I could have helped you somehow."

Cam slumped back against the door, loosening his tie and the words trapped in his throat. "There may be another way."

"Anything, Boston."

"A cop's daughter has disappeared."

"It's connected to your sister's case?"

"Maybe, but there are complications. The daughter's into some shit. The dad too. That's probably why she was taken—"

"Sounds like last spring," Nic said, putting it together.

Now Cam just had to make the ask. "Which is why I'm calling you. I need you to work your legal magic."

"That the only magic you need from me?"

Not by a long shot. He needed that magic voice live and in person, the magic taste that went along with it, and the very magic that somehow had made Nic the person who grounded him best. But with his family on edge already, Nic's professional magic was all he could ask for.

"You're the best federal prosecutor I know." Cam took Nic's silence for understanding, of all the things he'd said and not said. "I need the best on this case, Dominic." Cam said what he could, urging Nic for this favor.

It was enough, thank God. "I'll be there tomorrow."

———

Nic slurped another spoonful of Mary's homemade cioppino, cursing himself for staying away for so long. He'd had his reasons for avoiding his childhood home—namely his father—but that had come at the price of missing Mary's cooking. The native San Franciscan was not easily outmatched in the kitchen. He'd stayed in touch, visiting with her at least once a year, but these sorts of home-cooked meals were sorely missed.

As was the woman herself, the last of his father's household staff.

She sat across from him, making sure he ate every bite. Motherly as always. He'd only planned to swing by on his way to the airport to make sure Mary had all his contact numbers in case the worst of any variety should happen and to issue a *behave* warning to his father. The last thing he needed was for his father to incite an incident with Vaughn while he was clear across the country. But his father wasn't home yet, and Mary had insisted on feeding him while he waited.

"Tell me about him."

Nic almost sent a clam flying across the kitchen. "Him?" he said, bobbling the shell and dunking it back in the seafood stew.

"Whoever you're flying off to Boston for."

"It's a case." He pretended to focus all his attention on wrenching the morsel loose from its shell. Not on the excitement that was trilling through him at the certainty of seeing Cam again tomorrow.

He'd been disappointed to deliver bad news to Cam earlier, but that disappointment had vanished with the opportunity to help more tangibly and in person. He'd jumped at the chance, even if there was still something niggling in the back of his mind. Cam hadn't let him be there for him personally, but he'd let him be there professionally. Cam had been the one pushing for more and then he hadn't. Was he giving Nic the space he'd asked for? Or was there another reason he hadn't initially wanted Nic in Boston?

He hoped it wasn't guilt or embarrassment that had made Cam push him away. He had plenty of that of his own, and he'd bared those scars, memorialized in ink, to Cam. He hadn't told him the full story, but Cam knew he wasn't perfect. Nic didn't expect him to be either. In fact, he craved those imperfections along with every other part of the man he—

He gulped down another spoonful of stew, forgetting to blow on it and scalding the roof of his mouth.

Mary snickered. "See, that's what you get. Now, tell me about him."

He looked into her knowing green eyes, which had always had the power to make him spill it, even as an adult it seemed. "He's an FBI agent."

"Ooh. Handsome?"

He nodded. "And funny. Smart, very by the rules, but he'll bend them if it's for someone he cares about. We have . . . friends in common." Family had been on the tip of his tongue, but he still struggled with the concept.

"You like him," Mary said with a smile, and Nic had to set down his spoon. He hadn't admitted this to anyone, not fully at least. Hell, he was only just admitting it to himself.

"I haven't felt like this about someone since . . ."

He couldn't finish, name and words stuck in his throat. He cast his gaze outside to the cypress trees in the back-yard, the sight of which only made the words harder to come by. Made the branches on his back seem like they were extending and wrapping around his throat, strangling him.

They receded a little when Mary laid a hand on his fore-arm. "You can't let what happened almost thirty years ago hold you back from love again."

Love.

That emotion, that connection, that trouble that Nic didn't want to attribute to what had been brewing between him and Cam.

"Look what love got me and the people I cared about last time."

He'd loved, as true and deep as his eighteen-year-old heart could go. He'd loved a boy he shouldn't. A boy who would have become his stepbrother, his mother engaged to Curtis. Garrett had become his best friend and shared this house with him for three years. The best three years of his life. In part because Garrett's mom, Victoria, with Mary's help, and with Nic's father frequently away on business, had made this awful cavernous estate house seem like a home.

Until Curtis had come back from a trip early one day and found Nic and Garrett twined beneath the cypress trees, arms around each other, lips locked as they shared a dance in the warm spring afternoon.

Things had gone downhill from there. Victoria had taken the blame because God forbid Curtis Price's son have been the one who seduced the boy. Who loved Garrett.

She'd taken a hit intended for Nic, taken the slurs and the emotional abuse and blame Curtis heaped on her, and when Curtis had moved to hit her again on Nic's graduation day—because she'd packed their bags, including Nic's, daringly intending to take him with her—Nic had taken the hit instead. He'd stood between them and Curtis, shouting at his father that he was gay, had always been gay, and would always be gay. He'd threatened that if Curtis laid another hand on them, Nic would kill him.

His stand against Curtis, together with Mary's threat to call the cops, had been enough to allow Victoria and Garrett to escape.

To disappear.

Having been fleeced by his prior wife, Curtis was happy to have dodged a potential bullet. He hadn't even looked for them. If he had, he wouldn't have found them. Victoria and Garrett Scott had ceased to exist. Nic could find no legal record of the woman who had almost become his stepmother or of her son. Nic's first and only love.

Until Cam.

"You got them out," Mary said, squeezing his arm. "You saved them."

"After I put them in a position where they had to leave. I shouldn't have gotten attached to Victoria, I shouldn't have gotten involved with Garrett, and I sure as hell shouldn't have been fooling around with him here where we could be caught. Where Dad did catch us. But I couldn't help myself. I loved them too much."

"No such thing, Dominic." She shook her head, smiling sadly. "I didn't know your mother, but she'd be proud of you. For what it's worth, so am I."

He covered her hand, working the knot back down his

throat. "It's worth more than you know." He finished his stew, and she moved to take the bowl. He stood instead, taking it to the sink and washing it out himself. He turned and rested back against the counter, looking at one of the three women who'd raised him. "Who saved you, Mary? Why did you stay?"

"For you." Said simply, like a truth he didn't deserve.

He'd expected as much, but he hung his head, humbled. Grateful. "I can't thank you enough for that, but I've been gone twenty-seven years."

"Same answer, for you." She spread her knobby hands over the wood table, then lifted them, indicating the roof over their head. "To save this, for you. And to save him, for you. Otherwise, you'd feel guilty."

"But how, when he's run everyone else off? I'm worried, with him becoming more desperate . . ."

"He won't hurt me," she said, correctly reading his fears. "He tried once and then my husband laid him out." Nic's jaw hit the floor. Laughing, she stood and crossed over to him, grabbing a hand towel to dry the dishes. "You remember that spur-of-the-moment retreat he took to Palm Springs when you were ten? He was having the bones in his arm reset."

The backs of his eyes stung, and he didn't dare look outside. Not at the cypresses. Not when his father could walk in at any minute. "You didn't have to stay for me."

Mary finished drying the dishes, tossed the towel aside, and wrapped him in her arms, her head barely reaching his shoulder. "I love you like my own, Dominic. I'd do anything for you." She pulled back smiling and patted his cheek. "And working for your father paid for three of my own kids to go to college. One's a teacher, one's a doctor, and the other's a software engineer. Plus, I almost have enough saved up for me and my husband to retire someplace warmer."

He clutched her arms, not too tight but serious enough to make his point. "Please hear me, Mary. One, I'm not sure how much longer he can pay you. Two, more importantly, I'm worried for your safety, and I don't just mean from my father. He's not made the best decisions lately, and the people he's pissed off won't care who's in their way."

Her wrinkled skin blanched, and by the widening of her eyes, Nic thought maybe he'd finally gotten through to her.

"Thank you for trying to save this for me, but I'd rather you save yourself. You need to leave for that someplace warmer as soon as you can."

"Who's leaving?"

Nic spun to find his dad standing next to the table. He looked even more haggard than he had several months ago. More weight and blond hair lost, the bags under his eyes purple, and the briefcase in his hand empty, for show, if the way it hollowly thudded on the floor was any indication.

"I'm leaving," Nic said, covering because his father would not want him discussing family business with "the help," even though Mary had been privy to most of it over the years. "To Boston for work."

"Weren't you just in San Diego?"

"Yes, and now I'm needed in Boston." He turned back to Mary. "Would you give us a few minutes?"

She lifted on her tiptoes and kissed his cheek. "You go take care of your man."

His dad at least waited until she was out of the room before snidely mumbling, "Your man?"

"Yes, the man I'm involved with needs my help on a case, so I'm going to Boston to help him."

"You sure do have a type." Curtis threw his coat at the chair, missing it by a mile. He didn't bother picking it up off the floor, no doubt assuming Mary would do that. "You like to play hero, don't you?"

Every muscle in Nic coiled to attack, the insult cutting to the heart of him. He didn't play hero; he was someone who protected others. That was the man he'd become, the life he'd made, and his father wasn't going to take that away from him or bait him into tarnishing it by hitting a spiteful, defenseless old man. He curled his fingers around the counter and breathed through his nose, calming himself and getting to the conversation he wanted to have. He was in control here. "You mortgaged the house."

"You don't want it."

"You're right, I don't. I have my life, and this place doesn't factor into it. I would have deeded it to Mary, if she'd wanted it, or sold it and donated the proceeds to a battered women's or queer teen shelter."

"You will do no such thing with your inheritance."

Nic pushed off the counter, meeting his father in the middle of the room. "I don't want any of your damn money. I keep telling you and your fucking creditors that. And besides, what's even left?"

His father angled his face away, chin and nose held high, as if those alone could keep his bloated pride afloat.

"Whatever you've been hiding in that offshore account?" Nic said. Blue eyes, the same icy shade as his, darted back to him, alarmed. "If I can find it," Nic said. "So can Duncan Vaughn."

"You leave that account alone."

"What's it for?"

"Not you," his father spat.

Nic barely avoided the flying spittle, bending over to pick up Curtis's coat so Mary wouldn't have to later. "I didn't expect it was," he said, folding the coat over the back of a chair. "Don't know if you know this, but Vaughn's taken out an insurance policy on this place for twenty million dollars. That's twice its value. I don't want Mary to die in a fire because he's decided to collect." Nic stepped closer, forcing his father to look up at him. "So if you have to tap that not-so-secret slush fund of yours, you better damn well tap it."

"Go be a hero," his father said, defiant and prideful to a fault. "I don't need you to save me."

"It's not you I'm trying to save."

THIRTEEN

Soda cans spilled out of the recycling bin, candy wrappers overflowed the half dozen coffee mugs lying around, and a new color folder had been added to the rainbow files overnight—everything he and Jamie could gather, legitimately and otherwise, on Shannon Murphy and Officer William Murphy. They'd gone over the missing persons report with a fine-tooth comb, read and reread through the family statements and those of the last people to see Shannon, and hung another poster sheet with three columns for Shannon's case: *Timeline*, *Suspects*, and *Notes*.

The middle column was blank.

Cam didn't think it would stay that way for long—the guilt would eventually get to Billy if he and Jamie didn't get to the truth first. There was an equal chance the kidnapping had nothing to do with whatever had Billy torn up, just like Erin's kidnapping maybe had nothing to do with Cam and Bobby's activities that day—wrong place, wrong time. But if he'd somehow had a hand in that, like Cam had in Erin's disappearance, not being there when she needed him, then Cam hoped that would lead Billy to give them the full story. A detail in the full picture, no matter how small, could be the clue they needed to bring Shannon home.

Maybe also to learn what really happened to Erin. Sooner rather than later would be good. His mom was stable through the night, but she now had a second surgery scheduled for tomorrow. Another chance for things to go wrong. He wanted to give her answers before then, if at all possible. To put her mind and the rest of his family's at peace, if not ease.

Straightening from where he was bent over the long desk reviewing case files, he grabbed his and Jamie's breakfast bowls and took them to the kitchenette's sink. Jamie had made biscuits and sausage gravy before heading off to meet with his former graduate adviser at MIT. He'd offered to cancel but Cam had insisted he go. He never knew when they might need that connection or those skills that had been passed down to Jamie. And honestly, he'd needed some time to himself to process information and the general state of things before starting another marathon day.

Which was scheduled to kick off in twenty minutes or so with a lift from Quinn to the hospital. Their mother's doctors wanted to go over the details of tomorrow's surgery, and Cam wanted to give her a status update. Then he'd head to the station for a joint task force meeting with his old partner from the local FBI field office and Murphy and Smith, and Di's BPD team. Nic, scheduled to arrive at one, would meet them there. Cam needed more hours to get all the shit done and yet the hours couldn't pass by fast enough.

A knock sounded on the door, and Cam glanced at the wall clock.

Nope, no fast-forward button. He hadn't just sped up the space-time continuum or lost twenty minutes sleepwalking. "You're early, Q," he shouted at the door. "Give me a minute." He finished rinsing the dishes and was halfway to grabbing the coffee mugs when the knock sounded again. "All right, all right, I'm coming."

God help him if Quinn had forgotten the Dunkin' cause he had to binge that shit while he could. He yanked open the door. "I hope you didn't—"

"Didn't what?" Nic grinned. "Catch a direct flight and get here early?"

Speechless, Cam stood holding the door open, eyes feasting on the perfectly put-together man in front of him. The tailored gray suit, crisp white dress shirt, and another light blue tie that matched his eyes. Every brown and gray hair in place. A smile that was relaxed and gorgeous. No one would ever guess Nic had just come off a commercial red-eye if not for the sprinkling of overnight scruff and the rolling suitcase behind him.

"I hope you don't mind I'm early," he said. "I came straight here."

Cam shook his head and stepped back, opening the door wider. He was still struggling for words, not so much from surprise any longer as from the different directions his insides were tugging him. Head telling him that Quinn would be here any minute; he should catch Nic up on the case. Heart telling him that the person he'd wanted, *needed*, most the past four days—hell, the past five weeks —was right in front of him. Every muscle unknotting because Nic was here, then knotting right back up because

Nic was *here*. All of his blood racing south because Nic was here looking like that, and Cam's dick wanted more than the quick and dirty reunion they'd shared at his place.

So did his heart.

"My room won't be ready until this afternoon so if I can—"

Heart and dick on the same page for once, they teamed up and drowned out the rest, including Nic's words. Cam spun and pushed him up against the closed door, shoving a knee between Nic's legs and running his fingers under the lapels of his jacket and up his chiseled torso. "Did you wear this suit for me?"

"Yes." No hesitation, a truckload of gravel in that one word.

Cam coasted his hands over Nic's shoulders and then up his neck to his cheeks, dragging his thumbs over the reddish-brown scruff flecked with gray. "But you didn't shave?"

Nic angled his jaw, nuzzling against his hand. "Because you like it."

No argument there. Cam stepped closer, tasting it, lips on the prickly skin as he pressed every other inch of their bodies together. "Can I kiss you?" He needed to ask, not just take, because he was already asking so much of Nic. But fuck, he needed . . .

"Fuck—"

"Please say yes."

Nic's hands shot up, mirroring Cam's hold, the tips of his fingers tickling the nape of Cam's neck. Cam met his eyes, twin pools of scalding ice blue. "Will you let me finish?" he ground out, then ground down on Cam's thigh, rocking his hips and showing off how much he needed him too. "Fuck. Yes."

Cam fell into him. Into the kiss he'd missed. Into the arms that held on tight and kept him from shattering. Into love, more and more each day with this man. Slumping back against the door, Nic wound his arms around him, one hand diving into his hair, the other down his back, hauling him further in, kiss by kiss, breath by breath. Each swipe of the tongue another inch, each groan another mile. Cam ran with him, mouths and hips grinding, wanting to sprint to the finish but wanting the marathon reunion they'd denied themselves back in San Francisco.

Back in San Francisco. Not here in Boston. Where there was more than one race and where there was more than just his dick and heart involved.

Head kicking in, he knew that if they kept going like this, they'd both be naked in less than five minutes and Quinn would be here in ten. Fuck if they were going to be robbed of another reunion. As much as that potential reunion felt like Cam's whole world right then, it wasn't. There was a case, another girl missing, and possibly answers to the disappearance that had haunted his family for decades.

A family that didn't know he was bisexual, and his lover had just come on the scene. Would Nic even still want that, want him, when he learned Cam hadn't told his family? He'd been doggedly forcing Nic out of hiding while keeping a part of himself hidden from the other most important people of his life. Conversations needed to be had, several of them, and priorities reordered before their reunion became the top one.

He reluctantly broke the kiss but not the embrace,

resting his forehead on Nic's shoulder while he caught his breath and his bearings.

As if sensing his distress, Nic shifted his hold from desire to comfort, the tips of his fingers carding through his hair as he wrapped his other arm around him tighter. "I've got you, Boston. Just breathe."

And he did, easy for the first time since he'd been here.

After another minute, he stepped back and smoothed down Nic's dress shirt. "Thank you for coming."

Peeling off the door, Nic did the same for him, or tried, fluffing the hair he'd mussed. "I told you, you call, I'll be here. Whatever you need." He flourished his fingers in an abracadabra motion and Cam chuckled on his way to the kitchenette.

"Coffee?"

"Always."

He started the single-serve machine brewing, the strongest of the pods for Nic, who sidled up beside him, hand on his lower back. Cam wanted to purr like Bird.

"Are you sleeping?" Nic asked.

Cam side-eyed him. "Are you?"

Nic stepped closer, nuzzling his temple. "It's not a bed problem. It's a who's-missing-from-the-bed problem."

Head falling back, Cam's eyes slipped closed, reveling in the warmth and affection. "Are you trying to kill me?"

"I'm trying to tell you I missed you." Nic dropped a kiss on the hinge of his jaw, and Cam's knees were like putty, a fitting match to his insides. The assault on which Nic thankfully paused after another kiss, swiping his cup as the drip finished. He trailed his hand over Cam's hip as he stepped away. "Now, catch me up on this new lead."

He brewed himself a cup and launched into a debrief,

filling in the gaps of what he'd already told Nic and what they'd learned since yesterday. Their cups were empty by the time he finished. Cam added them to the collection by the sink. "I can bring this into the FBI's purview. We need to for resources, and the officer involved is from my old neighborhood. I can get him to trust me. I need you to rep the USAO so I can keep it contained."

"You don't anticipate any trouble with the local field office?"

"Not likely. One, it's my old office, and two, the SAC has a soft spot for missing children cases."

Nic lifted a brow, and Cam wanted to reach out and smooth it down. He settled for smoothing Nic's tie instead. "Her sister went missing too. Runaway, for certain in that case, but she knows what it feels like. She wants others to have a better ending than hers."

"You were a good fit for her team, then. But you left."

Cam's eyes clashed with searching, cautious blue ones. "I had my reasons." Being near his best friend to start, a job promotion for second, no more Boston winters for third. A certain AUSA for all the rest.

Nic let it go for now. "You think the US Attorney might object?"

"He's new since the admin change, so I don't have any leverage there."

"I'll take care of it."

That easy, and the calm washed over Cam again. Nic made him want to break all the rules, but at the same time, he made navigating so many of them easier. "Fuck, it's good having you here."

"Thank you for letting me help." Hand drifting from his

back over his ass, Nic drew him in for another kiss, like he couldn't get enough.

Cam could commiserate, getting so lost in those lips and mouth that he barely registered the knock on the door. Or was that the second one? "That's Quinn. He's giving me, us I guess, a ride to the hospital."

Caution and questions clouded Nic's eyes once more. "I can stay here, look things over, then meet you at the station as planned if that's easier."

Cam shook his head. "No, it's easier when you're with me. Always." He dropped a parting kiss on Nic's lips, then straightened his hair and clothes before opening the door.

"Don't tell me you got a girl in here?" Quinn said, waggling his brows and charging in.

Apparently he hadn't done a good enough job with the hair and clothes.

His brother drew up short, however, when he saw Nic by the table. Nic had done a better job setting himself to rights, looking his usual polished self, though Cam noticed his shoulders a tick higher than usual. "You must be Quinn," he said, hand extended. "Assistant US Attorney Nic Price. I work with Cam in San Francisco."

Quinn shook his hand. "You're here to help with the case?"

"Just got in. Cam was catching me up. He's been up all night working." Nic gestured at the wrapper-filled coffee mugs, the mess now working in Cam's favor.

"Well, that explains things," his brother said, seemingly satisfied.

Except it didn't explain things in the least, and by the look Nic was giving him, his brilliant mind was putting things together. Cam had a lot of explaining to do.

———

The car ride to the hospital was cordial enough, making getting-to-know-you small talk with Quinn. Nic asked about the fishing business. Quinn asked how long he'd been a lawyer, and once he found out Nic had been a SEAL, all the usual questions. When Quinn asked if he had any tattoos and Nic answered "A few," Cam, in the passenger seat, quickly diverted his gaze out the window and slapped a hand over his mouth, muffling laughter.

It was the only break in Cam's otherwise tense, uneasy posture. Nic had seen him like this once before, the night before he'd gone undercover with Becca's crew, anxious and worried that he would overstep the line from present cover to past reality.

This was not the relaxed, confident, could-talk-to-a-tree investigator and friend Nic knew. He couldn't easily write it off as family tension either. Yes, their mother's condition and digging into Erin's disappearance were causing a strain, but the family was still close. Angry maybe, awkward not. Nic couldn't help wondering if the tension had to do with something else. Like Cam not really wanting him here in Boston. And did that have anything to do with Quinn's comment when he'd arrived or with Cam's reaction to it? Nic had covered for him, out of habit more than anything, but to say he was confused right now was an understatement.

Back in San Francisco, Cam had been the one wanting to move in together, to take things public. Nic had conceded on the moving-in part. Not necessarily by choice, at first, but after missing Cam this week and after his talk with Mary, he was reconsidering.

Except had Cam now changed his mind about making their relationship public? Because there wasn't going to be one, kisses notwithstanding? Because he was going to move back here? It would be safer for him out of Nic's orbit, but Nic's chest ached at the prospect and disappointment left a funny taste in his mouth.

All of which paled in comparison to the life-and-death matters they had to deal with here and now. Squelching down his disappointment, Nic buttoned his coat as they approached the waiting room full of people he recognized from the pictures on Cam's desk.

Cam wanted to go over some questions with his mom, and he wanted Nic there for that in case he saw some connections Cam had missed. But the family was gathered for an update on Edith's condition first. Nic offered to wait in the cafeteria until they were done, but Cam, for all his awkward silence, shot that suggestion down like a dart. The pleading in his dark eyes was all Nic needed to see.

Though seeing a room full of dark furrowed brows over eyes glaring at him, the only other person besides Cam dressed in a suit, Nic thought maybe he should have trusted his gut and waited downstairs. His gut soured further when Cam, putting extra distance between them, introduced him formally. "Everyone, this is Dominic Price. He's a federal prosecutor I work with in San Francisco."

Bobby greeted him first, his blue eyes kind as he shook Nic's hand, thanked him for coming, and for having Cam's back last spring.

Keith, who Nic recognized from his bearing, remained standing apart in the far corner of the lounge. "Why are you bringing more people into this?" he asked Cam. "Jamie wasn't enough?"

"Nic's the reason your leave got extended. Show some respect."

Keith strode forward, arms over his chest. "My CO said it was a SEAL captain that got my leave extended, not a fucking suit."

From his conversations with Cam, Nic had expected Keith's attitude. He even expected the bite in his words, having dealt with more than a few hotheaded enlisteds. So he'd come prepared with his zippered case of ribbons and medals, and he'd clipped in two of the most distinctive pins, rank insignia Keith would recognize, as cuff links before they'd left the hotel.

Making sure his cuff was showing, he held out a hand to Keith. "Retired Captain Dominic Price, SEAL Team 3 and Navy JAG Corps."

Bobby whistled low, and Keith's startled blue eyes grew wide.

The sergeant snapped to attention with his next breath, as a well-trained Marine would do. "Apologies, Captain." Keith shook his hand. "This is a sensitive subject for our family. I'm not at my best."

"I'm aware of that, Sergeant," Nic replied. "Cam's also a friend. I know this is a difficult time for all of you. You're doing better than most under the circumstances."

"Who's this?" came an even thicker Southie voice behind them.

Nic turned, spying the man who could only be Cam's father standing in the doorway, two trays of coffees in hand.

Bobby relieved him of the coffees, passing them around, while Cam introduced Nic to his father, who greeted him warmly, expressing his gratitude for getting Keith's leave extended. "You're friends with Cam in San Francisco?" Nic nodded, and Ken slapped his back. "Be a good wingman and help my son find a wife who can get him to sleep."

Beside him, Cam jerked, and Nic flailed for a response, at a rare loss for words.

A *wife*.

Not a wife or husband. And back in the hotel room, Quinn had asked if there was a *girl* in there. Not a girl or guy.

Was Cam not—

Before Nic could finish his thought, a doctor appeared in the doorway.

"How's Mom?" Quinn asked.

"Why don't we all have a seat?" the doctor said.

"That don't sound too good, Doc," Ken said as the family scattered around the room, claiming chairs and sofas. If Nic had his way, he'd sit on the arm of the chair Cam had fallen into, but if his suspicion was right, that would be the last thing Cam wanted. So he took up a spot on the wall near him. Apart from the family but close enough Cam would know he was there for him and without causing him more distress.

"She's holding her own," the doctor said.

"With this many of us," Quinn said, "she's had a lot of practice."

Laughter broke the tension, but then the mood nosedived again with the doctor's next words. "That's good. She's gonna need all her strength as we go on. We have to clean out some arteries, but I need to remind you of the possible complications, including an increased risk of embolism and stroke."

Cam sucked in a breath, and Nic took a step forward,

the instinct to go to him automatic. Until Cam stiffened, his rigid posture as clear a *stay back* sign as any. The comfort wasn't welcome. Not here at least.

Because Cam wasn't out as bisexual to his family.

The rest of the doctor's words faded as Nic fell back against the wall and turned that revelation over in his head, a sandstorm brewing in his stomach and mouth and itching under his skin. Christ, the last thing Nic wanted to hide at this point in life was his sexuality. There'd been no going back after he'd made public that fact at eighteen. It had driven his every step forward. It was who he was, Garrett had helped him realize that. Serving during Don't Ask, Don't Tell, he'd had to be careful, to take his extracurricular activities off base, but Nic had never pretended to be what he wasn't. Embracing his sexuality was as much a promise to himself as a tribute to that first love and an atonement for what had been lost because of it. To be free and to love who he wanted.

If he and Cam kept building something, he wouldn't want to hide that either. While Nic had been reticent last spring to make their relationship public—to protect Cam from Vaughn, to avoid awkwardness with their friends, to avoid issues at work—those were all temporary hurdles that could be cleared. And they had nothing to do with him being gay or Cam being bisexual. Cam was too good a man for Nic not to want to live and love him openly. This, however, was a much different, much higher hurdle.

It wasn't a hurdle he could boost Cam over either. Coming out to his family was a decision Nic had made for himself. Granted, his hand had been forced, but he'd said the words, he'd made the final call. He wouldn't—couldn't —make that call for Cam, especially not in a situation that was already fraught with tension. And especially when he didn't know enough about the Byrne family dynamics to know whether Cam's coming out would be accepted. Sure, they'd accepted Jamie, but he wasn't their son or brother. Nic recalled his interview with Becca yesterday, how she'd described her family turning against her. Like Nic's father had turned on him. He didn't think that would be the case with Cam's family, but he didn't know. Only Cam did and he'd chosen not to say anything about the two of them being more than colleagues and friends.

Which was what Nic would have to be. And only that. Far short of what he really wanted with Cam.

FOURTEEN

As the doctor continued to go over surgical forms, Nic excused himself to make a call. He needed to make sure the ball he'd started rolling yesterday with Justice on Shannon Murphy's case was on track. He also needed a break from the mounting tension between the Byrne brothers and from the realizations he'd had about Cam and his feelings toward him.

He didn't have long to dwell, his call expedited to the Deputy Attorney General. "Price," he answered. "Tell me you're calling with an answer about San Diego."

"No, sir. I need to reserve that decision for the end of the week." Given this latest development and the strain Nic sensed Cam was under being away from his family, San Diego was still in play. "Unless your timeline's been moved up."

The Deputy AG chuckled. "Price, you know as well as I do that my timeline is always moved up. But for this I can wait."

"Thank you, sir."

"Now, what was it you needed?"

He gave the Deputy AG the thirty-thousand-foot view of the situation, emphasizing his experience handling delicate cases, Cam's experience as a K&R expert, and the potential connection Shannon's disappearance had to multiple cold cases. Federal prosecutors didn't usually go digging into those. Bad for the clearance rate. But Nic was willing to take the risk if it brought Shannon home and Cam's family peace.

"They're already overworked in the Boston office, and if the Bureau SAC there backs your and Byrne's involvement, that'll go a long way. I doubt they're going to object but let me touch base with them and get back to you."

"Appreciate it, sir."

"I've got hearings up on the Hill again this afternoon, so it might be my assistant or the Boston office you hear from."

"I'll be on the lookout for the call. And good luck with the hearings."

"Thanks." Not an amused chuckle this time. "I'll look forward to hearing from you Friday."

Call ended, Nic was calmer than when he'd started, the deep dive back into work and protocol grounding. It helped as he rejoined Cam and his brothers gathered outside Edith's room. Nic maintained a careful distance between them, close enough for friends and colleagues, nothing more. As it were, Keith was arguing strenuously and loudly against Cam and Nic speaking to his mother about the case. He understandably didn't want to upset her. Cam understandably didn't want her to think he wasn't doing as she asked.

The lady herself made them both understand she was

the one in charge. "Keith!" she called from inside the room. "Stop making trouble."

The younger man scoffed. "Me?" he said, looking back and forth between them. "We wouldn't be having this conversation at all if not for—"

"That's enough," Edye cut him off. "Let your brother in."

Nic couldn't see her from where he stood but that voice left no room for argument. Realizing he'd lost this round, Keith blustered out, shoving Cam's shoulder as he passed.

"We got him." Bobby snagged Quinn's sleeve and followed Keith into the elevator.

"Your father?" Nic asked, noting the older man's absence.

"With my sisters-in-law in the cafeteria. Mom insisted he eat and take his meds."

"And I insist you get in here," she called from inside the room.

"I can wait out here," Nic offered.

"No, I want you in there." With me, unsaid but said. Until he added, "In case there's something helpful for the case," and Nic wondered if he'd imagined Cam's true intention.

He nodded and stepped aside so Cam could lead them into the room.

Cam's hand coasting across his lower back was enough of an answer for now.

Inside, Edith sat propped up in the hospital bed, book on her lap, dark eyes sharp behind a pair of reading glasses.

It was clear who ruled the Byrne family.

"Who is this gorgeous specimen?" she asked, eyes

blatantly raking him up and down. It was also clear where Cam got his flirtatious streak.

"Mom," Cam groaned, the picture of an embarrassed child as he pulled a second chair next to the bed.

Nic laughed out loud as he avoided the IVs and wires and gently shook Edye's hand. "Nic Price, I work with your son in San Francisco."

"You're an FBI agent?"

"No, ma'am." He lowered himself in the chair next to Cam, not wanting to loom over her. He braced his forearms on crossed legs and leaned forward, keeping up the rapport. "I'm a federal prosecutor."

"He's being modest," Cam said, casting him a side-eye. "He's second in command at the local US Attorney's Office."

She straightened a little, catching on. "Are you here to help Cam? To help me?"

"I'm going to do whatever I can. He's made good headway."

Her gaze shifted to her son. "What've you found?"

Cam updated her on his findings, fully as to the cold cases, then more generally as to the Murphy matter. Enough to give her hope but not enough to compromise the ongoing investigation.

"What about all the other girls? In the books?"

"Most of them have been found."

"We actually ran into one earlier this year," Nic added.

"What about the ones who haven't been found? You said they fit a pattern? That Erin fits it too?" The heart attack clearly hadn't affected her mental faculties. She'd distilled all that down to the connections to her missing daughter.

"She does." Cam curled a hand around hers. "But don't get your hopes up, Ma. We'd identified most of these girls before and the trails were too cold to follow."

"But not this cop's daughter. You're going to help find her regardless?"

Cam nodded. "Yes, Shannon's the best lead we've got."

"Then what are you still doing here?"

"I wanted you to know that I—" He looked over at Nic, then back to his mother. "That we are doing everything we can."

She patted his hand, much like Mary used to do to Nic when he was being obtuse. "I always know that."

Cam hung his head. "I didn't that day."

It was everything Nic could do not to reach out to him.

Edye had the right words, though. "But you have, son, every day since, including now, even though your brothers don't want you to."

Unconditional maternal love and belief; it would kill Boston to lose her. "You want me to," Cam said. "I need to. And they need to know too."

She smiled and ruffled his hair. "You always were the smartest one."

Nic rolled his eyes dramatically. "Please don't encourage him."

Cam chuckled, and it was a good, much-missed sound. "And you," Cam said to him with a smile, "don't tell my brothers she said that."

Nic grinned back at him. "My lips are sealed."

He didn't miss the double play of the words, dark eyes flaring. Edye had his back too. "I like him."

Cam rose, bending over to kiss her head. "Don't encourage him either."

She smirked, splitting a look between them. "This is going to be fun."

———

By the time they left Tufts Medical and navigated midday traffic over to the station, Jamie was waiting out front for them. Cam had hoped to talk to Nic on the drive over— talk, apologize, fuck he didn't know what—but Nic had spent half the drive on the phone with the Boston US Attorney and the other half with an attorney from his office in San Francisco, making sure a motion on Friday was covered. Cam didn't want to interrupt, seeing as all those arrangements were for him, but he also didn't like the wall Nic had thrown up between them. Granted Cam had laid the foundation and Nic was only following his lead, but this was not what he'd intended to build together.

"Nic," Jamie greeted him, hand outstretched. "Thanks for getting here so fast."

"Was happy to help," Nic replied.

"We officially get jurisdiction?"

"I sure as fuck hope so," came another voice from down the street. "Otherwise, I'm in the wrong damn place."

Smiling, Cam turned toward the New York accent that was even thicker than his Boston one. Born and raised in the Big City, diehard Yankees fan Matthew Kim had somehow landed in Red Sox country after Academy. Cam couldn't have gotten luckier in the rookie partner draw.

"Matty-K," he said, arms spread wide.

His old partner walked into them, giving him a back-slapping hug. "You know, you're the only one who calls me by that fucking nickname. It's been such a peaceful year without it."

"Couldn't let you forget it."

"I heard about your mom," Matt said, smile dimming. "You wouldn't rather be at the hospital?"

"Climbing the walls while she has another surgery?" Cam shook his head. "No, and I'm doing what she asked."

"Need the distraction, I get that." He clapped his shoulder before turning to Jamie. "Whiskey, I heard you bagged a hot-as-hell Irishman."

Jamie side-eyed Cam, who shrugged. "Hey, you said it."

"Whole city full," Matt teased, waving his arms around, "and you had to go to San Francisco to get one."

"I got the right one," Jamie said. "That's all that matters."

Matt cringed dramatically, like he was smelling something foul. "Oh God, he's a lovesick fool. Keep him away!"

Cam laughed. "You have no idea." As if to cover his own current state of foolishness, he turned to Nic, introducing him formally. "Matthew Kim, this is AUSA Dominic Price."

The two men shook hands. "You overseeing this for Justice?" Matt asked.

Nic nodded. "I am now."

"We work together in San Francisco," Cam said. Nic didn't flinch but Cam saw that telltale lift of his broad shoulders. Cam talked over it, continuing to ignore his own foolishness. "The SAC filled you in?"

"She did," Matt said. "And now that we're official, I can speak freely." Leading them to one of the picnic tables in the station courtyard, Matt switched from jovial bro to the impeccable agent who'd always had Cam's back. "We know why Officer Murphy wants to keep this quiet." He pulled a file out of his messenger bag and dropped it on the table. "It's not just the daughter who's into some shit. He's knee-deep in it too."

"Trying to protect her?" Nic asked.

"She's a street dealer for Koehler." One of the local thugs that Cam knew all too well. "He's been using it as leverage against her dad," Matt said. "Favors from BPD. Looking the other way when shipments go missing and such."

"That's a tougher sell to DOJ," Nic said. Cam didn't do a good job of hiding the frustration on his face. Seeing it, Nic hastened to add, "I'll do what I can to sell it, but Murphy's law enforcement. He knows better. It'll go smoother if he cooperates."

"He hasn't so far," Jamie weighed in.

Matt eyed the bulging folder in the middle of the table. "We've got enough there to make that happen."

Cam's phone vibrated with an incoming text from Di. "We better make it happen soon," he said, looking back up at the group. "Murphy just got a ransom demand."

"Let's do this, then." Matt grabbed his file, standing with a grin. "Just like old times." He elbowed Jamie in the side. "You still aren't official."

Jamie shrugged, explaining to Nic, "I may have consulted a bit when I was at MIT."

Nic rolled his eyes, chuckling. "I would have never guessed."

He started to stand but Cam laid a hand on his knee beneath the table, keeping him seated. "Go on in," Cam told Matt and Jamie. "Need to check one more thing with Justice. We're right behind you."

Matt was about to say something, but Jamie pushed him on ahead.

As soon as they rounded the corner, Nic's attention whipped back to Cam. A blush stained his high cheekbones, highlighting his handsome, angular face, and made Cam want to do more than just talk.

But talk was what they had to do before moving forward on the case or otherwise. "Thank you for wrangling with DOJ," he said.

"You can quit thanking me. I told—"

Cam squeezed his knee, then inched his hand higher. "But I didn't tell you, not everything."

Nic laid a hand atop his, stopping it from climbing higher. He left it there, though, tangling their fingers. "You're not out to your family."

Of course he'd figured it out. He was one of the smartest men Cam knew. "It was never the right time and now . . ."

"I'm not going to ask you to, Cam. That's your decision."

Cam's gaze shot up from their hands. "I expected you to argue."

Nic shook his head. "Not about this. It's one hundred percent your call."

"I feel like a coward. You, Aidan, and Jamie, you're all out, and I—"

Nic squeezed his fingers. "There's no one right time, Boston. No one right way. It's different for each person. Sometimes a person comes out all at once to everyone, which was the case for me. Sometimes it's bit by bit, like Jamie, like you. In any event, it should always be by choice, not because they've been outed, issued an ultimatum, or had their hand forced. I'm not going to do that to you."

The conviction of his words and in his fierce blue eyes made Cam wonder and worry more about Nic's own coming out. There was more to it than he'd let on last spring, Cam was sure. And he was increasingly certain it had something to do with *GS* and the cypress tree inked on Nic's back.

Nic turned over their hands and put something in his palm. "But if you want to build something here, Boston, you're going to have to eventually. I'll give you time, but I don't want to hide forever. I can't anymore."

He withdrew his hand and slid off the bench, headed for the station's entrance. Cam waited until he'd turned the corner to open his palm. In it was a folded airplane napkin. He peeled back the corners to reveal a rough sketch of a new Gravity label.

Fighting Boston Irish. An imperial stout. Gravity's falling apricot logo was the top third of a Celtic clover.

Cam lost his breath, his heart too.

The future he wanted was right there—in his hand and walking into the station house to help solve a case that had haunted Cam for half his life. Yet it felt like the future he wanted—with Nic—was slipping away, the rope coming untethered and Cam floating farther out to sea.

FIFTEEN

"How'd the ransom demand come in?" Cam asked.

He sat on one side of the conference table—Nic on his right, Jamie and Matt on his left. Di was facilitating at the head of the table. On her other side, across from the federal contingency, sat Murphy, looking even more wrecked today, together with Smith and a BPD union rep.

Di pushed an evidence bag Cam's way, a generic burner phone inside. "Video on the phone. It was dropped off at Murphy's home."

"Anyone see the courier?" Matt asked.

Murphy shook his head.

Cam drew the bag toward them. "Evidence has processed?"

Di nodded, and he pulled the phone out. Flipping it over, he opened the photo app and pressed Play on the only item there. A single video.

Nic and Jamie crowded close, while Matt stood behind him, viewing it over his shoulder. They collectively noted details as they watched.

"Basement," Nic said, and Cam agreed, judging by the diffuse light coming from what looked like a sidewalk-level transom.

"Commercial building," Matt said. "Electrical panel's too big for residential."

"A garage of some sort," Jamie added. "The boxes stacked along the wall are from an auto parts dealer." The gearhead would know. Cam recognized them too.

A figure appeared on-screen wearing a ski mask. Given their size, it was a male. The voice confirmed it a second later. "I have your daughter, Officer Murphy."

Cam detected an accent not too far from his own. "Boston native."

"If you want her back, here's what you're gonna do . . ." The suspect went on to describe how Murphy was to steal evidence that was in the D-4 evidence locker. "You do this," the man said, "you'll get Shannon back."

The camera panned and rotated to the side of the room they hadn't seen yet, and in the corner, on a thin stained mattress, huddled a teenage girl. Legs folded against her chest, she'd buried her face in her knees.

"Smile for the camera," the man said, and the girl looked up.

Cam sucked in a breath. She looked so much like Erin. Dark hair, dark eyes, tears streaming down her face. In his periphery, he saw Nic's hand twitch, like he'd been about to put it on Cam's leg, but then his fingers curled around his own thigh instead. Cam shifted, brushing their knees together under the table. After their earlier conversation, after watching this and knowing that could have been Erin too, twenty years ago, he needed the connection. Nic didn't move away, and that link helped Cam stomach the rest of the video. Through a close-up of Shannon's tear-streaked face, another repetition of the kidnapper's demands, and where to meet them for a handoff later that night. When the video ended, Cam closed the app and slowly slid the phone back in the evidence bag, letting his adrenaline bleed out as he gathered his thoughts.

"Do you have any idea who might be behind this?" he asked Murphy once he'd passed the bag back to Di.

Murphy wiped at his own tears. "I didn't recognize the voice."

"That's not what Agent Byrne asked," Matt said, reclaiming the seat on the other side of Jamie. "Is Koehler behind this?"

Murphy visibly trembled. "We need assurances," the union rep said.

Nic withdrew a folded paper from his jacket pocket. He'd been on a call when Cam had come in from the courtyard. This must have been why. He slid the paper across the table to Murphy. "Immunity from federal obstruction charges."

"What about my job?"

"DOJ can't guarantee that," Nic said. "That's BPD's call." Murphy looked from the union rep to Di, then to his captain. "You're compromised, Billy," Smith said.

"This is your daughter." Cam drew Murphy's attention back to him, back to what was important. "Is your job more important than her life?"

He hung his head, chastened. "No, of course not."

"Do you have a pen?" the union rep asked.

"And a pad of paper," Murphy added. Di got him both,

and Murphy signed the deal, then started scribbling names on the legal pad. "Who I think might be involved." He pushed the pad across the table to Cam. "But like I said, I didn't recognize the voice on the recording. Or that place."

"But they know who you are." Cam handed the pad of names to Jamie. "Run these and let's see if we can also trace the call origin."

He nodded, already typing a mile a minute on his phone. "I'm on the boxes too."

"We can go at this from two sides," Matt said.

"Agreed. One team on the handoff, one team on the garage." Cam turned back to Murphy. "Can you handle the meet?"

"It has to be me," he said, voice shaking. "Me and me alone. No cops. That's what he said."

"You'll be wired."

Murphy shook his head. "He'll see that. I can't risk Shannon."

"He won't see the tech I've got," Jamie replied. "And I can make the evidence look like it's gone. Create a ghost of the record."

"And we can mock up something for the handoff," Matt said. "Embed a tracker."

"All right," Cam said, hearing all their bases covered. "The video said half past midnight. We've got work to do."

Everyone around the table stood and hopped to it. Matt off with Di to call in the FBI from Chelsea, Jamie off to tech, and Murphy, with his captain and rep, off to a holding room.

When it was just him and Nic left in the room, the last half hour came crashing down and the remaining adrenaline rushed out of Cam. Eyes closed, he rested back against the edge of the table. Heat hit his side and Nic's fingers brushed over his.

"Breathe, Boston."

He sighed, head falling back. "She looks so much like Erin."

"And yet we have a pretty good idea why she was taken, if not where."

Cam righted his head, brow furrowed. "What are you saying?"

"You need to be prepared for Shannon's case not to be connected to Erin's. This may just be a runaway who got caught up with the wrong people who are using her as leverage."

"Since when are you questioning the victim?" Cam made to snatch his hand back, and Nic held tighter. Forcing him to listen.

"I haven't heard from the victim in this case. I'm giving her and her father the benefit of the doubt." He glanced significantly at the immunity agreement on the table. "But I also talked to Becca—she looks just like them too—and she was a runaway, plain and simple."

He was right of course. The investigator side of his brain knew that was the more likely scenario. That this wasn't connected to Erin at all. But the brother and son part of his heart desperately wanted it to be.

Nic scooted closer, their shoulders brushing. "You need to be Special Agent Byrne with the FBI, not Cameron Patrick Byrne, grieving son and brother. Can you do that?"

Gazes locked, he reached for the grounding those blue eyes offered. "Regardless of whether she left voluntarily or was kidnapped, I don't want her family to go through what mine did. They need to know."

Nic smiled, small but satisfied. "So Agent Byrne it is."

He nodded, focused again. "I'll catch 'em."

"And I'll lock 'em up."

———

"Enough, Dominic!"

Cam yanked a Kevlar vest on over his head, and Nic wanted to grab him by the straps and shake him. He couldn't believe they were having this fucking argument again.

Within earshot of Jamie and other agents no less.

Cam reached for a helmet and Nic slapped down his hand, demanding his undivided attention. He was sure it drew others' attention too but fuck it. They were already eavesdropping. "Do not leave me in a fucking van again," Nic gritted out. Sidelined during the Kristić raid, listening as the op had gone south, had been maddening.

Dark eyes snapped to him, all business. "While it would have been unorthodox, you could have—maybe should have—led the team on the Kristić raid, but these agents don't know you. This is *my* team, *my* people. Not yours, not Aidan's. And this is my case, my specialty."

The agent voice rankled, even if every word Cam said was true. It also rankled that he'd been left out of the tactical planning. Cam had probably anticipated this argument and had hoped to avoid it. Tough shit. Even if he wasn't going in, he needed to know what Cam was charging into.

"Why are you leading *this* team?"

They were parked a block away from the garage they suspected the ransom call had originated from. Jamie had traced the call to a nearby cell tower, then had even better luck tracing the auto parts boxes to one of Koehler's South End garages. While they converged on the garage, Matt was leading a separate team across town at the supposed exchange site.

Cam uncrossed his arms, a measure less defensive. "I'm leading this team because there's nothing to suggest the people who took Shannon will actually hand her over at the exchange. She's too valuable as leverage. They want to see that Murphy is cooperating. Following their orders with no cops or feds involved. That's what that meet is about."

"But there are feds there."

Cam held up a finger. "One team. Because they're unlikely to show there, at least not until Murphy steps into the zone and proves himself. They'll call from a distance and ask to see proof. Then it's an easy snatch and grab of either Murphy or the evidence they think he has. Matt's team is there for protection and intercept."

"And the three teams here?" Nic asked.

"Rescue, if Shannon is being held here. And this is my old hood from when Bobby and I were teens. That's why I'm leading the team here."

Nic dragged a hand over his jaw, scruff growing in thicker while his patience thinned by the hour. He dropped his arm and lowered his voice, imploring, "I cannot be on the other end of the line again, listening and only half knowing what's going on. I don't need to be the lead. Just your backup."

"And I cannot watch you get tossed over the hood of a car again or worse." Stalemate, which Cam broke in dirty cheater fashion. "Besides, do you want to be the one to tell

Aidan you left his husband out here alone in the surveillance van?"

"Please, Jamie could drive this thing out of here before anyone ever caught him."

Cam smiled, and Nic realized the trap he'd stepped into. "Which is why you're staying in the van," Cam said, victorious.

"Fuck you," Nic spat back.

Cam leaned closer, voice a whisper. "If it keeps you alive so I can do that later, then fine by me." He turned on his heel, grabbed a helmet, and walked over to the bank of surveillance monitors where Jamie and the other agents were checking comms.

Nic stood in his corner, stewing. Cam's parting shot was the best thing and worst thing Nic could've heard right then. Cam still wanted him—good—but they were trapped in a fucking van with other agents in the middle of a time-sensitive op. He couldn't do a damn thing about the kiss he wanted to give Cam. He could have used the raid to channel some of that energy, but Cam was sidelining him again. Frustration assailed him from every direction, boiling over as he watched Agent Byrne go through the pre-op motions.

"Everyone in position?" Cam asked into the comm mic.

Beta and Charlie teams checked in, then Matt from the exchange site. "We're set with Murphy here," he said. "Just waiting for your mark."

"We're a go in five," Cam said, signing off.

Turning away before he did or said something he shouldn't, Nic ducked into the front cab, collapsing into the passenger seat and staring out the front windshield. The night went from dark to darker as it slipped into the next day, no sign of life on this industrial block in the wee hours of the morning.

After another couple minutes, Cam appeared through the dividing curtain. "You gonna stay mad at me?" he asked, dropping into the driver's seat as the curtain swung back closed.

"This argument isn't over."

"Says the attorney."

Nic rolled his eyes, not fighting his smile. The exchange, while frustrating as hell, felt like normal. Like them. Not like the weird limbo they'd been in earlier that day.

"You strapped under the coat?" Cam asked. Nic flicked back the front flap of his jacket, flashing his Beretta. Cam nodded. "Try not to get into trouble."

"Says the man in tactical gear."

Sliding forward, Cam angled toward him, brushing their knees together and dropping his voice low. "It's the only thing keeping me from jumping you right now."

Nic tilted his head toward the back of the van on the other side of the curtain. "That and your best friend in there."

Cam clicked his tongue against the back of his teeth. "Low blow, Price."

"Says the man telling me to stay in the fucking van. Again."

Cam glided his knee inside Nic's, higher up, pushing his legs apart. Doing what his hands couldn't in case anyone saw through the window. "You're my rope. I can't have it severed. So yes, I'm ordering you to stay in the fucking van."

Losing the battle to frustration and desire, Nic shot out a hand, grabbed a vest strap, and yanked Cam closer. Not all the way into his lap, because there was only one place that would lead, which was a no-go with other agents in back. But close enough to smell the lingering traces of Cam's soap, to feel the heat of him beneath the gear, to press his cock against Cam's knee between his thighs. "I'll stay in the fucking van," he growled. "But you hold tight to the rope."

Cam grinned, wicked. "Count on it."

SIXTEEN

"Half past," Jamie radioed, and Cam gave the signal for his team to move. On quiet approach, he was depending on Jamie cycling through position checks to gauge where each of the teams were, including Matt's across town.

Cam led his team down an alley a building over from their target. Peering around the corner, he looked for the gate in the target garage's back fence.

Every other building on this street was a garage and most of them had caged-in yards where cars were parked overnight. The fences around the garage yards usually had two entrances. A big rolling gate for cars to pass through and a smaller swing gate easier for people to enter and exit. A better-than-average B&E guy, Cam had always counted on those pedestrian gates for quick and easy access.

He spotted the smaller gate on this side of the target near the back of the garage structure. Good, they wouldn't have to expose themselves darting across the yard. He signaled his team to move again. They crouched low, sliding along the back of the neighboring building, hiding in the shadows.

At the near corner before they crossed the next alley, Cam signaled his team to stop and did a one-eighty sweep with his eyes and helmet cam, trusting Jamie to double-check the alley and target building.

He saw the problem as soon as Jamie did, the other man saying, "Hold." A flurry of keyboard strokes, then the security cameras at the corner of the target building dipped, their power light clicking off.

"Clear now," Jamie said, just as Matt radioed, "Murphy texted them a picture of the goods. He's approaching the drop location now."

They had to time this exactly right. Cam wasn't lying when he'd told Nic he didn't think the kidnappers would actually meet Murphy at the drop. At least not with Shannon. But he did think they would be in that vicinity, not too far from where they could claim their prize. That left Shannon here—potentially unguarded—while the henchmen were distracted.

Cam signaled his team to move again, and Jamie kept the others updated. "Alpha team approaching target."

"Car approaching the drop point from the west," Matt said. "Slow, lights off."

Jamie rattled off the car's specs, as seen through Matt's camera. A red nineties Camaro—something about the details of the car rang familiar to Cam. He made a mental note to follow up, then got back to work on the gate's lock, focused on his team's advance.

Matt counted down the approach in feet until the car was parked, and Murphy was at the driver-side door.

"Driver's in a mask," Jamie reported, and Cam bit back

a curse. Through the comm Murphy was wearing, he heard the conversation.

"Give us the goods," someone in the car said.

"Yeah, here."

"Murphy's handing over the package," Jamie reported. Forgeries of documents that were supposedly stolen out of the D-4 evidence locker.

"We'll be in touch with our next request," the same voice from the video replied, and then the roar of an engine blasted over the line, followed by Murphy's screams of "Where's my daughter?"

Cam's team had to move. Now.

He blocked out the burgeoning chaos on the other end —Matt ordering his team to converge, a gunshot, "Murphy's hit"—and charged forward with his team, through the gate to the back door of the garage. Holding up a hand, he counted down the breach with his fingers, making it all the way to one, then paused when the squeal of tires burning rubber echoed not in his ear but close by. On the same block as them and gaining speed by the sound of it.

"Alpha," Jamie said, "Unknown car headed your way. Charger, newer model."

No time left.

Bypassing the lock, Cam clutched the door jamb on either side, bracing himself to kick the door in by force.

Moisture seeped through his gloves, yet there'd been no rain or moisture in town for days.

Jerking back his hands, he flipped up his tactical helmet mask with the back of one and brought the other to his nose, sniffing.

He recognized that smell, the same one he'd gotten a

whiff of early Saturday morning outside the burning apartment unit in Nic's building.

Accelerant.

"Boston, get the fuck out of there," Nic's strangled scream came across the line. "He's got a Molotov."

Breaking silence, Cam shouted at his team, even as he braced again and lifted his foot, kicking at the door. "Everyone, get back! Move, move, move!"

"Cameron!" Jamie shouted. "Go with them!"

"Why the fuck aren't you moving?" Nic added loudly.

He kicked again at the door. "Shannon could be in there." The roar of the oncoming car grew louder, closer. "Jamie, get up front and drive. Follow the car!"

On the other end, the van's engine revved and Nic cursed first at Jamie, then at him. "Fucking hell, Boston, get out of there!"

"She may—"

"They're not going to sacrifice their leverage. She's not in there!"

Even if Shannon wasn't, something had to be if someone was willing to torch the place with a Molotov cocktail. Evidence, leads, maybe something that could connect the case to Erin. Cam had to get in there, save whomever or whatever it was before all hope went up in flames.

"Agent Byrne!" Nic clipped in a voice that cut through Cam's single-minded determination. It was not a tone he'd ever heard him use before; one Cam guessed had been more common in the desert halfway around the world. "Back off the target now!" Cam hesitated, his helmet and no doubt the camera attached to it shaking. Nic tempered the commanding tone when he added, "Nothing will be solved if you die. Don't do that to your family."

Don't do that to me.

"Fuck!" Spinning on his heel, Cam ripped off his accelerant-soaked gloves and ran for his team at the far edge of the yard. "Stay on the—"

His words were swallowed up by the spinning of tires, the shattering of glass, and a booming *whoosh* that drowned out everything but Nic's "Boston!"

A ball of heat blasted into Cam's back, lifting him off his feet and hurtling him against the gate.

———

"Turn the goddamn van around, Jamie!"

Nic's shouts from the back of the van went unheeded by the man up front who was whipping them around corners and speeding down the narrow streets of Boston. Traffic was light at this hour—they were moving fast after the Charger—but the streets weren't totally deserted, their mad dash drawing a cacophony of car horns. The only reason Nic wasn't puking his guts out on the wild ride was his prior experience getting tossed around tanks and boats. This was nothing new. But the tossing and turning of his insides . . . Now that was new and shaking him up far worse than the physical jostling.

"Get up, get up, get up," he mumbled, not that Cam could hear him. Audio had been blown by the explosion, but Nic still had visual. A sideways shot from Cam's motionless helmet cam showed the fire eating up the garage, creeping out toward the yard and an unconscious Cam. Why wasn't anyone pulling him back? Had the entire team been taken out? Or had Cam just lost his helmet? Nic couldn't see and the not knowing was driving him insane.

"We need to go back!" he shouted at Jamie. "We don't know what happened to the team."

"I need you up here!"

"Fuck!" Nic slapped the table with his open palm, frustration boiling over at being sidelined and pulled away from where he wanted to be. Again. But if he wanted to get back there, the quickest way was to help the driver.

Cranking up the volume on the wall speakers, making sure he'd hear Cam's call when it came through, he shot to his feet and charged up front. He'd just pushed through the curtains to the cab when Jamie slammed on the brakes, propelling him forward, fast. He went flying toward the dash, arms and hands outstretched to catch himself, but the speed and momentum were more pressure on his wrists than they could handle.

He was going to hit the windshield.

Later, Boston, was on the tip of his tongue, but Jamie saved him the sentiment and probably his life, grabbing a fistful of his jacket and yanking him back. He went down hard in the passenger seat, but he was still in one piece, as was the biker that had ridden out in front of a speeding van.

"Get out of the way!" Jamie yelled, and the biker, still wide-eyed from his near-death collision, hustled past. Foot on the gas, Jamie revved the van back into action, chasing after the Charger. "You okay?"

Nic straightened in the seat, checking his wrists and appendages. "Yeah, thanks."

Eyes still on the road, Jamie shot him a sideways grin. "Didn't think Cam would appreciate it overly much if I killed you."

"And I'm not going to appreciate it overly much if

something happens to him and I'm in this van with you," Nic replied as he buckled his seat belt. "No offense."

Jamie chuckled. "None taken."

"What do you need me to do so we can get back there?"

"If I get close enough, can you shoot out the tires?"

Yeah, he could. The Navy had trained him well, as an attorney and a sniper. He withdrew his Beretta and disengaged the safety. "Get me in spotting distance, and I'll nail him."

Grin wicked, Jamie kicked the van into another gear, gaining on the red taillights ahead of them. When the Charger hung a left a street ahead, Jamie took the next left, a block early. Sliding and correcting, he flew down the empty side street. Unbuckling and getting into position, Nic wound his left arm through the seat belt, securing himself, then levered the top half of his body out the window, ready to take aim when they emptied back out into the cross street, right on the Charger's tail.

Drawbridge lifting up ahead, the chase was on, the Charger racing to make it over the bridge before the two halves split. Nic lifted his firing arm, trying to get a clean shot, but the Charger's swerving motion was making it impossible. "I'm gonna need you to swing left to get a clean shot."

"We're gonna lose them if you don't hit it."

"I'll hit it. Do it now!"

Hand over hand, Jamie wrenched the wheel, sending the van into a left-drifting skid. Nic aimed and fired twice, hitting each back tire. The Charger lurched, slowing as it climbed the rising bridge, but even as its tires shredded, it continued racing ahead on metal rims.

"Fuck!" Jamie corrected the van to give chase, but they'd lost too much ground. "He's got run-flats on there."

"What are those?"

"Racing tires. Can drive on the rims."

Jamie followed him up the bridge but braked at the edge, saving them from going over. From his seat on the windowsill, Nic watched the Charger clear the widening gap and land on the other side, leaving a shower of sparks in its wake.

"Dominic!"

He whipped around, staring toward the back of the van. Cautiously believing what his ears had told him. Then throwing caution to the wind when the call came again.

"Dominic, Jamie, can you hear me?"

Sparks erupted inside Nic, relief brighter than metal on asphalt.

SEVENTEEN

"Price!" Jamie grabbed hold of Nic's biceps, yanking him back. "Wait until I put the van in park!"

Nic wrenched his arm loose, and as soon as they pulled to a stop in the lot across the street from the smoldering garage, he shoved the van door open and charged across the street. Traffic had been blocked in either direction, clearing a path for EMS. And for Nic to make his way directly over to the group of assembled law enforcement officers, a certain dark-haired, dark-eyed agent among them.

Nic knew Cam was okay. He'd reported in with him as Jamie had hung a U-turn at the bridge and aimed them back toward South End, but the conversation had been too brief, others on scene waiting for Cam's orders. Now at the scene himself, Nic needed to see Cam with his own eyes, touch him with his own hands, and kiss him with his own lips.

Registering his approach, Cam broke from the group and waited for him to close the distance. Nic held his gaze as he stalked past him, making the demand to follow clear. They circled around the back of an ambulance, finding a quiet spot among the chaos on the other side.

"You get checked out by the EMTs?" Nic asked.

"Yes, I'm fine."

Nic glanced left and right—no one in sight—then rounded on Cam. "Good, then I can do this." He grabbed the lapels of the jacket Cam had replaced the vest with and yanked Cam forward, kissing him hard. Desperate for the connection that had almost been severed again. While he'd been stuck in another fucking van.

He made his argument with his hands diving into Cam's matted hair, with his lips and tongue pleading his case by kiss, and with his body straining against Cam's, reaching out with a need he didn't bother to hide. No more being sidelined when it came to this man. Fuck that shit.

The *whoop-whoop* of a siren startled them apart, momentarily concerned the ambulance they'd fallen against was about to move, but then lights from another approaching firetruck cut across the shadows.

Chest heaving, catching his breath, Nic fell back against the side of the ambulance next to Cam. "That's what I wanted to do the second I heard your voice on the radio. And I was fucking across town."

Cam lolled his head to the side, eyes heavy-lidded as he reached for Nic's hand, tangling their fingers together. "I'm fine, baby."

"Barely." He rotated onto his shoulder, angling toward Cam, needing to stay close. "And I was no safer in the van."

"Jamie got you out of the blast radius."

"But we couldn't catch the car."

"Ditto on the car at Matt's scene," Cam said. "At least the shot to Murphy wasn't fatal."

"Warning shot." Nic surveyed the smoldering building again. With multiple FBI and BPD teams involved, EMS had been on alert and had converged quickly. They hadn't lost any personnel and enough of the metal garage structure had survived so that crime scene techs were scouring the scene. "Anything salvageable?"

Cam's hand spasmed in his and the tortured expression that crossed his face made Nic want to pull him back into his arms.

"What is it?" he asked.

Cam let go of his hand, and Nic instantly felt the chilly loss. "Follow me." The chill continued to creep through his veins as they tiptoed over soot-covered rubble to an open hatch door in the back corner of the structure. "We got the fire contained before it made it downstairs," Cam said. "This was what they were trying to destroy."

In the basement, halogen work lamps aided crime scene techs who were busy processing a workbench full of home-made explosives materials. Mingled in were burner phones and, Nic stopped to look, sheets of paper with BPD district phone numbers, addresses, and schedules.

"Price," Cam called. He stood at the end of the hallway, holding open the door to another room. Nic didn't want to go in there. A tremor ran up his spine and foreboding settled in every cell of his body. Nothing good awaited there.

His instincts proved correct.

It was the room from the ransom video, and with the bright lights shining, Nic realized how small it really was.

And how covered it was in blood. The mattress, the floor, the cuffs that had held Shannon Murphy.

And God knew who else.

"Someone was definitely held captive here."

"Maybe multiple someones," Cam replied.

Maybe also Erin he didn't say, but Nic heard it all the same.

"The techs will take samples and tell us." Nic stepped closer, shoulders brushing, and spoke low, comfort for Cam's ears only. "We don't know what they're going to find, Boston."

"No, we don't," he croaked. "But we have to find Shannon fast."

"No argument there."

Before either of them could posit next steps, Cam's phone rang, the "Sweet Caroline" ringtone sending another tremor up Nic's spine.

A family member was calling at two in the morning. Cam brought the phone to his ear, listening, and his face blanched ghostly white. The news couldn't be good.

"I'll be right there." Cam hung up the phone, moving stiffly, slowly, as if he couldn't quite believe what he'd heard.

Nothing good. "What is it, Boston?"

Cam's dark eyes were twin pits of misery. "Mom's had a stroke."

———

Cam had never been so grateful for Jamie's driving skills as he had been today. First, getting the van out of the blast radius, then getting him to Tufts Medical faster than humanly possible. At the hospital, he drove up to the drop-off curb and parked in the *24 Hour Reserved for Security* space. "I think we qualify," Jamie said.

"Works for me," Nic agreed.

Cam didn't argue. He was out the door the next beat, Nic and Jamie on his heels.

"Just in case," Jamie said, "I'm going to hit the front desk. Badges," he said, hand out. "As I'm technically not official anymore."

Cam drew his FBI badge out of his back pocket and slapped it into Jamie's palm, landing atop Nic's DOJ credentials.

"Go," Jamie said. "I'm right behind you."

Cam took off for the elevator at the end of the hallway, assuming Nic would follow. He punched the call button, and when the doors didn't automatically open, punched it again. As much for something to do with his hands as a target for his frustration.

No Shannon Murphy rescue.

No suspects in custody.

No leads on Erin.

And now his mother was taking a turn for the worse. Before he had anything to show for the heartache he'd caused, past and present.

No hope.

He lifted his hand to smash the button again and Nic intercepted him, grasping his forearm. "The button is not your enemy."

"Fuck off," Cam snapped, then immediately regretted it.

Nic thankfully didn't take offense. He stepped closer instead, sliding his hand down Cam's forearm to his wrist, fingers caressing the heel of his hand, soothing. "You need to breathe, Boston. Get yourself under control."

"One thing, Nic. She wanted one thing, and I've got nothing."

The doors to the elevator finally opened, and Cam moved to charge in. Nic's hand around his wrist held him back, making room for the couple of passengers to exit. Once they were clear, Nic led him in and pressed the button for ICU. The doors closed and Nic moved in front of him, forcing his gaze. "You're doing what she asked."

"We still don't—"

Nic closed the distance between them. "You have the first lead in how many years?"

"It may not be connected." Cam poked him in the chest. "Your words."

"But it may be." He covered Cam's hand with his and lowered it. "And it's not nothing. You're getting closer to saving one family the pain yours went through."

Cam searched for answers in his light blue eyes. "Did I cause my own more pain doing so?"

"Right now, that doesn't matter. Being here for your family does."

Cam closed his eyes and rested his forehead against Nic's shoulder. "I feel like I'm coming untethered."

A feeling that intensified when Nic let go of his hand. But then those long, strong arms wrapped around him, holding him together. "I've got the rope," Nic whispered in his ear.

Standing by him, even after he'd run hot and cold the past few days. After he'd pushed him away in favor of keeping what little peace was left with his family. "I don't deserve—"

A hand ran up his back and into his hair, holding him close. Cheek to cheek, Nic's warm breath fanned the side of his face. "I will not let go."

Cam's heart and lungs stuttered. "Please don't."

Nic angled his face in, brushing their lips together. It was a different sort of kiss for them. Not the rough, can't-get-enough-of-you claiming of mouths. Or the just-shut-up lip smash they were both so fond of. It was slow, gentle, full of silent words—*I trust you, I've got you, I'm here*—and every bit as claiming as all their other kisses. Maybe more so. And it was by far the most convincing argument Nic had ever made without saying a word.

The elevator dinged, arriving at their floor, and Cam didn't want to leave the safety of Nic's arms. Nic, however, was wise enough to step back in the nick of time, Bobby waiting for them in the hallway. They were still close enough for the dark brows above Bobby's narrowed eyes to snap together.

"Cam, what—"

"How is she?" Cam asked as he and Nic stepped out of the elevator. Bobby looked like he wanted to get back to his unfinished question, so Cam came at him with another request. "Tell me what happened, Bobby."

Conceding, his brother fell in step beside them. "She made it through the surgery and was in recovery."

That'd been the last Cam had heard too. "I talked to Quinn this evening before we went dark for an operation." They turned the corner to the ICU hallway. "He said she was waking up."

"She did wake up around midnight. Ate a little too. And then—"

"This is your fault!" Keith came barreling toward him,

pointing an accusatory finger. "She had the TV on, and they cut to a report about the blast in South End. You just can't quit, can you?"

"Is that what the doctor said caused it?" Cam asked Bobby, horrified and being towed under by a cresting wave of guilt.

His older brother shook his head. "Blood clot like they warned us."

"She was fine, then she wasn't!" Keith hollered in his face. "Because of you!" He reared back an arm, hand fisted, and before Cam could blink, Nic was between them, palm in Keith's chest, shoving him up against the wall.

"That's enough, Sergeant."

"Why are you even here?" Keith spat, eyes hard and angry. "This is a family matter."

"And Boston's mine."

Cam's heart skipped a beat, then lurched into his throat. He moved to break up the stare-down, but Jamie's hand around his biceps stopped him.

"I didn't have much of one growing up," Nic went on. "But your brother and his friends took me in. That's why I'm here, for *my* family, which by extension is your family. So, stand the fuck down. None of us needs this right now, least of all your mother."

"What's going on?" Everyone's attention swung the opposite direction.

Quinn stood in the doorway of Edye's room, arm around their tearful father. Cam's heart plummeted, all the way to the floor, the roller coaster making him nauseous. Keith looked equally green, raising his hands, and when Nic dropped his, Cam reached for his brother. Keith came to his one side, Bobby to his other. A hand coasted across his lower back, giving him the courage to ask, "How's Mom?" even as he feared the answer.

"No change."

The brothers sagged against one another. Cam broke first, going to his father and pulling him into a hug. "Tell me," he said to Quinn over Ken's shoulder.

"They may need to operate again. She's on blood thinners now to try and dissolve the clot less invasively."

"And the clot was an effect of the surgery," Bobby said behind them. "Nothing else."

"I'm sorry," Keith mumbled.

Cam dragged him into the hug too. "It's okay. We're all on edge."

"You should go see her, Cam," Quinn said after a moment.

Cam nodded, handing Keith and his father off to each other. He glanced back at Jamie and Nic standing beside each other. The latter nodded. "Go," he said. "We'll be here."

Taking a deep breath, he entered the dim room. And realized he hadn't inhaled nearly enough. Because all the oxygen vanished, whooshing out of him like he'd been punched in the gut.

Last he'd seen her, his mom had been frail but awake and sharp. Now, she was laid flat out, unconscious and breathing with the help of a ventilator. Knees going weak, he caught himself on the bed's foot rail, shaking the bed and drawing the notice of the nurse in the room.

He smiled gently, not seeming the least bit surprised. "Talk to her," he said. "There's still brain activity. She needs to know you're here."

The nurse slipped out, and once Cam got his legs back

under him, he moved to the chair at the side of her bed. He wanted to hold her hand, and the nurse had helpfully made a path for him through the IVs and wires. Her hand was warm, which was a small comfort, but the way it didn't move, didn't curl around his, wiped the comfort away.

He squeezed for both of them. "I need you to hang on, Ma. I'm getting closer. We found where the kidnapped girl was held. Maybe Erin too." He swallowed down the bile that rose up just thinking about Erin in that room and focused on his mother instead. "I'm going to find out what happened to her, I promise, but I need you to fight, Ma. I need you to fight like you fought for me."

EIGHTEEN

Nic sat at the table in Cam and Jamie's suite, dress sleeves rolled up, going over again the documents in the rainbow-colored file folders and on the poster sheets hanging on the wall. Real estate for additional notes on the latter had become sparse, three different sets of handwriting adding bits and pieces as connections and observations struck.

But for all their efforts, as the sun rose on Thursday morning, they were still no closer to finding Shannon or Erin. And the sleeping man on the couch was near to breaking, no matter how tightly Nic held on to the rope.

There was a click across the room, and Jamie's bedroom door swung open.

Spying Nic, he started to say something, but Nic held a finger to his lips, shushing him. He nodded at Cam asleep on the sofa, and Jamie smiled, keeping quiet as he made his way to Nic. "How long's he been out?"

Nic checked the phone Cam had left on the table. "Couple of hours."

Jamie, in sweats and a T-shirt, slid onto the stool beside him, looking him up and down. Nic knew what he was seeing. Same dress slacks from last night, wrinkled. Same dress shirt as well, likewise wrinkled. Scruff filling in as he approached three days without a shave. Not his usual look. "No, I haven't slept any," he answered before Jamie could ask. "And I already got the lecture from your husband"—he waved a hand—"so just no."

Jamie chuckled until his smile turned contemplative. "I heard what you said last night at the hospital."

"Walker."

"We've been telling you for months that you're family. Glad you're starting to believe us."

Nic rested his forearms on the table, gaze aimed out the window at the rising sun over the water. "Like I told Keith, I didn't exactly have a functional one growing up. It's hard to know what to do with one now."

"You think we're functional?" He slapped a hand over his mouth, trying and failing to contain his laughter. "Pssh."

Nic couldn't hold back his own laugh.

Seemed Jamie couldn't hold back his coaching-moment either. "You protect, Price. You've been doing that for our family for a while now, and you're doing it for Cam's now, even if they don't fully appreciate it."

He gestured at the folders and documents on the table. "I wish I could do more, somehow mold this into a case, but we have so little to go on."

"Or maybe not," Jamie said, eyes locked on the sheet of paper Nic had clipped to one of the folders. "What's this?" he asked.

Cam's torso popped up, hanging over the back of the couch. "What's what?"

"Sorry," Jamie said. "Didn't mean to wake you."

"How long have I been out?"

"Just a couple hours," Nic replied. "You needed it."

Standing, Cam ran a hand through his hair, making it a bigger mess than it was already. "What were you asking about?" he said, coming to stand beside Nic.

"The list Becca made." Nic nudged the paper toward him. "Names from the crew she used to run with here after she left home."

Cam tapped at the third name down. "This one looks familiar. I've seen it. I'm just not sure where."

"Laptop's in my room." Jamie stood and grabbed the list. "I'm gonna go run these again."

"And I'm going to make coffee. Maybe it'll jog the memory." Cam glided a hand over Nic's shoulders as he crossed behind him. The casual touch felt good, right again after not having the closeness when they'd needed it most.

Nic wanted more of it and with Jamie out of the room . . . Though hadn't Cam wanted to tell their friends about them, if not his family? And hadn't Nic effectively shown his hand to Jamie the night Bobby had called about Edith? Or last night in the van? At the hospital? No way the former investigator hadn't figured it out. Nic was tired of hiding if he didn't have to, especially when Cam needed every bit of support he could offer. He slid off his stool and followed him into the kitchenette. "How you feeling?"

Cam popped in a single-serve capsule, locked down the lid, and hit the Start button. Coffee brewing, he rotated and rested back against the counter. Nic was sure he was going to tell him to piss off. "I feel like this might just be the second worst week of my life," he admitted instead.

Nic didn't need to ask which week was Cam's worst. It was the very reason they were here, buried in old case files that led nowhere. Stretching out an arm, he circled Cam's shoulders and tugged him into his body. He was stiff at first but then relaxed into the hold. Nic dropped a kiss on his head. "We're going to solve it."

Relaxation vanished, however, when Cam's phone vibrated on the table.

Stiff as a board one second, darting over to the table the next, Cam either didn't notice Jamie standing in his bedroom doorway or didn't care that his best friend had seen them embracing. Nic hoped the latter, that he'd made the right call. Jamie's slight nod to him said as much, but Cam didn't notice their exchange, reading a text on his phone instead.

"It's Di," he told them. "She said to call in."

"So call in." Jamie crossed the room, setting his laptop on the table, while Nic moved to stand beside Cam.

Di answered Cam's call right away. "Morning, sugar."

"Need a good one, Di. Tell me what you've got."

"A burner phone just like the one Officer Murphy received. Only this one was dropped off at the station with your name on it."

"My name?" He stumbled back into Nic's waiting hand.

"A copy of your South Boston library card was attached."

A stunned shockwave rolled through him—Nic felt it in his hand—but then his spine straightened with determination. "We'll be there in twenty," Cam told her and hung up.

Nic's gaze shot over to the timeline of Erin's case.

"That's the same library Erin was at the day she disappeared."

Cam nodded. "And I haven't set foot in that library since. This has to mean something. The cases have to be connected."

––––––––

The station was bustling, triple the usual force crowding the bullpen, as Di's team waited with the D-4 cops and Matt's agents for a joint task force briefing. No arguing, as far as Cam could see, which was a good sign. With a cop's kid on the line, everyone seemed to understand they were on the same team. Well, everyone except Murphy and Smith, who'd wasted a day trying to handle this themselves. But he and Nic had brought them in line, and with the truth about his sister possibly on the line too, Cam needed everyone on the same page, now more than ever.

Spotting them, Di broke off her conversation with Matt and met them at the front counter. "You look like hell," she said to Cam.

"Love you too, sweetheart," he teased back with a smile.

Shifting from worried to mama-bear protective, she glared at Nic and Jamie. "You two were supposed to take care of him."

"Don't blame them, Di. With everything yesterday and then Ma taking a turn for the worse last night, it was hard getting much sleep."

"She gonna pull through?"

He swallowed hard, forcing out the truth. "I'm not as sure as I was earlier in the week."

"Oh, sugar."

"Need to keep busy," he said, shaking off the threatening break. "And we need to find Shannon."

Di followed his lead. "We're all set up in the big briefing room. Just need to usher everyone back there."

"I'd like to listen to the message first, without an audience."

"I've got the phone in my office." She led them around the outside of the bullpen to her office.

Cam followed her in, Nic and Jamie on his heels, which almost caused a four-body pile-up when Di suddenly hit the brakes.

"What's wrong?" Cam asked.

She tilted her head, eyeing her desk. "I had the phone right here."

She went one direction, Cam the other, searching all around the desk. She opened and closed drawers, Cam got on his hands and knees and peered under it, and Nic and Jamie were scouring the rest of the office.

They all came up empty-handed. "It's gone," Cam said.

"That's impossible." Brow knitted, Di marched to the door. "Hey, Owens," she called to the uniform at the desk right outside her office. "There was an evidence bag on my desk. Did you see anyone take it?"

"Smith from South End. Said you wanted it for the briefing." Murphy's captain.

"Fuck!" Cam shot past Di into the bullpen. No Smith or Murphy there. He hung a right and sprinted down the hall to the briefing room.

Just some other D-4 officers lingering around, waiting to get started. "Where's Smith?" Cam demanded.

"On his way here," one replied right away. "He's bringing Murphy from the hospital."

He reversed course, hightailing it to surveillance, where Di was already directing the duty officer to pull up the security footage. As Owens said, Smith approached Di's office, told him that he was taking the phone to the briefing, then walked right past the briefing room and out the back door.

"You got outside cameras?" Nic asked.

A couple clicks later, a view of the back door and lot appeared on-screen.

The duty officer rewound the tape, and sure enough, Smith snuck out and into a cruiser with Murphy, who was identifiable by the stabilizing sling around his arm. Once they hit the street, they turned on the lights and sirens and sped away.

"They're trying to handle it themselves," Di said.

"How long ago was this?" Jamie asked.

The duty officer toggled down, popping up the time stamp. "Ten minutes."

"Fuck!" Cam just stopped himself from ramming a fist into the wall, frustration and lack of sleep almost getting the better of him. Nic moved to contain him, and Cam's gaze snapped to his. He was causing a scene but better here than out in the bullpen. He needed to rail, and Nic, seeming to understand, nodded, making himself the target. "My name was on the fucking phone!" Cam shouted. "That was our best shot at finding Shannon." And it might have been his only shot at finding his sister.

"We can ping the GPS on the cruiser," Di said.

Jamie slid into the chair next to the duty officer, opening his laptop. "Did your techs make a recording of what was on the phone?" The officer nodded. "Drop it to me. I'll be on your network in less than a minute."

"How?"

"Don't ask," Nic said, then to Cam, "Better?"

"Depends what's on that recording."

"Boston."

Cam took a deep breath, forcing himself calm. "I'm good. Thank you." Nic stepped aside, and Cam moved behind Jamie, telling him to hit Play when a voicemail window popped up.

"Hey, Twenty-four, I got something you want. Let's make a deal. Meet—" The recording cut out, fading into static.

"Fucking hell!" Cam roared.

Before he could grab something to throw or ball his fists, Nic clasped his biceps from behind. "Breathe, Boston."

He vibrated in the other man's hold. "He knows me."

Jamie twisted in his chair. "The nickname?"

"My jersey number in high school."

"If you wore it at BC too . . ." Nic said, but Cam was already shaking his head.

Jamie answered for him. "He wore twelve at BC, same as me at Carolina."

"You recognize the voice?" Nic asked, still holding him, only lighter now.

He was the only thing keeping Cam grounded. Keeping him from flying off in a million directions. "No, but it was a big fucking high school."

"Can you—" Nic started.

"School rosters, got it," Jamie said before he even finished, whipping back around, fingers flying over his keyboard.

"You can search back that far?" the tech asked.

"Don't ask those questions," Jamie said, at the same time Cam snapped, "I'm not that old."

Jamie lifted his fingers off the keys a minute later. "That's why you recognized the name."

"The name from Becca's list?" Cam and Nic asked together.

"Yep." Jamie highlighted a name on the screen. "Reid Porter. He went to your high school."

NINETEEN

Cam was in an unmarked BPD Mustang with Jamie, racing after Smith and Murphy. They'd traced the Camaro from the botched exchange last night to one of the chop shops where Reid Porter worked doing the books—or cooking them. If Reid thought he was getting a meet with Cam, that he might leverage Cam's past against him, then, taken together with that smug-sounding voicemail, it stood to reason that Reid would actually show up for this meet. He'd think it in his benefit, a power play, which Cam hoped would leave Shannon relatively unguarded at either the chop shop or Reid's residence for Nic and Matt to rescue.

They were on their way to check those out while Cam and Jamie led two other teams to the meet. Cam had had to firmly and finally trample the instinct to sideline Nic for his protection. They needed Nic's deft touch with abuse victims on the rescue end of this one, and Nic could protect himself, no doubt. Didn't make Cam any less anxious about sending him into a potentially dangerous situation. The difference this time, though, was that Cam had accepted his nervousness as being more about himself than Nic. He couldn't lose Nic, not when it was increasingly apparent he needed Nic to ground him, to remind him not to compromise Agent Byrne when Cameron Byrne, brother, was clawing beneath the suit.

"He's more than capable," Jamie said, reading him like a book. "And Matt and his whole team are with him."

"I know that." Cam drummed his thumb on the passenger windowsill. "Still too many variables."

"You've dealt with more before."

True, except Cam hadn't dealt with the variable of being in love before. Of sending the object of his affections into the line of fire. He propped his elbow on the windowsill and stared out at the passing landscape.

"You ready to talk about what's really going on?" Jamie asked.

"Me putting my family through hell again," he deflected. "No thanks."

"We can talk about that. Or we can talk about you being in love with Price and not knowing how to tell your family."

Cam dropped his arm and leaned his head back, eyes closed. "Daily cursing myself for recruiting you into the FBI."

Jamie chuckled. "What are friends for?" Jamie shot him a side-eye then focused again on the road, weaving in and out of traffic at a breakneck pace, closing in on the red dot displayed on the phone. "He makes you happy?"

"And frustrates the hell out of me."

"Sounds about right."

"Before, it was him who wanted to hide."

"But Price is out."

Cam shook his head. "Not about that," he said, drawing a raised brow from his friend. "Reason that isn't mine to tell, which he's translated to a need to protect me."

Jamie scoffed. "Fuck, y'all are perfect for each other." He shifted the car into a higher gear, throwing Cam back against the seat and interrupting the middle finger he'd been about to shoot at him. "So, your family, then?"

"Not exactly the time to spring this on them."

"Maybe not, but you had to know it could go this way. That you might have to have this conversation with them one day."

"But it could just as easily have gone a different way."

"But it didn't." Jamie smiled, the lovesick-fool grin that meant he was thinking of Aidan. "Love doesn't care."

Would his family though?

The police radio unit crackled, positions reporting in.

"How can you drive like a bat out of hell and have this conversation?"

"This is all muscle memory." Jamie's grin morphed from lovesick to sly as he kicked the Mustang into sport mode, revving it faster. Someone was having fun with the souped-up police vehicle.

Cam was mid-eye roll when Jamie swerved around a slow-moving Prius, and the back end of a fire-engine red, mid-nineties Camaro came into view three cars ahead. Not the police cruiser they'd been after, but Cam knew this car. From the footage of Murphy's meet last night and from high school.

"That's Reid," he said. "He's had that car since high school."

"What do you want to do?" Jamie asked.

"Stay on them." Cam reached for the police radio. "Murphy, Smith, pick up!" He tried to raise them twice more with no luck. "Beta team, this is Alpha. In pursuit of suspect Porter. Beta, intercept Murphy and Smith."

"Roger that," Di confirmed. Beta Team was approaching from the opposite direction, the original plan to box the meet in. Looked like they'd be boxing in their target instead.

"Reid's spotted us," Jamie said, and Cam's gaze whipped up, just as the Camaro sped forward, weaving across lanes of traffic, aiming for the exit a mile ahead. "Moving that fast, he's jacked the engine."

"Can we catch them?"

"From this close, hell yeah." Jamie swerved over onto the shoulder, speeding ahead.

"Alpha in pursuit," Cam radioed, then hit the lights and sirens. No use hiding now and better to get the civilian traffic out of the way.

Jamie drove the Mustang faster, and Reid shot the other direction, no longer aiming for the off-ramp they'd planned to intercept him at.

"Shit!" Cam cursed.

"There's a left exit two miles ahead." Jamie cut back into the scattering traffic, narrowly missing a bumper.

"Alpha, Beta, this is Charlie." Nic's voice came over the radio. "Shannon's not at either location."

"Copy that," Cam replied. "Alpha still in pursuit." He flipped the radio off. "She could be in the car," he said to Jamie. "We have to be careful."

"We need to get in front of him, then. Tell me where I can make a move." Cam surveyed the road ahead while Jamie remained focused on Reid's Camaro and dodging the cars between them.

"There's another exit a half mile up on the right, before the left one."

"On- and off-ramps? Lights at the intersection?"

"If I remember correctly, yes to both."

"You make the call," Jamie said.

If anyone could thread that needle, it was Jamie. And they couldn't lose Reid again.

"Do it," Cam said.

Jamie zoomed back onto the shoulder, laid down metal, and they sped past the Camaro and onto the exit ramp, Jamie blasting the horn. Cars were already braking and moving out of the way, which was a good sign. The steep incline, however, was not. "I can't see if it's clear up ahead," Cam said.

"I'm gonna go right. More room to cut across the inter-section, and less likely to hit a car turning across." Jamie pressed and held down the horn, speeding up as they approached the crest of the intersection. "Hold on!"

Cam grabbed the oh-shit handle and squeezed shut his eyes, *Sooner, Price* drifting through his head. Praying that it wasn't *Later* instead.

Tires squealed and horns blared all around.

But there was no crunch of metal. And no deceleration.

He opened his eyes, and they were headed back down the on-ramp. "We're not telling Aidan about that," Jamie said, swerving back into traffic.

"Or Nic." Cam twisted in his seat. "Camaro's four cars back on the left."

"Plenty of time." Jamie cut across lanes of traffic, zigzag-ging in police maneuvers to keep other traffic back. Reid had nowhere to go. His only option was to try and outrun them, a race he was never going to win.

The Camaro jumped into the left median, and Jamie hurtled ahead. At the last second, he swerved left, drifting and sliding the Mustang so that it perfectly blocked the ramp. Reid jerked the Camaro right, trying to get back onto the freeway, but he couldn't maneuver fast enough, ramming sideways into the rail.

Cam prayed Reid and anyone else in the car had on a belt or was otherwise secured. He shoved open his door, weapon drawn, and hustled to the driver's side of the Camaro.

"FBI! Hands up, Porter!"

Cam didn't see anyone else in the car. Just Reid, his headful of straggly blond hair lying on the steering wheel, the rest of him shaking.

Jamie circled around the back of the car. "Clear."

Cam closed in, shouting again, "I said hands up, Porter!"

Reid raised his hands, the nail beds black with grease, and fell back in his seat, laughing. "That was fun." Was he high? Judging by the rail-thin form, sagging yellowish skin, and missing teeth, Cam wouldn't doubt it. "Hey, Twenty-four. Just the man I was looking for."

"Where's Shannon?"

"Shannon who?"

Not seeing a weapon, Cam yanked the car door open and hauled Reid out onto the pavement. "Check the car," he ordered Jamie as he holstered his weapon, cuffed Reid, and turned him over. He had at least fifty pounds on the guy. He wasn't getting away or putting up a fight.

"Nothing inside," Jamie called.

"Check the trunk."

Jamie reached across the seats from the passenger side

and pulled up the lever. The trunk popped open, and Cam's heart sank, not hearing anything. Jamie ducked out and around to the back of the car. He raised the trunk lid the rest of the way and slumped.

Cam held his breath, fearing the worst.

"It's empty."

Not the very worst but a close second.

———

Nic stood on the observation side of the two-way glass, watching as Cam and Matt questioned Reid.

"Where's Shannon?" Matt asked for what had to be the tenth time. "Who are you working with? There was a second voice."

Reid squirmed in his chair, but he still wasn't talking.

"You were blackmailing Murphy," Cam said. "To steal or destroy evidence from a case implicating Brian Koehler. When Murphy didn't work out, you were going to try and blackmail me using my past because you knew I used to run in those circles."

"How long have you been on Koehler's payroll?" Matt said. "Since he started dealing meth to you?"

"Or is it blow?" Cam said. "We'll have the drug tests back later today."

"Wonder how your boss feels about one of his shops getting blown up last night?"

It would be great if they could ask him, but Koehler was in the wind. Security footage from Logan yesterday had him boarding a flight to Doha with fake papers. The footage showed him alone as did pictures of him in a half dozen other places the past week. They had no reason to think Shannon was with him. Hell, it was unclear if he even knew about any of this. It might have just been Reid trying to earn stars, and when he'd gotten a whiff of it, Koehler bolted on the first flight out to a nonextradition country, escaping the pending charges against him and the idiocy of the flunkies on his payroll.

Wait . . . "Koehler's payroll," Nic murmured.

"What's that?" Jamie asked behind him, pausing his warp speed typing.

Nic rotated, leaning back against the glass. "Can you pull up the payroll for Koehler's businesses?"

"The legitimate ones, yes. The others, not as quickly."

But not a no. Nic couldn't help but chuckle. "Let's start with the legitimate ones. Cross-check them with the list Becca gave me."

Jamie nodded, and Nic turned back around, eyes tracking Cam around the room. From the whispers he'd heard, Cam and Jamie were lucky to be alive after the car chase this afternoon. He'd been waiting at the station when they'd returned, but there had been so much activity—from booking Reid, to throwing Murphy and Smith, whom Di had apprehended, into temporary holding, to running all manner of traces on Reid's phones and personal data—that Nic hadn't gotten a minute alone with him before Reid was ready for questioning. As much as he'd wanted to kiss and hold Cam in his arms, reassure himself that Cam was in one piece, there was no time to waste.

For Shannon's sake or Cam's mother's.

At last check-in, her condition hadn't worsened but she hadn't improved either. Her not waking up yet was starting to concern the doctors, which in turn was putting Cam even more on edge. His questions were clipped, his patience thinned, his orders sharpened—more than anyone here was used to from Agent Hard-Ass.

Proving Nic's point, he smacked the table in front of Reid. "This is a girl's life on the line, Porter! Who's holding Shannon?"

"Two hits," Jamie said, and Nic spun back around. "Both have records." Nic moved to stand beside Jamie, who'd pulled up two rap sheets on-screen. Petty crimes, possession, breaking and entering, except the one on the right for Timothy Harper also had numerous domestic violence charges filed against him by an ex-wife.

"That one." Nic tapped the right side of the screen. "Now search against—"

"Got it, cross-checking." Jamie pulled up the list of missing persons on the left side of the screen. Zero matches. "Aside from being in the Boston metro area, nothing," Jamie said. "No known associates or associations between Harper and any of the missing persons."

"Look at the dates," Nic said. "The domestic violence incidences and the missing persons reports line up. A few days apart, each time."

"Fuck," Jamie cursed, no doubt seeing it too.

"He can only go so long before he erupts." And attacked his family, and when that wasn't enough, a brown-haired, brown-eyed girl. Someone who looked like Erin Byrne, and if those dates matched up . . . "Jesus Christ, Erin was the first."

Nic yanked out his phone, speed-dialing Lauren.

"Hey, stranger," she answered. "It's quiet here without you and Cam. Just Aidan blustering around. And—"

"Lauren," he cut off her ramble.

Practiced at reading him by now, she snapped to professional attention. "What do you need?"

"Has Becca been transferred out of local lockup yet?"

Rapid-fire typing on the other end of the line. "She's scheduled to leave in thirty."

"Transfer me to the warden now." Nic circled the table and double-tapped the glass. Cam was excusing himself as the warden answered the other end of the line.

"Price, what can I do for you?"

"I need to speak to Rebecca Wright before you transfer her."

"That's highly unusual."

"Two minutes, warden. She's been instrumental in helping us on a case, and I need to confirm something with her. A girl's life is on the line here."

The warden cleared his throat. "All right, just a minute."

Cam entered, closing the door behind him. "What've you got?"

Nic switched the phone to speaker.

"Attorney Price," Becca said, and Cam's eyes shot to his, surprised. "You going to save me from gen pop for another few days?"

"Help me save a girl's life, and I'll do my best."

When she didn't answer right away, Cam interjected. "Becca, it's Cameron Byrne."

"Oh-ho, Hot Stuff. Should've known this involved you."

"Becca, you help us out here, and I swear I'll be the first one to speak on your behalf at your parole hearing."

"I'm never getting out of here, boys, let's be honest."

"But I can try to get you someplace more pleasant," Nic said.

"Please, Becca," Cam added.

Only a second of hesitation this time. "What do you need to know?"

Cam sagged with relief, bracing a hand on the table.

"That list you provided has been invaluable. There's a name on it we're particularly interested in. Timothy Harper."

"He's the reason I left that crew," she said, making no attempt to disguise the disgust in her voice. "Creepy fucker, always staring and skulking around. He gave me the wiggins."

Cam leaned more of his weight onto his hand, and Nic gave him a supportive nudge. Harper was their guy; Cam knew it too. The end of all this was rushing up to meet them. But where?

"Do you have any idea as to his whereabouts?" Nic asked.

"No, I only ever saw him on jobs. I'm sorry I don't know more."

Nic believed that she was. "No, Becca, this is good. Thank you."

"I hope you find her, Hot Stuff."

She handed the phone back to the warden, and Nic negotiated for her to stay a few more days in local lockup. Maybe by then this would all be over, and he could file the paperwork to move her out of maximum security. By the time he finished with the warden, Cam had steadied himself and was headed back into the interrogation room.

"Does Timothy Harper have her?"

Reid froze. No squirming, no cute answers, no deflections. Just utterly still.

And ghostly pale.

"Does he have her?" Cam roared.

"I want a deal," Reid squeaked.

Cam lunged across the table, grabbing Reid by the ragged collar of his T-shirt. "This is a girl's life, you weaselly fuck!"

There was a traffic jam at the observation room door, Nic and Jamie both trying to rush out at once, but Jamie had the size advantage, which Nic needed right then for Cam's sake. He let Jamie out first and followed him into the other room. Jamie and Matt wrestled Cam off Reid, who looked smug, like he thought he was getting off easy, Nic the smaller of the three men. He wasn't so smug once Nic grabbed him by the arm, wrenched it behind him, and slammed him face down against the table.

"I can't grant you a deal," Nic growled.

"Then I'm not telling you shit," Reid said, struggling.

Nic wrenched his arm higher. "If you don't tell us where to find Harper, I can assure you this. I'll make it so you go to Cedar Junction. Maximum security. Do you know what they do to people who hurt or help hurt little girls in places like that? And just think, how many people does your boss have up there? Think he'll let you live? Will he trust a useless shit like you to keep his mouth shut? Or will he decide to shut you up permanently?"

With Cam wrapped up in Jamie's arms, Matt crouched on the other side of the table, eye-level with Reid. "It's in your best interest to cooperate, Porter. Where does Harper have Shannon?"

"At his grandparents' old farmhouse. Out in Lincoln."

TWENTY

Cam wanted to move on the house in Lincoln as soon as they could suit up. But Matt showed him an aerial shot of the property, and he knew it would be sundown before they could move. A big old house in the middle of big open fields—dense forest two hundred yards behind the house, a two-lane state highway in front of it, then a thin buffer of trees on the other side of the road before the land opened up again into another field. No way they could get at the house from either direction without being seen in broad daylight.

Especially if Harper was on the lookout for them via the security cameras on each corner of the structure and on the door.

They mapped out the approach, moving in through the property across the street. Down the drive with its line of trees, thick with foliage from the summer, to the gully behind the copse of trees across the highway from Harper's house. The backyard was a more direct route but converging from across the street provided the most cover and the least amount of exposure.

Less time for Harper to detect them, become desperate, and possibly injure himself or Shannon.

Mother Nature helped a little, bringing in a late afternoon storm that darkened the skies and poured down visibility-obscuring rain.

An hour ahead of schedule, Cam lay in the gully across the street, target in view.

"Lights on. No movement," Matt said beside him. "No cars either."

A surveillance drone dropped out of the low clouds right over the house, out of the range of the cameras. "Drone isn't picking up any heat signatures," Jamie reported through the comm in Cam's ear. His visit to MIT had certainly paid off.

"Lights on in the subbasement too," Nic said on his left side. He pointed at the half windows visible just above the ground.

"Drone can't detect below grade," Jamie said.

Rain pounded Cam's back, pouring off the vest and FBI windbreaker, flowing under his arms and down his neck. It was a hot, suffocating, late summer rain, and he could barely get in a breath that didn't weigh him down more.

Fingers nudged his left hand, Nic's tangling with his. Cam was done asking him to stay in the van. He needed him here. Visor up, Cam looked him in the eyes, the icy blue calming, solid, pushing back the humidity and giving Cam the fresh air he needed to breathe.

To act.

"Visors down and move on my count," he said.

The agents and officers lined along the gully snapped

their gear into place. "Whiskey," Cam said. "Ready to kill the cameras?"

"On your count. If he's watching, you won't have long."

"Roger that." He moved into a crouch and the others followed suit, ready to cross the road and converge on his mark.

"Three, two, one."

"Cameras are down," Jamie confirmed.

"Go, go, go!" Cam ordered, and the line of LEOs in tactical gear moved in a dark line across the street.

Still no movement in the house.

The same sinking feeling Cam had had when they'd pulled Reid over settled deep in his gut again. Was this going to be another dead end?

They fanned out around the house, checking the exterior for explosives. Whispered calls of "Clear" echoed over comms, one position after another. Hearing the last "Clear," Cam reached out and tested the front doorknob.

Locked.

And there were five additional deadbolts on the door.

Harper might not be here but something worth protecting was.

He could take the ten or so minutes he'd need to pick them all. Or he could signal for the battering ram, which would take care of the wooden door in seconds. It would make a racket, sure, but at that point, if Harper was even here, he'd know they were too.

Signaling for the ram, Cam grabbed one set of handles as it was passed up, Nic across from him took hold of the other. They reared back, he counted it off—"Three, two, one"—and they heaved. The door shattered in concert with all the first-floor windows, shouts of "FBI!" and "BPD!" ringing out as they stormed inside.

Cam entered ahead of Nic, gun drawn, prepared for battle, only to be greeted with calls of "Clear" from each room.

Visors flipped up, the team heads met in the middle of the kitchen. "First floor empty," Matt confirmed.

"You go up," Cam told Matt. "Di, take your team out back. We'll take the basement." The teams broke, Cam and Nic leading a group of agents toward the basement stairs that led off from the kitchen.

More locks. The battering ram came back out and they were through it in seconds.

To shouts of "Help! I'm down here!"

Cam made to run, but Nic grabbed him by his jacket, holding him back. "She might not be alone. Don't run to your death."

"Shannon Murphy?" he shouted.

"Yes, please, help!"

"Are you alone?"

"Yes, please, get me out of here before he comes back."

"Slow, Boston," Nic cautioned.

Cam took his advice, and they crept down the stairs, weapons at the ready. At the bottom, the other agents fanned out around them. "Shannon, where are you?"

"Back here!"

They turned, spying another passage beneath the stairs.

"Flashlights on," Cam said, and they followed the short hallway back.

"Here! Here!"

Cam shone his light toward her voice, and there in the beam of his flashlight on a grungy mattress was a handcuffed Shannon Murphy. He swept over the area with his light, Nic doing the same beside him, and once they confirmed the small, confined area was clear, Cam moved closer. "FBI, we're here to help."

"Oh, thank God." She started sobbing into the oversized T-shirt she wore, and Nic approached her other side slowly, taking off his rain jacket and wrapping it around her.

"We've got you. You're going to be okay."

"Somebody find the lights," Cam shouted.

"Located," one of the other agents called, and flicked the switch.

Shannon squinted at the sudden flood of light, burrowing into Nic's side. Her dark hair was matted, the T-shirt dirty, and Cam didn't want to contemplate the stains on the mattress. But for as pale as she was, Nic suddenly blanched whiter.

"What is it?" Cam asked.

"Turn around, Boston."

He whipped around, then fell on his ass on the end of the mattress, all the wind knocked out of him.

The entire back wall was covered in pictures.

Of Erin.

Taken outside her school. On the playground. At the library. At the docks.

Hell, in front of their house.

In this room.

His stomach lurched, and if not for Nic ripping his helmet off at the last possible second, he would have doomed the tactical gear to retirement.

Instead, he managed to roll off and empty the contents of his stomach in the corner.

Nic was by his side when he uncurled, kneeling and

heaving for breath. He looked over his shoulder, seeing one of the other agents carrying Shannon out. "Fuck, I'm sorry."

"Nothing to be sorry for, Boston."

"Contaminated the scene."

"One tiny corner of it. And you didn't hit any evidence."

Evidence.

He started to look again toward the wall, but Nic grabbed his chin, forcing his gaze to him instead. "Can you stand?"

Cam nodded but kept a hand wrapped around Nic's as he wobbled to his feet. "Don't look," Nic said, putting himself between Cam and the wall of pictures as they walked past.

"But it's evidence," Cam argued. "It might tell us where she is. We have to—"

"You have to breathe first."

Air, however, continued to be in short supply as they reached the main floor to a grim-looking Matt and Jamie. "There's something you need to see," Jamie said. "Drone picked it up out back." He moved to his other side. "Hold on," he said, whether to him or Nic, Cam didn't know.

In the end, it applied equally. Cam needed them both to hold him up when they reached the door, looked out over the big open field, and counted the flags the agents were sticking in the ground. A single stone sat atop each mound of dirt that was being cleared of weeds and flagged.

"Are those . . ." Cam couldn't finish, the reality, the horror, too much to bear on top of everything else the last few days.

Nic gripped him firmly as Jamie confirmed the morbid truth. "Graves."

———

They waited on-site for the medical examiner and two teams of techs—BPD and FBI—to arrive, working in concert to find out just how many victims Harper had claimed. Nic counted the flags once more as they prepared to leave. Ten, and he expected the number to grow. More bodies to examine to determine if any of them were Erin. Before they left, they spoke with the ME, Cam giving him as much identifying information as he could about Erin at the time of her disappearance, including braces on her teeth, a childhood break to her pinky finger that had left it crooked, and the St. Andrew's medallion with its inlaid topaz she always wore. They left with the ME's promise to contact them as soon as they found anything or made any determination as to whether one of the graves might be Cam's sister's.

From there, they swung by the station where Matt was already questioning Reid again on Harper's possible whereabouts. Reid claimed not to know any other places Harper might be. Claimed not to know Harper that much at all, including that he was a serial kidnapper and murderer. According to Reid, Harper had hopped around the South End garages for decades, had had a nasty divorce, and mostly kept to himself. He also occasionally ran jobs for Koehler, so that was why Reid had roped him into helping take Shannon to gain leverage on Murphy, an impressionable young cop from the same neighborhood who'd been under their thumb, and to win points with his boss. It was only supposed to be temporary. Harper had disappeared with Shannon after the garage fire, and Reid had thought Harper was just securing her elsewhere, maybe at the house in Lincoln, not disappearing with her for good. And certainly not adding her to the morbid collection in the backyard that Reid claimed to have no idea about.

It was well into the night by the time they made it back to Tufts Medical, and Nic had a feeling the night was far from over. They stopped to check on Shannon in the trauma unit, leaving Jamie in the hall as he tried to hack his way to some trail on Harper. He was no further when they rejoined him to head up to Edye's room, and he stopped the search altogether, pocketing the phone, when they turned the corner onto the ICU ward. Good thing as walking-zombie Cam came to life at the sight outside his mother's room. The entire family was gathered, together with a priest. It took both Nic's and Jamie's hands around his biceps to keep Cam from charging angrily forward. The crowd parted, and Bobby slipped away from the group.

"What's going on?" Nic asked, as Cam demanded to know, "What the fuck is Father Patrick doing here?"

"Her blood pressure and temperature dropped a couple hours ago."

"Why did no one call me?" Cam said. "We didn't know—"

"They're giving her last rites, just in case." There was no hope in Bobby's voice that Nic could detect, and by the way Cam crumpled, he'd heard the absence of the same.

It took everything in Nic not to step forward. Not to wrap his arms around the man he loved and try to ease his suffering.

Loved.

He loved Cam, plain and simple, and that's what people did for those they loved. What he'd done once before and held himself back almost three decades from doing again. Until Cameron Byrne had walked into his life and not given him an option. Fuck, why had he ever wanted to hide this? How he felt about Cam was real, and the ache in his chest was as real as the pain he'd felt after the fall that had ended his SEAL career.

Real and life-changing.

But he was held back, first by his own fear and now by a choice that wasn't his own to make, one he had to respect.

He shot Jamie a pleading glance, desperate for someone to do the thing he couldn't without potentially exposing more about their relationship to Cam's family than Cam wanted out there. With a slight nod, Jamie moved to Cam's side, drawing him into his long arms, and Nic wasn't the least bit jealous.

Yes, he wanted to be that person, but right now, he was just grateful Jamie was here to do what he couldn't.

What he could do though was check on the status at the scene. Maybe bring Cam and his family peace another way. He excused himself, stepping back around the corner and dialing Matt.

"Matt, this is Price," he said when the agent picked up. "Have we heard anything back from the ME?"

"Just got off the phone with him. Based on his preliminary inspection, none of the remains match the hallmarks Cam provided for Erin, and he doesn't think any of the graves date back far enough to be hers."

"Fuck. We need to know something soon."

"Cam's mom?"

Nic braced his hand against the wall, leaning his forehead into it. "It's not looking good."

"We'll keep processing. ME could be wrong. I'll let you know if anything changes."

"Wait," Nic said, catching him before he hung up. "Any leads on Harper's whereabouts?"

"Nothing yet. We're going to let Reid stew for a couple hours, then question him again."

"Okay." Nic dropped his arm, looking up to find Jamie and Cam rounding the corner. "Keep us posted." He ended the call and dropped the phone back in his pocket.

"What'd they find?" Cam asked.

"Doesn't look like any are Erin."

Cam looked gutted but not all that surprised. "She's the first kill. She's probably someplace special. I need to go."

He was already turning for the elevator when Nic shot out a hand, grasping his wrist. "No, you need to be here with your family. I'll go."

Cam's "No!" was loud and just this side of desperate.

"I'll go," Jamie said. "Keep you both updated."

Nic clasped his shoulder. "Thank you."

Jamie nodded. Then to Cam, "Whatever you need."

"I need you there."

And by the death grip Cam had on Nic's wrist, he needed him here. The ache in Nic's chest eased a little.

TWENTY-ONE

Cam slumped on the end of his hotel bed, shower-damp ends of his hair dripping water down the sides of his face and neck and over his chest, the latter heaving every so often. Whenever he remembered the wall of pictures of Erin in that basement or all those graves in Harper's backyard or the fact that his mother could die at any moment.

He'd still be at the hospital if it hadn't been for his nieces and nephews who'd refused to leave unless Uncle Cam left, thinking he knew best. That if Uncle Cam thought it okay to leave, then Nonna would recover, or at least hang on until they came back. Uncle Cam didn't know that. What Cam knew was the kids needed sleep and the least he could do for his family was encourage that, seeing as he'd brought them nothing else but misery this past week. While it looked like Harper had likely taken Erin, they didn't know where he or Erin were, what he'd done to her, or why she'd been taken in the first place. He had nothing to tell his mother, who was in a coma, barely hanging on, as if she was waiting for an answer he still didn't have.

"You should lie down for a few."

Cam shifted his gaze from the darkness outside the window to Nic standing in the doorway, coffee cup in hand. Hair likewise damp, he'd swung by his room, showered, and changed into jeans and a T-shirt. Further than Cam had gotten in just his boxers.

"You shouldn't have brought me coffee if you mean for me to sleep."

"I didn't actually believe you would." Nic crossed the room and sat next to him, handing him the cup with a smile.

He drank, but the warm beverage failed to chase away the cold that had settled inside him. "Any word from Matt or Jamie?"

Nic shook his head. "Checked in with them while you were in the shower. Still chasing down leads."

"We should get going." Cam threw back the rest of the coffee and started to stand.

Nic's hand on his shoulder pushed him back down. "You need to breathe, Boston."

"I'm breathing just fine." He tried to shake off Nic's hand, and when that didn't work, tried forcefully pushing it away.

In moves too swift for his exhausted brain and body to keep up with, Nic knocked the cup from his hand, grabbed his wrist, crossed his arm in front of Cam's body, and swung a leg behind him. The end result was Cam locked in Nic's arms, his back to Nic's chest. He tested the hold, and Nic tightened it. He wasn't going anywhere.

Cam growled in frustration. "Dominic, we need to go—"

"Do you remember what you said to me last April in your kitchen?"

"I said a lot of things that night."

Holding Cam's right wrist with his left hand, arm stretched across his body, locking him in, Nic slid his right hand free and caressed the lower right quadrant of Cam's torso. "Do you remember what you said about the tattoo I have on me here?"

Cam's skin there was bare, but in the same place on Nic, a rainbow-colored frog held a SEAL trident. He'd gotten the tattoo when Don't Ask, Don't Tell had been repealed. "We don't celebrate the victories enough," Cam said, recalling the words. "But you' re the one who said it."

"You made me realize it." Nic slid his hand the rest of the way over Cam's stomach and around his waist, pulling him back tight. "You rescued Shannon Murphy. You saved her, Cameron. That's a victory and not a small one. I know there's a lot of darkness right now but there's light too. Shannon's safe."

Cam heaved a giant breath, remembering the way Shannon's mother had arrived in Lincoln and wrapped her daughter in her arms, crying tears of joy.

He heaved another breath. And choked on it, realizing his mother would likely never have that moment.

Chin on his shoulder, cheek pressed to his, Nic whispered, "I've got you" in his ear. "Let it out."

"Mom will never have that," he croaked out through another stuttered breath. "I let her down as a kid and now I've let her down as an adult. She may die without an answer about her only daughter, my sister, who I should have protected that day." He squeezed his eyes shut, leaning his head back on

Nic's shoulder, tears leaking out and joining the other tracks of wetness on his face. "Oh God, she'll never know. I tried . . ." His words drifted off, trapped behind the lump in his throat.

Nic clenched him tighter, and Cam swore it was the only thing keeping him together. That and Nic's faith in him. "She knows, Boston. That you dedicated the rest of your life to atoning for that day. That you help other families so they don't lose their loved ones too. That you're here trying to give her resolution."

His breaths came shorter now, not quite sobs, Nic holding him too snug for that, but the tears, exhaustion, and frustration he'd been fighting for the past week were bubbling up and out. "If she has to go, I wanted her to go . . ." Three gulped breaths later. "To go to heaven and know Erin was there waiting for her."

Nic shifted around to his side and lifted a hand, lightly grasping his chin and turning his face toward him. Cam startled at seeing tear tracks on his face too. "You wanted her to know that?"

Cam swallowed hard, admitting the truth. "I needed to know that." He reached up, brushing the wetness from Nic's face. "Why—"

"Because I can't stand seeing you hurt like this when I know you've damn near killed yourself to make it otherwise."

God, this man. Behind that cold, hard mask, it was nothing but fire and feeling inside. So deep, so loyal, so self-sacrificing that Nic had stood by his decisions all week, even as he disagreed, even as he almost broke himself on this case. Like he'd done for someone else nearly thirty years ago and been disowned for. Because he'd do anything to protect and help those he cared for. That's the man he was—the man Cam was in love with. And fuck if he didn't want everyone to know it.

He leaned forward, forehead resting against Nic's temple. "You know what else I regret?" he whispered hoarsely.

Nic wiped again at his face, then trailed the hand over his back, soothing, as he rested the other on his thigh. "You have nothing . . ."

"I regret that she might die not knowing I've fallen in love."

Nic gasped, the hinge of his jaw opening under Cam's lips, the hand on Cam's back freezing while the other on his thigh tensed.

"She might never know that her son had found a smart, beautiful man, a soldier and lawyer, who would stand by her son's side even when he didn't deserve it."

"Boston," Nic rasped.

He drew back and framed Nic's face in his hands, senses firing at the thicker than usual scruff prickling his palms. "I'm so sorry, baby. I realize now how much I want her to know you, to know you've made me happier than I've ever been, that I love you." He tilted forward, dropping a kiss at the corner of his mouth. "I'm so sorry I was too much of a coward to tell her."

Long, soothing fingers trailed up his back and carded through his hair. "You don't owe me an apology."

He shook his head. "I love you, Dominic. The last thing I want to do is hide that love from anyone. Can you forgive me?"

"Nothing to forgive."

"Do you love me?"

Nic's lips trailed across his cheek, nuzzling, as the hand on his thigh inched higher. "More than I should."

"Then I'm ready to present our case."

Nic pulled back, meeting his gaze. His pupils were blown so wide hardly any of the blue showed, but the dark brows across the top of them were knitted. "What are you saying, Boston?"

Cam smoothed over them with his fingertips, then down Nic's face. "No more hiding, from anyone. Family, friends, the fucking Federal Building. I don't want to regret not telling anyone how much I love you."

Nic gripped his wrists. "You're putting yourself in the line of fire. I need you to understand that."

"I'm already there, baby."

The fingers around his wrists convulsed, then constricted, Nic's face taking on the determined look he got right before he went into a courtroom. The look that made Cam's blood boil. "I won't lose you."

"We can't be sure of that," Cam said. He was a law enforcement officer, Nic was an officer of the court—anything could happen, that was their reality. So was the fact that he loved this man. "But I don't want to waste another minute of loving you."

"No objections."

Nic captured his lips, the same sort of deep, claiming kiss from this morning. Only this time he wasn't making an argument. And neither was Cam. The case was closed. Another victory, seemingly small but huge for them. Back to building what they'd started months ago, the both of them on the same schedule.

"Need you," Cam mumbled against his lips. "Too long."

Nic dropped a hand onto his thigh again, but it didn't

stay there long. He glided it up and over his erection, palming him through the cotton of his boxers. Cam groaned, thrusting into it. "Let me take care of you," Nic whispered, stroking him as he ran a tongue up the side of his neck and shifted back behind him. "I just want to be here for you."

All the tension of the past week bled out of him. Relaxing back into Nic's body, Cam laid his head on his shoulder, baring his neck, and threw his legs over Nic's knees. Spread wide, he rolled his hips and shoved his dick into Nic's grasp. "Take me, baby." Away from it all, for the space of a moment, to celebrate this victory they so badly needed.

Nic's hands disappeared, but only long enough to strip off his shirt, then his warm, bare chest was against Cam's back and his hands were on his body again, traveling two different directions. One cutting a path to his nipple, the other diving below his waistband. Cam lifted his hips, encouraging Nic to push his boxers down farther so it was easier to stroke and fondle. As Nic pumped him, Cam writhed back against the erection nudging his backside. His ass clenched in anticipation, wanting Nic inside him. The prosecutor preferred to bottom, but he'd been willing to switch on occasion when the urge hit Cam. And it was hitting him hard tonight, wanting that connection and more.

Needing to grab hold of every part of Nic.

He turned his head, mouthing the underside of Nic's jaw. "Want you to take all of me tonight. Want to feel all of you inside me."

Nic swiped his fingers over the tip of his cock, collecting moisture, then closing them back around him, easing the slide. "Whatever you want tonight, I'll give you all of it. Everything." Using his knees, he spread Cam's legs wider and dipped his hand lower, down the seam of his balls and under to tease his taint. Cam groaned and shoved his ass back against Nic's erection, practically riding him. Grabbing his chin, Nic angled his face around and plunged a tongue into his open mouth, renewing that connection.

Cam poured it all into their kiss—all of this week's fear and frustration, all of his guilt from the past two decades, and all of his love for Nic that had been building for months.

They kissed and rocked, wrapped up in everything, in each other, until Nic lifted his legs and tumbled them backward. He slithered out from under Cam, ditched the rest of his clothes, and climbed onto all fours beside him. He leaned over him and took his cock down his throat in one swallow.

"Ah fuck, yeah." Eyes scrunched closed, Cam arched his back off the mattress. Every bit of him, every thought, every weight and worry, was being sucked out of him, Nic taking the darkness away and just leaving him with light. Pure white scorching light.

It brightened more when Nic eased off his dick, mouthed each of his balls, then, hand on his hip, rolled him the opposite direction, onto his side. He spread his cheeks and speared his hole with his tongue, teasing and licking.

"Yeah, baby, that's it," Cam panted. "Get me ready for you."

Nic rimmed him into a writhing mess before backing off his hole and nipping his ass cheek. "Tell me how you want this."

"Bare. I want to feel all of you."

Nic groaned and took another bite of his cheek. "I'm negative. It's only been you since my last test."

"Same," Cam moaned, the one word drawn out as Nic reached an arm through his legs, grasping his dick. Cam dropped a hand over his, stroking him together.

"Keep jacking yourself," Nic said after what felt like hours but was probably less than a minute. Withdrawing his slick hand, Nic rubbed it down Cam's crack, around the wet rim, and pushed a finger inside.

Cam stroked himself through the burn of one finger, then two, and finally a third. Nic did his part for distraction as well, licking and kissing over Cam's shoulder, his neck, and up to his ear, groaning there when he began to stroke and coat himself.

"Get that dick in me," Cam ordered on a growl. "Now."

"Tell me to stop if I need to," Nic said. "I'm taking care of you." His kisses were soft, gentle, a sharp contrast to the hard length pushing into him, spreading, burning.

He grimaced, the sting sharp without extra lube, and he couldn't keep a hiss from escaping his clenched teeth.

"Okay?" Nic asked, and Cam nodded. "Short breaths," Nic said, winding his arms around him again, holding him tight across the chest like before.

Cam relaxed into the strong, sure hug, held together, safe.

Nic thrust gently, once, twice, taking care as Cam got used to the fit again. "Harder," Cam pleaded, and Nic rolled them so Cam was sprawled on top of him, dick saluting the ceiling. He hiked their legs up, sinking deeper, hitting Cam in just the right spot.

"Jesus, fuck," he cursed, never feeling so wide open nor

so safe before. His arms flailed and Nic was there, catching him, tangling their fingers.

Wrapping one combined grip around his dick, working him together, he laid the other across his chest, splayed over his heart.

Holding all of him.

It was all so bright, blinding white, not a speck of darkness in his world, all of it focused on the man beneath him, inside him.

He came wrapped up in love, Nic's "Love you, Boston," a whispered exclamation in his ear.

TWENTY-TWO

Nic cleaned himself off and wet a second washcloth for Cam, wringing out the excess water before he grabbed a dry hand towel, killed the bathroom light, and crossed the room back to the bed.

Cam was sprawled on his back, phone held high above his face, avoiding the mess on his torso.

"Any updates?" Nic asked as he wiped Cam clean.

"No change on Harper's whereabouts. Mom's condition has improved. Priest may have been premature."

"That's good." Nic glided the washcloth over his cock, and Cam shuddered, bobbling the phone. Nic caught it and set it on the bedside table. "Sensitive?"

"Wonder why?" Cam grinned, and Nic's world righted the rest of the way with that smile.

He slapped Cam's hip. "On your side, Boston, so I can finish cleaning up the mess I made."

Cam shimmied on the sheets. "I don't know. I kind of like it."

Chuckling, he gave up and pushed, not giving the agent an option. "Until you wake up in a wet spot."

"Why must you always be the voice of reason?"

"Um, lawyer."

Lawyers also asked questions, and as the sky had begun to lighten outside and the outline of Boston harbor appeared out of the dark, a particular topic, a worry, had weaseled its way back into Nic's brain.

"Why'd you leave Boston?" he asked.

"The job, to be Aidan's partner, to be in the same place as Jamie. And there was this AUSA who'd caught my eye."

"Oh, is that right?" He rolled Cam back onto the mattress and tossed the cloths off the bed. He propped himself on his side, one leg thrown over Cam's, head in his hand. "That the only reason?"

Cam snagged his free hand, tangling their fingers and laying them on his chest. Nic could feel his thundering heartbeat underneath.

And the rumble of Cam's words. "Bobby almost caught me with a guy. I was out at this place in JP—Jamaica Plain—and Bobby was there late, upgrading their security system. I'm on the dance floor with two guys, hands down the pants of the dude in front of me, riding back on the one behind me, and my brother walks by not ten feet away."

A wave of jealousy burned through Nic's veins, making him see red.

Cam's hand on his cheek pushed the haze away. "I'll only be dancing with you from now on."

"I don't dance."

Cam smirked. "We'll see about that."

"Dream on, Boston." Nic kissed his palm, then wound their fingers together again, unable to shake his doubts completely. "But this is your home, Cameron. You've got a good partner in Matt and the SAC shares your professional interests. All of your family's here."

Cam's fingers tightened around his. "Don't you want me in San Francisco?"

Nic listed forward, stealing a kiss. "Of course I do, more than I should. But you'd be safer here."

Cam glared. "We gonna have this argument again?"

Nic laughed, happy to hear Cam sounding more and more like himself again. "No. We're not. I just want you to be happy, whatever, wherever that is."

Cam rolled onto his side, bringing them front to front. "You know what makes me happy?"

He smoothed a hand over Cam's hip and around to palm his ass, bringing their cocks back into rutting contact. "What's that, Boston?"

Cam laid a line of kisses over his collarbone. "Being in the same town as my best friend. Working with the best agent I've ever known. Finding the person who grounds me like no other. Drinking my man's beer and then kissing the taste of it off his tongue. You gonna tell me more about that FBI stout?" Cam tongued the groove at the base of his neck and Nic shoved him onto his back, rolling on top of him.

"It's a work in progress, but I think it's gonna be our best brew yet." Smiling, he kissed Cam long and leisurely, imagining how good the new beer was going to taste on his boyfriend's lips.

When they broke for breath, Cam was gazing up at him, a touch forlorn again as he played with the hair at his temples. "Why do you want me?" he asked. "I'm flat broke, especially living there, I pick arguments with you for the fun of it, and our sports allegiances are totally incompatible."

Nic stared down at the man he loved, who'd bullied his way through three decades of hardened defenses. "You rescue lost people for a living. Is it any wonder you found me?"

"But you're still hiding parts, aren't you?"

Damn investigator, too good at his job. "Yes, because they're not my story to tell. Will that stop you from rescuing me?"

"Me?" he said with a rock of his hips. "Rescue the Navy SEAL?"

Nic framed his face, thumbs brushing his cheeks and soaking in the dark gaze swirling with more love than he'd ever hoped to have again. "I need you to keep holding on to that rope, Cam, even when I try to cut through it with a KA-BAR."

Cam laid his hands over his and locked his legs around his thighs, caging him in. "I'll hold on, baby, with everything I got."

———

A buzzing sound roused Nic from sleep. Turning his head and seeing his phone lit up on the bedside table, he threw out an arm, silencing it before it could also wake Cam. The big body half on top of his shifted, but the snores maintained their steady rhythm. They'd only been out a couple hours; enough for Nic but Cam could use an hour more. Seeing no messages on Cam's phone, he slipped carefully out of Cam's arms and out of the bed, smiling as he pulled the sheet up over Cam.

His phone buzzed again in his hand, and he shot a text back to Mel that he'd call her in five. It was early there, but she ran according to her own clock most of the time. Not wanting to put his suit back on, he snagged a pair of Cam's jeans, just a couple inches short, and—God help him—a BoSox tee, covered it up with Cam's BC hoodie, shoved his feet in Cam's boots, and pocketed a room key on the way out the door. First, he looked up the nearest Dunkin'—Cam seemed to think he needed to eat them as often as possible here, like they hadn't just opened one up by the airport back home—then once he'd placed a mobile order and started the right direction, he dialed Mel back.

"Price," she answered, "how are things there?"

"We rescued the vic and confirmed this case is connected to Cam's sister's disappearance. But we haven't found her and the suspect's still at large."

"Yet no loss of life. Count that a win."

This was why he got along with Mel so well. They saw the world in much the same way. "That's what I told Cam last night."

"And his mother's condition?"

"Improving, thankfully." It'd been a punch to the gut to see the priest at the hospital last night, but the news this morning that she was improving was no doubt why Cam had finally wound down enough to sleep.

"Another win."

Nic smirked, even though she couldn't see it. "Since when are you the team optimist?"

"Blame my husband." There was a smirk in her voice too.

He turned the corner and spotted the orange and pink sign up ahead.

Pleasantries were nice, but she'd called for a reason, and he wanted to get back to Cam sooner rather than later. "You called at five in the morning your time. What've you got?"

"A bit of a mixed bag here too."

"Give me the win first."

"Now who's the optimist?" They shared a laugh before she went on and Nic got in line for the walk-up window behind a woman and child. "I just got off the phone with your contact in naval admin. The burner phone was bought at the local Walmart. We traced the purchase to a Nicolette Sare."

He racked his brain but came up blank. "I have no idea who that is."

"So far, I've just got a North Carolina driver's license and a social security card. Twenty-seven-year-old unmarried female. I'm in the process of pulling everything on her."

Nic ran a hand over his scruffy jaw. "That was the good news?"

"Vaughn's upped the insurance on the mansion and the family office."

"Fuck!" The woman in front of him spun, green eyes glaring, and Nic mouthed *I'm sorry* before he darted out of line and around the corner of the building. "I need to set up that meet with Vaughn."

"Let's not do anything rash."

He ignored the warning and continued to pace and plan. "Somewhere neutral, but I don't know how much longer we'll be here."

"I put extra security on both the house and office already," she said, likewise ignoring him. "What else can I do until you get back?"

The green-eyed woman from the line flashed across his mind, followed by thoughts of the one back home who meant the world to him. "Mary."

"Your father's housekeeper?"

She was so much more than that to him, but he didn't have time to explain. "I talked to her before I left. Told her it might be time to retire."

"Or I could hire her away."

That would work too. "Whatever we need to do to get her out of that house."

"I'll take care of it. And your father's assistant?"

"Assuming Vaughn hasn't realized we turned his own nephew-in-law, I don't think he'll risk him."

"Just in case, I'll talk to Aidan. See if there's a reason we might hold him. Otherwise, we'll keep an eye on him too."

They double confirmed operational details before hanging up, and Nic stepped back in line, the calm of the hopeful morning shattered. He needed to bring Cam up to speed on all things Vaughn but had no business being his focus right now. Between Cam's mother, an at-large Harper, and the bodies and shrine to Erin found at the farmhouse, Cam had enough on his plate.

Better that Nic focus on helping Cam clear that crowded plate as quickly as possible, then they could get back home and deal with cleaning his. Because they were going to need to before he could truly settle the way he wanted to with Cam, safe and with the future ahead of them.

The mobile order line moved fast, and he was almost back to the hotel, mind whirring on both the case here and matters at home, when he sensed someone following him. He glanced in the side-view mirror of Jamie's rented Jeep up ahead and spotted none other than Timothy Harper skulking behind him. The way Harper was staring down his back, Nic was clearly his target, and judging by the rate at which Harper was gaining on him, Nic had ten seconds at most before Harper made his move.

Ten seconds to decide how to play this. He ignored the heat prickling his skin, the dryness in his mouth, and worked through the scenarios.

The guy looked rough. Not a meth addict like Reid but like a man on the edge whose whole fucked-up, twisted existence was hanging on by a thread. Nic didn't doubt that he could outrun him or that he could wait for Harper to get close enough to take him down and into custody. But would either of those paths lead them closer to finding out what had happened to Erin? Maybe this was the break they needed. He looked down at the box in his hands—doing what he needed for Cam—and made the decision to keep doing the same.

He played dumb when Harper shoved a pistol into his back a few seconds later. "Don't make a sound."

He glanced back at Harper, eyes falsely wide. "What do you want?"

"You know who I am?"

"Timothy Harper."

"You're the attorney, right?"

Nic nodded.

"Good. Then you're who I need."

Harper nodded toward the box. "Leave the shit. And put your phone in the box."

Digging his phone out of his pocket, Nic put it in the box, then slid the box on top of the Jeep. Right where Jamie or Cam would see it, and with his phone inside, they'd realize something was amiss.

"Get in the Charger," Harper said, nudging him with his weapon toward a sedan with fresh tires several spots over.

"What do you need me for?" Nic asked.

Harper shoved him into the passenger seat, then came around to the driver's side. "I need to know how I can legally get out of this."

"You can't."

Nic didn't like the cold, callous look in Harper's eyes one bit. "Then you're my insurance."

"For what?"

"To make sure I get out of it another way."

TWENTY-THREE

"Where is he?" Cam slammed his palms on the metal table. "You must have some idea."

Reid tried to scoot back, away from the unhinged man Cam seemed.

Was.

The back of Reid's chair hit the wall, cutting off his escape. "I told you, man. The garage and the place out in Lincoln were the only two places I knew about. Tim's wife took the house in South End."

The door swung open, and Cam whipped around. Matt slid into the room, taking up a spot on the wall next to Jamie. "Di just cleared that house. No one's there. Wife moved to Arizona, rents it out. She hasn't spoken to Harper in years."

Fuck!

Turning back to his suspect, Cam started forward again but Matt spoke first. "He never talked about anyplace else? Another family member's or friend's place he might crash at?"

Reid shook his head. "No, I swear."

Cam splayed out the pictures the ME had handed him when he'd come charging in. "These are Harper's victims."

Hand over his mouth, Reid angled his face away from the gruesome tableau.

"Twelve in all. They were buried at the farmhouse."

"I swear I didn't know." He sounded pitiful enough for Cam to believe him, but his guilt wasn't Cam's problem right now.

"Do you know what else was there?" He pulled out the last picture in the folder and slid it across the table. When Reid kept his gaze averted, Cam slammed a palm on the table again. "Look, you fucking asshole!"

A hand wrapped around his arm. "Ease off," Jamie said.

Cam ignored him, all his focus on Reid, whose eyes were wide as saucers, staring at the picture of the shrine to Erin on Harper's wall.

"That's his first victim. You recognize her, don't you?"

Reid covered his mouth again, nodding.

"Erin Byrne. My little sister."

"I had no idea. I'm sorry, man, but—"

"Now he's got someone else I love, and let me be clear, I will do anything and go through anyone to get him back."

An hour ago he'd woken to banging on his bedroom door. Every minute since had been a fucking nightmare. Jamie showing him the box of doughnuts he'd found outside on the Jeep. Nic's phone inside.

Nic gone.

He'd had a terrible notion of what might have happened and the hotel's parking lot security camera proved it. Harper, gun to Nic's back, shoving him into a car.

Cam was never eating fucking Dunkin' again.

Once at the station, Jamie had tried to track him on traffic cams, but in morning rush hour, it had been impossible to follow them. The man who'd kidnapped his sister, who'd kidnapped thirteen other girls, now had the person he loved most in the world. There was some small comfort in knowing Nic was more than capable, could likely get himself out of the situation, but would it be in one piece? All bets were off when dealing with an unhinged serial killer.

The rope was pulled taut, on the verge of shredding. Cam just had to hang on, hold the strands together. Find Nic so he could breathe again and get rid of this awful drowning feeling in his chest and head.

Fuck, he couldn't think like this.

And right now, he needed to be Agent Byrne, the Bureau's best K&R agent, otherwise Cameron Byrne was going to lose the man who was looking more and more like the love of his life.

He closed his eyes and breathed deep. A phantom touch across his back, the remembered taste of pilsner on his tongue, inked memories on pale skin, a whisper in his ear, *You catch 'em, I'll lock 'em up.*

Nic's icy blue eyes, warm and grounding, the last time they'd exchanged the familiar words, right here at the station. Before they'd raided the garage.

The garage . . .

Fingers tangling with his outside the farmhouse.

The farmhouse . . .

What else did they have in common? Something else a third place might?

He pictured both in his mind, viewing them from the inside out. Starting with a close-in shot of the containment rooms, then expanding the field of vision out to the bigger picture. The entire house, inside and out.

Outside.

He opened his eyes, staring right at the camera in the corner of the interrogation room.

Bingo.

Calmer, grounded, determined, he slid into the chair across from Reid. "You ran the books at the garage?"

Reid paled again and started to shake his head.

"I don't care," Cam said. "You paid the vendors, yes?"

Reid hesitated, and Cam just barely stopped himself from slamming a palm on the table a third time. "Listen, you're not here for whatever you may or may not have cooked. Now, answer the goddamn question."

"Yeah, yeah, okay, I kept the books."

"Who'd you pay to do the security upgrade?" He pointed at the camera behind them. "The surveillance."

Reid gulped audibly. "Your brother."

Cam wasn't surprised. Bobby was the best, and while he might not be in that life anymore, those guys trusted him. "He sell to any of you direct?"

"Yeah, occasionally."

"Sit tight." Cam pushed back from the table. "Keep an eye on him," he said to Matt, then beckoned Jamie out into the hallway with him.

Jamie handed him his phone, already ringing Bobby. "Whiskey, what's—"

"It's me, Bobby," Cam said shortly.

"What's wrong?" he asked, at once alert.

"Case took a turn," Cam replied vaguely. "I don't have time to get into it, but I need your help."

"Anything, brother."

"You installed the security system at Koehler's in South End? Cameras and the like?"

"Yeah, I did most of the garages around there."

"One of the guys there, Timothy Harper, had you install a similar one out in Lincoln."

"That's right. His grandparents' old farmhouse out in the sticks and his stepdad's old place that backed up to the library."

"Which library?"

"South Boston Public."

Vertigo struck, and Cam had to shoot out a hand to brace himself. He missed the wall and Jamie grabbed him, holding him steady. "The one Erin was taken from?"

"The same. That was my least favorite job ever."

"Send us the address."

"Cam, what's going on?" Bobby's voice was back to concerned, worry ratcheting up.

"I promise to explain everything," Cam assured him. "Just send me that address."

"I'll go look it up right now."

"Thank you." He hung up, insides churning. Had Erin been right there all along? Was Nic there now? He was excited and nauseous at the same time. He swallowed both down, looking up at Jamie. "I know where they are."

He barely had the sentence out when his own phone rang, a Boston area number lighting up the screen.

"This is Agent Byrne."

"Reid always called you Twenty-four," a thick Southie accent replied.

"Harper," Cam said.

Grabbing him by the sleeve, Jamie hustled him down the hall to the techs. "I'm gonna make this short and sweet," Harper said. "Because I'm sure you're trying to trace me."

Jamie scribbled on the whiteboard. *Keep him talking.*

Cam shook his head and snatched the pen. *Don't need to. Trace the address Bobby texts you. Get ready to move teams there.*

"You're going to get me a ride out of here if you ever want to see your pet lawyer again."

Jamie's phone buzzed and he flashed it at Cam, showing the address from Bobby. Cam knew exactly where that was, and it made all the sick sense in the world. She had been right there all along and now he'd bet his last dollar Nic was there too.

Go! he mouthed and flashed an open hand. *Five minutes.* Jamie went in motion, not needing to be told twice.

And since this might be the only chance he ever had to talk to Harper again—because if it came down to Harper's life or Nic's when they got to the scene, Cam would do anything and everything to save Nic—he asked the question that had haunted him for two decades. "Why'd you take Erin?"

"I used to watch her from my window, always reading outside in the library courtyard. I had to have her." The wistful tone of Harper's voice made Cam's stomach roil. "She was the start of my collection. None of the rest were ever as perfect."

Cam balled his hand into a fist. "So you took her that day? When I didn't pick her up."

"I was waiting at your house. With a gun. I would have taken her that day whether you were with her or not. I was done waiting."

Cam gasped at the bolt of unexpected relief—Erin's disappearance wasn't on any of their shoulders. If he or

Bobby had been there—or worse, his mom or Keith—then there would have been more tragedies.

A gun cocked on the other end of the line and Cam's relief vanished, replaced with fear. "I'm done waiting now," Harper said. "You meet me at Fish Pier tonight with the keys to one of your family's boats if you ever want to see your lawyer again."

Fear dissolved, anger burning it away. Cam was done waiting too. He'd be seeing Harper—and Nic—sooner rather than later.

———

Nic didn't know Boston all that well, but he didn't think they'd actually ended up far from where they'd started. They'd driven away from downtown, over another channel, then crisscrossed through blocks, at least twice passing the same spot. Like Harper was either trying to lose a tail or waiting until no one saw him drive into the little alley.

He let himself be manhandled into a dilapidated old house and to the basement stairs. Playing the attorney, not the SEAL. They'd found Shannon in a basement like this. The garage holding area had been in a similar basement. Maybe the clues he needed to find Erin would be in this one.

"Get in there." Harper shoved him forward, and Nic stumbled down the first few steps. "I'm gonna call Twenty-four and tell him if he ever wants to see you again, he's gonna get me a boat out of here."

Harper threw the door closed, plunging Nic into total darkness. "Fuck!" He took the stairs slowly and moved carefully into the room.

Not carefully enough, crashing into something a step later.

And on the heels of the racket came a whimper.

He froze. "Is someone in here?"

Another whimper, then stifled as if a hand was blocking the noise.

"I'm here to help." He slowly inched forward, testing the area with his feet and hands, trying not to knock anything else over. This sure as shit was easier with night vision goggles. "My name's Nic."

Movement to his right, someone shuffling away from him.

Shit, he needed to find the light. Whomever was down here was likely traumatized and wouldn't know if he were friend or foe. He'd have a better shot convincing them in the light.

He moved forward again, even as his mind whirred. Was it Erin down here? What he wouldn't give to be able to give Cam his sister back, but like this? After being held hostage for twenty years? She would never be the same person, maybe never recover.

His left hand hit a table corner. He patted around for a lamp, and when he didn't find one, reached farther back, hit the wall, and slid both hands along it until he found a switch.

He flipped it.

Under-cabinet UV lights clicked on one at a time, and when they reached the end of the row, they illuminated the young girl huddled on a thin, dingy mattress in the far corner.

Not Erin. But another lookalike.

Relief and sadness warred but only for a second before

instinct kicked in.

He had to focus on the priority in front of him.

The girl cowered, trying to huddle even farther into the corner. Battered and beaten, the side of her face bruised, her clothes ripped and stained, her ankles and hands tied, a gag wedged between her lips, stretching her mouth and the bruises. That had to be killing her.

Lowering into a crouch, Nic drew her gaze and raised his hands, palms out. "I'm here to help." He reached for the collar of his shirt and yanked it down, exposing his SEAL tattoo. "I'm a Navy SEAL captain," he said, using one of Cam's tricks and combining it with proof, the rank and emblem always seeming to assure people.

She relaxed a little, watching him closely.

"And my boyfriend is an FBI agent," he added for good measure. "He's on his way here." Nic was sure of it. Cam would figure it out. He was the Bureau's best at rescuing people.

Had already rescued him.

The girl twisted, letting her knees fall to the side.

"Can I help you?" he said. "I can take that gag out of your mouth. It can't feel good."

She eyed him another few seconds, then nodded.

He approached slowly, checking with her every step of the way until he was by her side. He held up his hands again for her to see, then moved them toward her face, carefully, no sudden movements, until he pulled free the gag.

She coughed and sputtered, working her jaw, wincing.

"What's your name?" he asked.

"Emma." He moved to untying her hands next, and she started to shake. "Am I gonna die?"

"Not if I have anything to say about it."

"He keeps going back and forth. Saying he's going to take me to the farm. Then saying he's going to bury me in the back with her."

Erin *was* here.

Oh God.

"I don't know who her is," Emma said. "But I don't want to die like her."

No, she didn't, and Nic wouldn't let that happen either. He finished untying her hands, wrapped the hoodie around her, then moved on to unbinding her ankles. "How long have you been down here, Emma?"

"Since yesterday."

Which was why she hadn't been reported as a missing person yet.

"I was cutting through the alley from the library," she carried on between sniffles. "Ma says I shouldn't, but I was late leaving, and—"

"I'm sure she'll just be glad to see you."

Harper's voice a floor above boomed, shouting at someone, and Emma flinched, staring up at the ceiling.

Nic grasped her hand, squeezing. "We're gonna get out of here."

Her big brown eyes shot to him. "How?"

Straightening, Nic stood in the middle of the room and made a three-sixty turn, looking for any other exits or windows.

None.

"Have you seen him go in or out any way but the stairs?"

Emma shook her head.

He searched the table for potential weapons. Wrenches,

anvils, sockets. Something he could make work for an attack.

Emma moved, trying to stand, and fell back against the wall.

The *thump* echoed.

He brought to mind the outside of the house, having paid close attention when Harper had driven the car around back. He considered the arrangement of windows and the approximate dimensions of its footprint, then surveyed the basement again. It was smaller than the building footprint. Or at least this part of the basement was. He stepped around the mattress, knocking gently on the wall Emma had fallen against. Hollow, with only a few studs. Plenty of room to go through.

"Okay, Emma, I'm going to need your help, if you're up to it."

"What are you gonna do?"

"This is a false wall," he said, laying a hand on the wall in front of them. "There's a room behind it. Maybe an exit." He picked up the mattress, and when the waft of putrid smells assaulted his nose, he forced the rising bile down his throat. "Can you hold this upright? It'll muffle the crash." He patted the corner of the mattress where he wanted her to hold it. "Now when I hit it, you let go, okay?"

She nodded, standing back already, but holding it up like he asked.

He backed up as far as he could in the space, then ran full-tilt, shoulder first, at the wall. He crashed into the mattress. And through the wall.

The mattress fell to the floor, sending up a cloud of dust, and Nic landed on top of it, almost retching from the smell.

Then almost retching from the waking nightmare he'd fallen into. The walls were covered.

In pictures of Cam's sister.

Every inch of wall space, at least several years' worth of pictures, highlighted by the light streaming in from above.

And beneath him, beneath the mattress, the ground wasn't flat. It was mounded, like a grave.

He closed his eyes, hoping to wake up in bed with Cam, hoping this was all just a nightmare that would fade in the light of day.

Light of day.

Eyes popping back open, he scrambled up and whipped around.

There was a subbasement window, definitely big enough for Emma to crawl through, and maybe even big enough—

"What's going on down there?" Harper jiggled the lock on the basement door.

Emma burst into the tiny room and almost fell, letting out a yelp. "He's coming," she cried in Nic's arms.

Nic looked around for something to use to bust through the window.

Finding nothing, he hiked up a foot and thanked all that was holy that he'd slipped into Cam's heavy-ass boots this morning. Tearing off one, then the other, he didn't waste time or try to be quiet, heaving them through the window and opening up an escape route.

Steps thundered down the stairs.

"Give me the sweater," he said to Emma, hand out. "Then stand back."

She tossed it to him, and he wrapped it around his fist,

using it to punch out the rest of the glass, careful not to cut his bare feet on it.

Warm summer air wafted over his face, and on it, the sound of sirens, growing louder.

"No!" Harper roared, clearly having caught on to what was happening.

"Okay, Emma, time to go."

She was both nodding and shaking her head. Not altogether convinced with this plan but not wanting to stay here either.

"The cops, my boyfriend, I can hear them coming," Nic reassured her as he swiped at the thin trickle of blood by his hairline. He wiped his hands off on his pants and made a brace with his hands. "You're going to put your foot here, I'll boost you up and out, and you run to them."

"What about you?"

"I'm a SEAL, I'll be fine, sweetheart," he said, even drawling a little like Cam did, hoping to put Emma more at ease. "But I need you to get to safety. And tell my boyfriend where I am, okay?"

She nodded, biting her bottom lip.

"Okay, on the count of three."

"No, you can't let her go!" Harper shouted, on their level now.

Nic glanced over his shoulder, seeing the other man running toward them. "Go, Emma! Now."

Her eyes grew wide, seeing the bogeyman closing in on them, and she planted her foot in Nic's hand. He heaved, tossing her through the window. Her bloody foot had just cleared the frame when a flash of metal caught the light in Nic's periphery.

He ducked, spun, and righted himself as Harper came

barreling at him again with a wrench. Nic shot up a hand, diverting the wrench Harper was trying to bring down on him, while lifting a leg and landing a kick to his stomach. Harper stumbled backward out of the tomb, and Nic advanced.

Out in the open, he heard the thunder of footsteps overhead. As did Harper.

He was trapped, and by that desperate gleam in his eye, foolish enough to think he could take Nic and use him as a hostage. Steadying himself, he gripped the wrench firmly and hurled himself at Nic. This time, with more room to maneuver, Nic grabbed his wrist, forced it out wide, and slid under his arm before yanking it back.

The wrench dropped from Harper's hand, and Nic dropped him to the floor, knee in his back.

"Dominic!"

"Here, Boston!"

What sounded like an army barreled down the stairs, and it looked like it too, as agents and officers led by Matt and Di spread out around him, weapons trained on Harper.

A pair of cuffs appeared over his shoulder.

He wanted to look over it, to the dark eyes that he knew were scared and eager for him, but as soon as he did that, he was going to have to bear witness to something dying inside Cam. A hope that someone you cared for deeply was still out there, alive somewhere. Nic hoped that for Victoria and Garrett. A part of Cam still hoped that for Erin even though the bigger part of him knew it was unlikely. That bigger part was going to be proven right today. Nic wasn't ready to bring that kind of pain down on Cam yet.

So he stalled. He took the cuffs from Cam, snapped them around Harper's wrists, and heaved him up to standing. He handed Harper off to Matt, and Cam yanked him into his arms.

Nic hugged him back, not a care for the agents or officers around them.

Cam had said no more hiding, he seemed to mean that, and Nic didn't want to hide either. But he did hide Cam's view of the room behind him, grateful for the couple of extra inches he had on the other man right then. "Emma?" he asked.

"She's safe." Cam leaned back, wiping the cut at his hairline clean for him.

Fuck, he wanted to kiss him, then wanted to turn him around and walk out of this room. But he also wanted to bring Cam peace, and he was here to hold him through the pain of getting there.

"Dominic, what's wrong?"

Nic cupped the side of his face with one hand and tangled the fingers of the other with Cam's, squeezing hard. "I found Erin."

TWENTY-FOUR

Cam stared at Nic's slowly seeping head wound, the blood a thin trickle that Nic wiped away every few minutes. Right then, it was the only thing holding Cam together. Worrying about something small, an incidental injury easily cared for, not life-threatening or life-shattering, was easier than thinking about the injury that couldn't be fixed. And the news of it he had to deliver to his family.

The hospital elevator continued to climb, and when next Nic lifted his hand, Cam intercepted it, slipping free the wad of tissues and cleaning the wound himself. "We should've gone by the ER to get you checked out."

"It's just a scratch." Nic wrapped a hand around his, lowering it and prying the tissue from his fingers. "And you need to tell your mother while there's still time."

He was right of course. They'd called Bobby from the field, and while his mother's condition hadn't worsened, she hadn't woken up either. Every minute her coma stretched on, the less likely she would wake. But if some part of her was still in there, still here with them, she needed to know.

He'd promised.

"Thank you," he said, then glanced across the cab to his best friend. "Both of you."

"Sometimes the answers hurt," Jamie said. "But it's better than the not knowing. Your family will see that now."

"I hope so." He took Erin's necklace out of his jacket pocket. It would be as sure a sign as any to his family if they hadn't already realized why he'd had Bobby call them all here.

The doors opened, and Cam claimed Nic's hand again. "No hiding," he said, repeating his pledge from last night. "More than that, I need you."

Nic's blue gaze didn't waver. "Then I'm here."

After that, his hold didn't waver either. Not when Jamie came to Cam's other side, hand clasping his shoulder. Not when the three of them turned the corner and found all of Cam's family gathered in the hallway outside his mother's room. And not when their eyes darted first to his and Nic's clasped hands, then to the topaz medallion hanging from his other.

The reactions were varied and each one pummeled Cam.

Bobby's "Oh God," as his wife Josie gathered him into her arms.

Quinn's dark eyes glassy with tears, before he buried his face in his wife Elena's hair, their teenage kids hugging him from the other side.

His dad lumbered toward him. "You found her?"

Cam nodded, and the next instant his father crashed into him, heaving.

Hands wrenched apart, Nic stepped back beside Jamie but still close enough Cam felt his presence. Knew they were both there for him.

But it was Keith that Cam needed to be there for most.

Over his father's shoulder, his younger brother stood shell-shocked, unmoving and pale. "She's not coming back?" Voice thin, trembling, he sounded closer to eleven, the age he'd been when Erin disappeared, than the thirty-one-year-old Marine he was today.

Cam untangled from his father, handing Ken off to a waiting Jamie, and moved to stand in front of Keith, lightly grasping his biceps. He vibrated in Cam's hold, wrought thin by emotion, a glass on the edge of breaking.

Cam understood. A little of him had died today too when they'd opened the grave Nic had found and saw the tiny skeleton clutching the familiar medallion. The last shred of hope that maybe Erin was out there somewhere had vanished. And that same little bit of Keith, though a bigger piece for all that his big sister had meant to him, was dying too, right here in the hallway.

"I'm so sorry, brother."

The trembling became full-on quakes, and Cam drew his brother all the way into his arms. Cam felt every hiccuping breath, every tear, every shudder, right down to his soul, which was shattering too, but he had to hold it together. He'd been the one to bring this down on them. He had to be the strong one as he delivered the news he'd so relentlessly pursued. Including to the person who'd set him on this path, if he wasn't too late.

Later, after he took care of his family, he'd fall apart in the arms of the man he trusted to hold him together.

Eventually, Keith's tremors subsided and he quieted, breaths evening out. He pulled back, blue eyes damp, but without the daggers of long-held resentment. "I know I didn't make it easy on you," he said. "But thank you for finding her."

"Thank Nic," Cam said, taking another step back and extending an arm toward the man with his chin ducked, clearly not wanting to draw attention to himself. But he deserved it, deserved all their gratitude for bringing peace where it had been missing for so long. "He risked his own life to go with the culprit and find where Erin was buried."

"Why would you do that?" Ken asked.

Nic glanced up, looking first at Ken, then at Cam, a question in his eyes that Cam answered with a nod and an outstretched hand.

No more hiding.

Nic stepped to his side, tangling their fingers together. "Because I'm in love with your son."

There were some surprised faces, at least one very happy face, several realization-dawning faces, and then there was Bobby's face. Smug, no other word for it.

"Something to say?" Cam asked him.

"I've been telling 'em this since April."

"Our phone call about the case?"

"When you told me about Nic working with you, there was something more in your voice. More than when you talked about your FBI partner. Or anyone else for that matter."

He glanced around again at his family. None of the faces

were angry, disgusted, or what he'd feared the most, disappointed.

"He obviously loves you," Quinn said. "And you him. As long as you're happy, brother, that's all we care about."

"And Mom got to meet him too," Keith added.

"I wish I'd told her though," Cam said quietly, echoing his sentiment from last night.

"She's still here." Bobby stepped forward and wrapped him in another hug. "Go tell her. Tell her to stay. To be here to see you get married."

Nic's hand spasmed in his, and Cam swallowed his half chortle, half choke behind a "Whoa now."

Laughter improbably rippled through the group until his dad approached again, hand patting his cheek. His eyes were misty, and there was resignation there, mixed in with peace and hope. "And tell her if she needs to go, Erin's waiting for her."

Cam swallowed down the lump in his throat and blinked away the threatening tears. Just a little bit longer. With Nic by his side, he entered his mom's room, no longer shocked by her condition but terrified in a whole new way. He'd promised her this truth, and if she needed to move on, he had to let her, as his father had said, but he hoped to God that what he was about to tell her wouldn't push her that direction.

"I'll be right here," Nic said, leaving him at the side of the bed. He took a seat in the chair, giving Cam a moment with his mother but not leaving him alone. His presence filled the room, wrapped around him like a blanket as the chill of the truth settled on his shoulders and in his gut.

As he put words to that truth and had the hardest conversation he ever had with his mother.

Completely one-sided.

"I found her, Mom," he started, then told her everything. She'd want to know. Would need to know, if she were to find Erin waiting for her. It ended on a high note, however, Cam also telling her about Nic, who stood and wrapped an arm lightly around his waist.

When he was done, *goodbye* and *I love you* said in case God forbid the worst did happen, exhaustion began to creep in and fill the void dogged determination and two decades' worth of guilt had left behind. He leaned heavily against Nic. "I'm ready to go."

Nic kissed his temple, then reached out a hand, lightly grasping his mother's forearm. "I promise to take care of him, Edye."

Tucked beneath Nic's arm, they were halfway to the door when the heart monitor beeped off rhythm. Cam turned, expecting the worst, and found the best.

His mother's dark eyes were open, and she was smiling at the both of them. "'Bout time you caught a good one."

TWENTY-FIVE

Nic recognized Cam's shock setting in as they left the hospital.

It had been another few hours after Edye woke before they'd given everyone goodbye hugs and finally made their way to the elevator. Hours during which Cam had held it together remarkably well despite the swing from low to high to low again. He'd held his mother's hand while she cried in grief and relief over the news of Erin. Nic hadn't drifted more than a few feet away from Cam at all times, even when the nurse had insisted she treat the cut on his head. He'd had her clean it and butterfly it shut while he sat in the chair behind where Cam stood by Edye's bed, always within reach, ready to catch Cam's trembling hand or to lay a steadying hand on his back whenever he needed the extra support.

In the elevator though, on their way down to the ground floor, the slight tremble in Cam's hands and knees spread to the rest of his body, leaving goose bumps in its wake. And when the doors opened, Cam's dark eyes stared ahead, unseeing.

"Hey, Boston," Nic called gently, grasping his hand. "Exit's this way."

He tugged him out of the elevator, trailing behind Jamie through the hospital lobby and out to the parking lot. Jamie glanced over his shoulder periodically, expression increasingly worried as the chatter of Cam's teeth grew louder despite the warmth and humidity that hung heavy in the air. When they reached the Jeep, Jamie opened the back door and Cam practically fell inside.

"He's in shock," Nic murmured low to Jamie.

"Should we take him back in?" Jamie asked, eyes cutting to the hospital entrance.

Nic considered it. Considered how Cam would be admitted and he'd be left outside in the waiting room. Not family technically. He shook his head. "I think what he needs most right now is a good night's rest. It's been days."

"Agreed." Jamie shrugged out of his jacket and shoved it in Nic's hands. "Get in there and wrap him up."

Nodding, Nic removed his own coat and slid into the backseat with Cam. Jamie closed the door behind him, climbed in the front, and started the car.

"Can't stop shaking," Cam chattered.

"You're in shock." Nic wrapped him in the jackets, then in his arms, holding him close.

"We'll get you warmed up," Jamie said, blasting warm air out of the vents.

With it eighty degrees inside and outside the car, it was sweltering, but the slight easing of Cam's tense frame was worth it. Nic ran a hand through his dark hair, down his neck, and over his back, coaxing the relaxation through the rest of him. "That's it, Boston." He pressed a kiss against his temple, breathing in his own moment of calm.

The tears came not long after. No giant heaving sobs, no audible whimpers. Just short breaths and wetness that seeped through Nic's shirt. The shock worn off enough, the time for responsibility passed such that Cam could grieve. Nic held him closer, whispering "Let it out" and "I've got you" as Jamie slowly wove the Jeep through the lingering rush hour traffic.

By the time they hit South Boston, Cam's tears had dried and he was snoring in Nic's arms, the week-long roller-coaster ride having finally caught up to him.

"I hope you don't mind a bedmate who snores," Jamie said.

Nic's eyes shot up, catching Jamie's blue ones in the rearview mirror, the corners crinkled, somewhere between exhaustion and a smile.

He pulled Cam closer, resting his chin on his head. "I was in the military. Impossible to ignore it in the barracks. You learn to tune it out. And I was probably one of the loudest."

Jamie chuckled. "Get a pug and you'll be a symphony."

"Don't think Bird will take kindly to that."

"That cat could probably take down a German Shepherd."

"It's fucking huge. And that name . . ."

"I tried to rename it Jordan."

They both laughed, and Nic marveled at the ease and oddity of the mundane yet momentous conversation. He'd basically just agreed to move in with Cam. To Jamie, of all people. The mind boggled.

The silence was surprisingly comfortable the last few

minutes of the drive, and Cam didn't stir as Jamie idled the car near the hotel's entrance. "Go ahead and take him up. I'll park."

Nic tried to rouse Cam, only to have him burrow closer. "Will he wake and pull his weapon on me if I carry him?"

Sympathy clouded Jamie's face as he regarded his sleeping friend. "That's twenty years of guilt and grief off him." He glanced again at Nic, face softening. "I think he'll sleep through just about anything right now. Besides, doesn't look like he's letting go."

No, he was still holding tight. Hiding from the world now, and Nic was happy to continue to shield him. "Okay, then, help me out?"

Jamie nodded and got out, while Nic, unwrapping Cam, put his jacket back on and pulled out his room key. He hauled Cam into his lap, one arm around his back, the other under his knees, and when Jamie opened the door, climbed out with Cam in his arms, still nestled against his chest.

"You got him?" Jamie said, closing the door.

"Got him," he said, readjusting and securing his hold. It had been a while since he'd carried someone so solid, but he wouldn't have Cam anywhere else right now. "We'll be in my room, if anything—"

"I'll see you in the morning." The trust and friendship in Jamie's smile pushed the last of the water under the bridge out to sea for good.

Even brought a smile to Nic's face, but it fell as they entered the hotel lobby and heads turned their way. He glared off every person who looked like they might approach and ignored the rest of the stares as he stalked past the front desk on his way to the elevator.

It opened as he reached it, a young couple on their way

out. The one man looked concerned, the other like he might swoon. Concerned shuffled Swoony out of the way and stretched an arm in front of the elevator doors, holding it open for Nic. "Can I hit a button for you?"

"Top floor," he replied gruffly, then softer, added, "Please."

The man reached in, hit the button, then backed out. "I hope he's okay."

"Me too."

As the doors closed, he heard Swoony mumble "relationship goals" to Concerned, and Nic chuckled lightly.

He made it up to his suite and inside, walking swiftly into the bedroom and sitting on the end of the bed with Cam. He didn't wake as Nic rid him of his outer layers, and when Nic laid him out on the bed, he rolled onto his side and buried his face in the pillow Nic had used. Standing, Nic worked free his shoes then spread the blanket at the foot of the bed over him, gazing down at him a few moments before he headed into the living room to turn off lights and lock up. He was on his way back to the bedroom when the phone in his pocket vibrated.

Nic recognized the DC-area number lighting up the screen and suddenly remembered it was Friday. He owed someone an answer. "Sir," he answered, "I apologize for missing our call today."

"I was afraid you'd forgotten about me," the Deputy AG replied.

"No, not at all. I'm still in Boston working that case. We just wrapped it."

"I heard. Nice work. Cleared more than one case off the board."

"Including my boyfriend's sister's."

"Boyfriend?" Said not so much in judgment—the fact that Nic was gay had long been in his file—but in surprise. "I didn't realize there was someone serious."

Nic leaned against the bedroom doorjamb, admiring Cam sleeping soundly in his bed, curled around his pillow with a smile on his handsome face, finally at peace. "We recently made it official."

"By the smile in your voice, I guess I know your answer on San Diego."

"It's a no, sir," Nic confirmed. "I appreciate being considered, but I'll be staying in San Francisco." Though the Deputy AG wasn't completely correct as to the reasons. Cam was a big part of the reason, but Nic also had a brewery to run and friends and family in San Francisco who he didn't want to leave any more than Cam did. Even if it would be the safest thing for them. His list was in ink now, as good as if he'd etched it on his skin with the other names he cared about.

"Okay, then," the Deputy AG said. "That's what I needed to know. Bowers is lucky to keep you."

Nic's bitter laugh snuck out.

Laughter sounded on the other end as well. "*San Francisco* is lucky to have you."

"Now *that* I'll believe," Nic said. "Thank you again for the opportunity."

"You're one of our best, Price. Don't let anyone tell you otherwise."

"Thank you, sir."

Hanging up, Nic felt oddly settled. He'd just made a decision that would make his day job hell, continuing to work for Bowers when he could have had his own office. But at home . . . His gaze fell again on Cam's sleeping form.

He wasn't foolish enough to think it would be easy. There was so much open still and Nic needed to make certain provisions to protect those he loved, but *there were people he loved*.

And the one he loved most was in his bed right now.

He tossed his phone on the bedside table next to Cam's, toed off his shoes, and flung his jacket into the chair, then crawled under the blanket, spooning his boyfriend.

Cam scooted back in his arms, as if seeking more heat. Nic wrapped his arms around him, tightening his embrace.

"Did you carry me up here?" Cam mumbled, still sounding half asleep.

"I did."

"Shit," Cam cursed. "I missed it."

Smiling, Nic kissed behind his ear, whispering, "I promise to do it again sometime later when you're awake."

"You better, and sometime sooner." Cam twisted and kissed the underside of his jaw, then burrowed back into the pillow with a mumbled, "Love you."

Nic smiled against the nape of his neck. "Love you too, Boston."

———

"A celebration of life," his mother had insisted. They'd grieved Erin enough. Now that they knew she was at peace, it was time to celebrate her life and the second chance at life Edye had been given too. So as soon as she was discharged from the hospital, they'd made it happen, Nic leading the effort.

They'd had case wrap-up to handle the past few days as well, but when they weren't at the station house or the courthouse, Cam had worked on getting his mother resettled at home while Nic had gone into captain mode, Keith his second in command, readying their father's biggest boat for the occasion. And a spectacular job they had done. Tables and chairs covered in Erin's favorite blue dotted the deck, and from wires strung between the masts and rails dangled black-and-white photos of Erin. Cam had helped his mother pick them out, and Nic had had them reprinted and displayed, a gallery of Erin's life for family and friends to remember and enjoy. Erin reading one of their mother's romance novels, Erin playing the fiddle, Erin double-fisting cream horn pastries, her face a mess.

Guests mingled on deck, looking at the photographs, sharing stories, visiting with his mother, and eating Erin's favorite foods that Jamie had prepared from Edye's old recipe cards. It was exactly the celebration Cam's mother had wanted, and she laughed far more than she cried from her bench seat along the boat's stern.

Leaning against the wheelhouse wall, sipping from his bottle of Gravity Belmont Red, Cam tracked his lover's silver-tinged head, higher than most. Nic circulated among the crowd, checking to make sure all the photos were properly displayed and that everyone had what they needed. He frequently stopped to check in on Edye, and each time he did, she'd grab his hand and proudly introduce him as Cam's boyfriend to anyone who was near.

He deserved all the attention. He'd helped make this happen on multiple counts—standing by him, working his legal magic, finding Erin, and pulling this celebration together in only a few days. He was amazing, and Cam was head over heels in love with him, now more than ever.

"I think Mom has a new favorite." Quinn stepped out of the wheelhouse, a beer bottle in hand.

"You complaining?" Cam said with a nod to the beer.

Smiling, Quinn clinked his bottle against Cam's. "Not in the least. Your man makes a good brew. Nice catch."

Nic and Jamie were right. He hadn't given his parents or siblings enough credit. "Never thought I'd be the best fisherman in the family."

Quinn chuckled. "I wouldn't go *that* far. How did you catch him?"

"I argued with him nonstop until the day he dissed Brady."

"How the fuck did that lead to you two being together?"

"I kissed him to shut him up."

Laughing, Quinn playfully punched him. "You should have told us sooner. I feel like an idiot for not having put it together."

"You left for college when I was eleven. I hadn't put it together yet either about my bisexuality."

Tension crept back into Quinn's tall, muscular frame. "Maybe I should have stayed. Helped you out in that, maybe also kept you out of the chop shop. If I had, maybe—"

"Don't go there, Q." Cam threw an arm over his shoulders and hugged him to his side. "You don't bear any of the blame for what happened to Erin. None of us do." He'd given them the full story last night—how Harper was determined to take Erin that day, even if he had to kill—but shaking twenty years of guilt wasn't going to come easy for any of them.

"I always felt . . ."

"Let it go, brother." Cam leaned his head against

Quinn's, temple to temple. "We all have to. It's over now, and turns out, none of us were to blame. She's at peace. She'd want the rest of us to be too."

Quinn was silent a few minutes, then rasped out a hoarse chuckle. "I don't know, Cameron, maybe you're the catch."

"Don't tell Nic that." He pulled back, smiling, and Quinn's gaze drifted back out to the deck. Cam's followed to where Nic and Keith stood by his mother. "Keep an eye on Keith, though, yeah?" Cam said. "I think he'll be better now, less angry, but I'm not sure what will fill that place for him. Hopefully something or someone good, but . . ."

"We're on it, brother."

The harbormaster radioed then, letting them know their lane would be clear shortly. Only the immediate family would remain onboard as they rode out to sea to scatter Erin's ashes. There was already an empty casket buried at the cemetery; no one wanted to go through that again. Returning her to the sea, the lifeblood of their family, was the celebration she deserved. Quinn went about powering the boat back up while Cam signaled Nic and Keith that it was go time.

Fifteen minutes later, all the guests had disembarked and Cam was passing his best friend around for hugs. Jamie had been invited to stay for the journey out, but already green on the docked boat, he'd declined, not wanting to mar what should be a beautiful moment with his seasickness.

Nic moved to follow him off, and Cam jerked him back by their twined fingers. "Where do you think you're going?"

"This is for family."

"And you're mine."

Bobby clasped Nic's other shoulder. "Your words, brother."

The look that bloomed on Nic's face—wonder, gratitude, and love—made Cam's chest ache in a good way. He'd gotten so lucky with the man he loved and his family.

"Besides," Keith added, "do you really think Mom's going to let you out of her sight?"

"I have to agree with my boys," Ken chimed in. "Ride out with us, son."

Nic's Adam's apple bobbed as the normally eloquent prosecutor struggled for words. "I'd be honored."

That settled, everyone snapped into motion, getting the boat unmoored and into its channel lane. The ceremony at sea was quieter than the one at the docks but no less joyful, and even a little funny, as Irish wakes tended to be. Edye read from the book about the old family dog that Erin had written in second grade, each of them adding their own memories and anecdotes. Then each member of the family, Nic included, tossed a handful of her ashes into the water. They dissolved in the foam of the ship's wake, and the seagulls that swooped alongside the boat cawed and rose higher, lifting up each bit of her soul that was set free.

She and his family were finally, truly at peace.

They drifted and told stories, remembering their sister for another hour or so before aiming the boat back to shore. Ken sat with Edye on her bench, surrounded by their grandchildren, while Quinn and Bobby, with their wives and Keith, toasted to the future in the wheelhouse.

Cam went looking for his future, finding Nic standing at the front of the boat. Arms spread along the rail, hair swept back by the breeze and sea mist, he looked at home out here on the sea. Cam, however, wanted to talk to him about making a different sort of home, with him.

Coming up behind him, Cam wound his arms around his waist and rested his chin on Nic's shoulder. "Quinn wanted to know how I became the best fisherman in the family."

"I've never even seen you catch a fish."

"He meant catching you." Cam dropped a kiss behind his ear, and Nic hummed contentedly.

Then spun, bringing them front to front and pinning Cam against the rail, reminding him of the strength and training that lay beneath the suit, or scowl as it were just then. "It sure as fuck wasn't your taste in sports teams," he said, flicking Cam's green Celtics polo in exaggerated disgust.

Cam returned the gesture, flicking the collar of the maroon shirt Nic had borrowed. "Says the man wearing my BC polo."

He smirked. "We can't all be perfect."

Cam grabbed a handful of his shirt and jerked him forward. "Come here, you smug bastard." Off balance, as Cam intended, Nic stumbled into him and Cam sealed their lips in a rough, hard kiss.

A round of wolf whistles sounded behind them, and they broke apart, grinning.

"Thank you for asking me to come with you," Nic said.

Letting go of the shirt, Cam smoothed his hands up Nic's firm chest and around his neck. "You said I'm your family."

Nic circled his wrists, squeezing. "Last time I'll ask, I swear, but are you sure you want to risk all this, your old life here and your new one in San Francisco, for me? With all the shit swirling around with Vaughn and my father, I wouldn't blame—"

Cam leaned forward again, a quick kiss to stop Nic's careening arguments. He pulled back but stayed close enough to feel Nic's stuttered breath on his lips. "You risked your life for me. For the peace my family here needed. Now if I want to do the same for the man I love, let me."

The kiss Nic laid on him then wasn't quick or chaste, and they won more applause and Edye's laughing shout of "get a room."

Cam came up for air, smiling wide. "Come home with me, Dominic."

Nic's usual confidence bordering on arrogance vanished, eyes darting from his shoes to their hands and back. He was laid bare before Cam and an audience. "Are you saying the offer still stands?" He swallowed hard, summoning what he could and meeting Cam's eyes. "To move in with you?"

Cam breathed a sigh of relief, a sigh of pure joy. "There's no place I'd rather you be."

TWENTY-SIX

Sitting midway down the first baseline at the ballpark, Nic stared out over the field, past the giant mitt and Coke bottle slide to the tankers and sailboats crowding the rippling waters of the Bay. Indian summer was still going strong—bright sun, warm temps, a good breeze. Not much had changed during his time in Boston or during the week since returning.

But it had been more than enough time for Nic's whole world to change.

Mostly for the better, which scared him far more than the leftover bad parts. He had so much to lose now—a new home, a family of trusted friends, a lover he didn't want to hide from. The mess with his father and Vaughn could steal all that good away at any second, which was why he was here today.

That and the killer craving for caramel corn that always struck him this time of year, right before the season ended as if his taste buds knew the sticky sweetness was about to disappear again for six months.

"That shit will rot your teeth out."

Nic glanced right, down the empty club level row—a day game the last week of a losing season didn't draw a crowd—and saw Aidan shuffling toward him, tie gone and already half out of his suit coat.

Grinning, Nic bent the opposite direction and came back up with another box of freshly popped, gooey-tossed goodness. "So you don't want the one I got for you?"

Aidan smirked as he tossed his coat over Nic's on the seat backs in front of them. "I didn't say that." He dropped into the seat beside Nic, rolled up his sleeves, and claimed his prize. "Nice seats," he mumbled around a bite.

"Perks of being a shiny new vendor."

"Gravity brews at the Park?"

Nic nodded. "Just signed the contracts for next season."

"You won't be able to tear Cam away from here."

He waved a hand in the air. "I'm hoping it'll mellow the BoSox of it all."

"No chance."

Nic hid his groan behind another mouthful, and Aidan laughed until a grand slam on the field drew their attention momentarily away, both of them standing to cheer on their hometown team.

"You settled in at the house?" Aidan asked once they were seated again.

"Yeah, all good."

Aidan bumped his shoulder. "I'm happy for you two. Jamie is too."

"That's good. I know how important he is to Cam."

"And he knows the same about you. And you've saved his best friend at least four times now by my count."

Nic angled toward him and lowered his voice. The likelihood of being overheard was minimal but caution dictated. "But what if I'm the one who gets him killed? Or any of the rest of you?" Stomach revolting at the notion, he set the caramel corn aside and wiped off his hands, wringing the napkin so hard he shredded it. "I couldn't live with myself if—"

Aidan clasped his arm, cutting him off. "We're going to nail Vaughn. You're going to get your happy ending too, Dominic."

But not every story had a happy ending, and until recently, the chapters of Nic's life had not ended on high notes. He hated to be a pessimist, especially when almost everything else seemed to be going right for a change, but he was a lawyer. And a soldier. Evaluating risks, expecting the worst, was what he'd been trained to do.

Just like the players on the field, he had to cover all the bases. Not let a line drive or fly ball slip through, because now, improbably, he found himself on a team. He couldn't leave the game or his team to chance when it was more than just his life on the line.

He reached forward to the seat backs in front of them to where they'd tossed their jackets and pulled his out from under Aidan's. From the inside pocket, he withdrew a sheet of folded paper. "In case I don't," he said, handing it to Aidan.

Aidan tossed his empty box aside, cleaned off his hands, and took the paper. His warm brown eyes scanned the sheet, brow furrowing. "This is an insurance certificate for the house." His eyes continued down, then grew wide when they reached the bottom. "For double the value."

"The report came back on the apartment fire. Arson."

"Shit." Aidan fell back in his seat like he'd been

punched in the gut. Nic could commiserate. "You think it was a warning?"

Nic nodded. "I can't be sure what's going to happen, and I can't risk your house. I know what it meant to you. What it still means to you even if you don't live there anymore."

"This is too much, Dominic," Aidan said, trying to hand the paper back to him.

Nic refused to take it. "Peace of mind."

Their stare-off lasted one crack of the bat before Aidan conceded with a huff, leaning forward and slipping the paper inside his jacket.

"I also need you to do me another favor," Nic said.

"Whatever it is, you know I will."

"You've said before you used to help with your family's estate docs."

"That's right."

"I need mine updated."

Aidan's brows snapped together and he shot forward in his seat. "Dominic—"

He held up a hand. "I should have done it years ago once Gravity was up and running, but now I have even more to protect."

"I agree they should be updated, but for this reason, Nic? Why are you so sure things are going to take a turn?"

Insides twisting, he turned his face away, staring back out at the field. Remembering how his dad had first bought season tickets as a means of distracting him. How he'd taken delight in sneaking off with Garrett to games at the old stadium. What it had felt like to lose him, to lose it all. Like the imagined sensation of the tree branches on his back twisting, knotting, and breaking. "I was happy once and I lost it all with two words and a fist."

"Your father," Aidan surmised, pity and fury wrapped together in his rumbling Irish burr.

"I don't trust it won't happen again by either his or Vaughn's hand, and I need to protect what's mine better than I did then."

Aidan grasped his shoulder. "You were eighteen."

"And I'm forty-six next week. With combat training, a legal degree, and a hefty bank balance, thanks to the brewery and a military pension I invested well. I have the means to provide and protect." He covered Aidan's hand with his. "Help me do that, please."

Aidan squeezed his shoulder, then slid back in his seat. "What are you thinking?"

"I want the brewery insulated and for it to go to Eddie, free and clear."

Aidan nodded, and Nic snagged another paper out of his coat and handed it to Aidan. On it, he'd written two account numbers.

"Offshore?" Aidan asked.

"Offshore," Nic confirmed. "If something should happen, there's enough in the first one to pay off Vaughn. If that's unnecessary, then I want it to go to Mary Del Selva." True to her word, Mel had "stolen Mary away" to work a couple days a week for her and Danny as Mary wound down to her full-time retirement. Nic wanted to make sure that retirement was secure.

"Okay," Aidan said. "And the second account?"

The second account was twice the size of the first one. His retirement nest egg, which he contributed to monthly. "For Cam," he said, blood heating and chilling at the same time. He never thought he'd have someone in his life like this again. That he had to provide for that person in the event of his death, sooner or later, was both heart-lifting and heart-wrenching. "That and everything else I have," he added.

"I figured as much."

"You'd do the same for Jamie."

One corner of Aidan's mouth hitched up. "I have."

Nic absently rubbed a hand over his left hip, thinking of the ink he'd started to pine for there. He knew exactly what he wanted it to be, a version of the label he'd already sketched, and he hoped like hell it would be inked in celebration, memorializing a victory. Not a tragedy. But in case there was one, and in case he was on the losing end of it, Nic didn't want Cam to regret the decision he'd made to leave the rest of his family behind and tough it out in San Francisco. For him.

"I don't want him to want for anything ever again."

"I understand, and I'll do this for you, of course." Aidan folded the paper into quarters, all the accounts and figures hidden, and tucked it into his dress shirt pocket. He sat back, arms folded, glaring intently. Knowingly. Like the best friend he'd improbably become. "But I think what Cam wants most is for you to stay alive."

Nic glanced out at the field again, hoping things went differently this time. Praying for the happy ending he wanted. That Cam deserved. "I'm going to try my damnedest."

But if it came down to it, he'd always save the man he loved. Even if it meant a fist to his jaw. Or a bullet to his heart.

———

Reviews are an invaluable tool when it comes to spreading the word about great reads. Please consider leaving an honest review for *Craft Brew* on your favorite review site.

Thank you for reading!

ALSO BY LAYLA REYNE

For the most up-to-date list of titles and a helpful reading order, please visit www.laylareyne.com.

Agents Irish and Whiskey:

Single Malt

Cask Strength

Barrel Proof

Tequila Sunrise

Blended Whiskey

Angel's Share

Trouble Brewing:

Imperial Stout

Craft Brew

Noble Hops

Final Gravity

Fog City:

Prince of Killers

King Slayer

A New Empire

Queen's Ransom

Silent Knight

What We May Be

Perfect Play:

Dead Draw

Bad Bishop

King Hunt

Best Play

Redemption Inc:

The Accidental

The Bounty

The Martyr

The Boss

Guard Duty:

High Winds

Rough Waters

Wild Type:

Variable Onset

Affinity Drift

Matched Pair

Soul to Find:

Icarus and the Devil

Jason and the Storm

Paris and the Reaper

Atlas and the Traitor

Table for Two:

The Last Drop

Dine With Me

Blue Plate Special

Over a Barrel

The Sweet Spot

Sigh of Relief

Changing Lanes:

Relay

Medley

Freestyle

Three Sticks:

Barn Burner

Dirty Dangle

ABOUT THE AUTHOR

Layla Reyne is the author of *What We May Be* and the *Agents Irish and Whiskey, Fog City,* and *Perfect Play* series. She writes sexy, intense LGBTQIA+ romance featuring competent adults in kitchens, sports arenas, car chases, and other high-stakes situations. Whether it's adrenaline-fueled suspense, rival athletes, vampires and shifters, or love mixed with mouth-watering foodie goodness, queer folks finding happily-ever-afters is guaranteed.

You can find Layla online at laylareyne.com and at the following sites:

BB bookbub.com/authors/layla-reyne

facebook.com/laylareyne

instagram.com/laylareyne

tiktok.com/@laylareyne

bsky.app/profile/laylareyne

www.ingramcontent.com/pod-product-compliance
Lightning Source LLC
Chambersburg PA
CBHW070526310726
48976CB00002BA/546